LAST HOUR

EMMA LAST SERIES: BOOK EIGHT

MARY STONE

Copyright © 2024 by Mary Stone Publishing

All rights reserved.

No part of this book may be reproduced in any form or by any electronic or mechanical means, including information storage and retrieval systems, without written permission from the author, except for the use of brief quotations in a book review.

❦ Created with Vellum

This book is dedicated to those who have been coerced or intimidated into paths not of their choosing. Your stories, struggles, and resilience in the face of fear and pressure are inspirations for us all.

DESCRIPTION

The first cut is the deadliest.

Special Agent Emma Last is finally ready to confront the 'Other' side of her life—the part filled with ghosts that only she can see. However, her supernatural abilities must take a back seat as a real-world crisis demands her urgent attention.

Ghosts or not, the clock is ticking.

The D.C. Violent Crimes Unit joins forces with the Bureau's Safe Streets Task Force to investigate a perplexing double homicide in the gritty underworld of gang territories. The crime scene bears an unusual signature—a bizarre, multi-bladed knife—suggesting a murder too peculiar and personal for a typical gang war. Besides, if the gangs wanted a war, they've had plenty of time to start one.

So why now?

As tensions simmer and the body count rises, a gifted but elusive graffiti artist seems pivotal to the investigation. But little does Emma know that unmasking the artist might unleash a torrent of danger, jeopardizing not just the case but also the lives of the entire team, with one member standing on the edge of a treacherous precipice.

Last Hour is the eighth book in the compelling new Emma Last FBI series by bestselling author Mary Stone. On the streets, there's no rest for the wicked or the good.

1

Charlie "Rux" Rucker bopped his way down the sidewalk outside the Night Trips Strip Club, earning him laughs and jeers from the ladies at the door. They did their own little dances to get people interested in sampling the wares inside, and he threw them a wave.

Rux rolled his eyes when he saw Jax still hanging around the entrance.

He don't stop flirting, the kid's gonna get hurt. They don't want nothing to do with his young ass.

Jax was just about legal drinking age, but not quite. Didn't stop the liquor flowing when Rux was with him. They ran with the Drivers, and Trips was a Drivers bar.

But they'd had their fun. It was damn near two in the morning, and it was time to get going. Rux had work in the morning, finishing up laying the tile in his mom's new bathroom. He just had that to do, then put the toilet back down, and he'd be done. They could finally sell that place and buy her something nicer.

Shit, with the money we're earning from selling, I'm buying two houses next time.

"Hey, Jax! Let's go."

The kid didn't budge, just kept flirting.

"Jax. Did I say time to go? I think I did."

He came over and joined Rux, finally. Soon as Jax had his head turned, the girl he'd been flirting with started waving at some dude across the street.

Rux put his arm around his baby brother's shoulders and pulled him away so he wouldn't get his heart stomped on. "You gotta learn when they mean business, and when they *are* business. Girls at Trips are always the second kind."

Jax kicked at a bottle as he ducked out from under Rux's arm. "I almost had Amber's number, man. You couldn't give me another five minutes?"

Here he goes again.

Rux moved down the sidewalk and let the kid ramble on about all the things he was gonna do with Amber someday. But something nagged at Rux's mind, like he should've remembered it before leaving the club.

Mighta stopped at three drinks instead of four. Or was it five? Shit.

It hit him. Their driver, Snake, was supposed to meet them out front. Snake knew the deal, being the NKOTB. Sure, he'd been running since they came down from Baltimore, but he was still one of the youngest and didn't do much more than paint a few pictures on the wall.

Not like Rux and Jax, working corner crews, keeping track of all the product.

Rux tapped out a text to Snake.

Your ass better not be where I think it is.

Nothing came back, and Rux tried again. After five more texts and five more minutes, he gave up.

"Jax, c'mon. We're walking."

"Walk? Why the fu—?"

"Because Snake's busy dipping his slithery tail where it doesn't belong. Now let's go."

He led them down an alley that ran along the back of Night Trips. It would take them to the next neighborhood over, and from there, they could get home easy enough. At least to Jax's little dump of a duplex.

Rux kept a better place across town, near his mom's, but no way was he walking that far in the dark, especially after drinking. And since Rails, the leader of the Drivers, had forbidden them from using rideshare, his only choice was to crash at Jax's.

Rails thinks we leave footprints using those apps, even though we all got burners at the ready. But the man said don't, so we don't, because "that's what Snake is for."

After this, Rux'd have to talk with Rails. Tell him Snake didn't get the memo.

"Rux, you serious? We walking all the way to your place?"

"No. We're walking all the way to yours."

Rux pulled up short when he heard Jax's footsteps stop behind him. He turned around but continued walking backward. "What're you doing? C'mon, now."

They made it to the end of the alley, with Rux and Jax trading jabs. Rux was about to step onto the sidewalk when Jax tapped his arm.

"What's up with Snake making us walk like this? Something's going on, right?"

Rux sure as hell wasn't gonna mention Snake's new girlfriend. She was a Powders girl, and that news did not need spreading around. Bad enough one of the Trips dancers knew about it, but Celine knew better than to run her mouth.

Least, she better. She doesn't want to find out what happens if she flaps her lips.

"Snake's busy, like I said."

"Yeah, dipping it where he shouldn't."

Rux rounded on him, backing him up a step.

"Jax, I told you, leave it the fuck be. Snake's got a new girl, okay? If he likes her enough to lay off the clubs, more power to him. He's a punk for making us walk, though, and bet I'm bringing this up to Rails first chance I get. Now let's move."

He stepped out of the alley and was about to cross the street when he spotted a girl from Night Trips walking down the block. "Hey, ain't that Celine?"

Jax had a hand up and was shouting at her before Rux could stop him. The girl startled and looked their way. But then she shook her head and sped up.

Slapping Jax on the arm, Rux followed Celine. "C'mon, let's see what she's doing. Maybe get another dance from her, off the clock."

The kid's footsteps slapped the pavement as he kept pace with Rux.

"Hey, Celine," he called, "you got time for another dance?"

Jax hollered his own invitation her way, but all she did was flip them the finger and turn around the next corner.

Rux shrugged, moving faster now, and Jax was right there at his shoulder.

They followed her another block, calling her name, offering a good tip for a bit of her time. They didn't usually hassle the girls at the club because Rails told them not to. But Rux was having fun with it, and he could tell Jax was too.

They had to be on the lookout, make sure the place didn't get a bad reputation, because that could bring the cops around.

But out here on the streets? Nah, this's our territory. Ain't no reason we can't have a little fun.

"Celine. Hey, I'm talking to you, girl. C'mon."

She kept moving, walking faster, almost running now. Rux and Jax started jogging.

They were getting close to her, nearing the next corner, but Rux froze in his tracks when he heard a scraping sound like metal on concrete. He drew his gun and turned, scanning the street, the darkened doors, the fire escapes, and the shadows under the moonlight.

Celine was out of sight now.

Nothing moved.

Rux held his breath, listening. The world was quiet, but the tiny hairs on the back of Rux's neck rose, telling him they weren't alone.

"C'mon, Jax. Get ready in case shit goes down."

The kid had his gun in hand and shifted his weight side to side. He followed fast when Rux moved down to the next block.

The scraping sound followed them, and Rux kept looking up at every fire escape they passed, expecting somebody to come jumping down on them at any minute.

At the next street, he took them into an alley that turned away from where he'd been heading.

Somebody's fucking with us. All right, then—let's fuck around.

The alley ended at a major street, two blocks ahead. He could already see the crowds up there, spilling out of another club and staggering toward cars lined up along the curb. Music played loudly, beats rattling windows and echoing down the alley.

Rux was ready to keep going but froze when he saw the blue-and-white bubble of the Powders gang marking the nearest wall.

Shit. Shit, shit, shit.

He stuffed his gun back in his pants and slapped Jax's arm, telling him to do the same, but the kid didn't budge.

"Isn't that a Powders tag? We're going down there without guns in our hands? You serious?"

"Deadass. Like Rails said the other day. Nobody starts

nothing. Just keep your head up and be cool. We'll be off their streets before—"

A whoosh of air put Rux back a step.

He went for his gun as a figure wearing all black flashed by him, grabbing Jax along the way and slamming him into the alley wall.

The kid let out a high-pitched wail of pain that turned guttural.

Rux spun away, firing blindly behind himself as he ran back the way he'd come. He dodged behind a dumpster and checked the alley, hoping the attacker's body was all sprawled out.

What he saw was his baby brother, the kid Rails told him to watch out for, sliding down the brick wall. Jax slumped sideways before falling face-first into a slimy puddle.

Run! Jax is dead. You always thought that peace treaty was bullshit, and now you got proof. Just get back to Rails and tell him.

Stumbling to his feet, Rux hit the alley wall hard before taking a lunging step toward freedom. He spun to flee, but the muscular, lightning-fast fighter leaped and landed on his back, tackling him to the ground and stealing the breath out of his lungs.

His gun went flying. Rux twisted sideways and rolled, trying to force his attacker off his back. Metal scratched and sparked against the asphalt, right next to his face.

Rux squirmed and thrashed, heaving under his attacker's weight. He was on his back now and brought one arm up to cover his face while he struck out with his other fist. The impact was brutal. He'd struck some kind of body armor or something, and it felt like he'd broken every knuckle. The dude on him batted his bloody hand aside and secured his knees around Rux's ribs.

He struggled to take in a full breath and punched upward

again with his other hand, then brought both arms together in a cross to block the knife in his attacker's grip.

He caught it just as it came down toward his chest. All he could see was a mass of darkness above him.

The attacker pressed down, trying to push the blade straight into Rux's heart.

Rux grunted, fighting back as he struggled to keep air in his lungs. He pushed with all his might and got a clearer view of the weapon. And what he saw about made his heart stop.

It was no knife. But there were multiple blades, emerging from the attacker's hand like long, sharp, curved talons.

And they were dripping in Jax's blood.

The figure hissed at him, straight up hissed, and leaned closer, putting all his weight into bringing those blades closer to Rux's eyes now.

"Driver. You think you can walk these streets and mess with my family? Just like a slimy snake you know?"

The attacker's rasp almost made the words run together. Rux heaved in a breath, desperate to get the dude off him.

"Who you talking about? What family?"

"Celine's my family, like all the Powders."

"She's..." Rux fought to take in enough air to get the words out. "She ain't no Powder. She dances at Night Trips."

"Uh-huh. And that's where she saw you with that slimy little snake, slithering around. Now two more Drivers going six feet underground."

Rux realigned his grip on the guy's arm, pushing him up and away, but the attacker swung his other hand straight into Rux's solar plexus, landing a punch that stole his strength.

He opened his mouth to inhale much needed air, but blades drove through his neck, cutting it off. Rux spasmed as his throat filled with lightning-sharp pain. Blood fountained from his throat as the blades pulled free. Hot and wet, blood gushed over his chin, cheeks, hands, shoulder, chest as he fought to stop his life from rushing away in a torrent.

The killer shifted, pressed on his chest for leverage, and stood up and away from the bubbling gore pouring from Rux's body. "Where's your snaky friend tonight, Driver? Huh?" The words seemed to come from afar, echoing with a cruel irony that Rux couldn't grasp.

Sirens screamed into the night, somewhere far away, like a sound Rux remembered from childhood as the last of his life spilled from his throat, making another puddle in the alleyway.

Memories flickered like old film, snippets of laughter, faces of loved ones, fragments of dreams unfulfilled. The time when he was seven, and his mom took him away from the lights of the city so he could see the stars shining in the sky for the first time.

The cold of the alleyway seeped through him, yet it was the chill of his own ebbing life that froze him to the core.

So many regrets. So many mistakes.

Lying there, the world receding, Rux's thoughts drifted to the absurdity of it all, how life's end could be so mundane, so unceremonious. As darkness encroached, his last conscious thought was a whisper, a wish to have seen the stars with his mom one last time. To have one last hour. One last minute…

2

Special Agent Emma Last stretched into child's pose, imagining Oren's rumbly voice encouraging her, his lower hand hovering above her back. He would remind her to breathe evenly, filling her lungs from the bottom to the top. Then emptying herself with a steady, complete exhale.

Oren wasn't there—the air hadn't chilled with any sign of the Other—but she felt like he could be, and that was what mattered.

Around her, the city park was a green expanse of calm. Trees rustled in the early morning breeze, and birds chittered about, searching for their breakfast. Other city dwellers had picked out their own spots to exercise or were walking and jogging along the park's paths—but the simple calm that came with morning time offered a solitary peace she'd been craving.

Cherry blossoms scented the air with a sweetness that meant spring had arrived, and a couple of squirrels squeaked at her from nearby, more interested than concerned. Emma was as far from death and the Other and the FBI as ever.

She inched her arms farther up the mat, imagining Oren's

hand settling onto her lower back, gently pressing, as she stretched her warmed-up muscles. The grass beneath her mat made for a soft, comforting surface. Feeling it beneath her, and the life in the park all around, she only wished she and Oren had gotten a chance to do yoga here together.

He'd have enjoyed this. He'd enjoy seeing me here, too, like this. Calm and at ease, with his help.

She'd woken up early for yoga in the park and found herself pleasantly surprised to see other lone yoga practitioners sprinkled around the green lawns. Even the couples exercising together hadn't gotten her down.

Nearly a week had passed since she'd seen Oren's ghost at his studio, but true to his word, she'd felt watched over since then. As if she weren't quite alone, even when she was.

Almost like a normal person feeling watched out for by their loved one. What a miracle that was compared to her normal life.

Yet, of all the ghosts who might've appeared to her, Emma's mother remained conspicuously absent.

Pulling herself to kneeling, Emma took deep breath after deep breath. Eyes closed, she let her body rest before coming back to the realm of the city and the life at the Bureau that awaited her. When she stood up and collected her mat, she felt both the buzz and the peace sweep over her from her yogic practice.

Oren would've been proud. He'd encouraged her, so often, to prioritize inner harmony to help her stay grounded when the realities of her life and her work threatened to overwhelm.

And they so often did. Whether it was a literal axe murderer hell-bent on vengeance or a twisted killer targeting impoverished children, Emma's professional life put her in touch with the worst of humanity on an almost daily basis.

Yoga, and her memories of Oren's teaching, helped her stay connected to the immediate moment. And she was better for it.

But now it's time to get started with your Monday, Emma girl.

The trip back to her place wasn't a long one. Within minutes of leaving the park, Emma was jogging in place at the intersection near her apartment complex, a stitch in her side begging her to stop.

The bakery across the street backed up that sentiment with a solid display case of fresh croissants and honey-toasted pastries, but Emma ignored both. She was finally back on track to a healthy routine, and she'd be damned before she'd let the demons on her shoulder win the morning.

I won't turn down a doughnut if Leo brings them in again, though. I've earned one, dammit.

The walk light signaled go, and she jogged forward, relishing the warmth in her muscles against the chilly morning air. She'd missed this. And at just after sunrise in late March D.C., her run was nearly perfect.

At the door to her complex, she adjusted her yoga mat under her arm as she swiped her key card, then pushed herself to keep up a jogging pace as she went down the hall and up the stairs. Her cooldown would come while she fixed herself breakfast since, miracle of miracles, she'd actually gone to the store and stocked her kitchen with healthy options to add to what Neil Forrester, her old boss, had ordered for her when he visited the previous week.

Inside her apartment, Mrs. Kellerly's familiar ghost hovered near Emma's Keurig, her frizzy white hair as puffy as ever. "There you are. And with a healthy glow to you too!"

"Morning, Mrs. Kellerly." Emma settled her yoga mat in the little alcove behind her front door, working to catch her breath. "You should be outside watching the city wake up. It's a beautiful morning."

She stretched her arms above her head, turning to see the ghost smiling. Her white eyes no longer bothered Emma, nor did the little chill to the air that came whenever the Other pushed its way into her corner of existence.

Mrs. Kellerly was practically family at this point.

"This is your third morning in a row, getting up to exercise." The ghost shuffled around the counter, eyeing Emma with a hint of approval in her voice. Oddly, it made Emma all the warmer. "It's good to see you like this."

"I like getting up before the sun, so I can watch it rise and call the city back to life." Emma pulled low-fat strawberry cream cheese, eggs, and a container of fresh mixed berries from the fridge, taking the haul to the counter. "Seeing other folks exercising, out enjoying the morning. This is the best time of year here. The cherry blossoms in the park smell heavenly."

With eggs on the stove and a whole-grain bagel toasting, Emma separated out some raspberries, blueberries, and strawberries to wash.

Mrs. Kellerly nodded her approval, wishing out loud that she could smell the breakfast.

Emma tossed her a smile just as her bagel beeped, then began preparing her plate. By the time she'd spread out the cream cheese and berries, her eggs and coffee were done.

At the island, she took a deep breath before digging in. Oren had always told her to treasure every moment. Every bite of every meal. Every sunrise and cloudy day. Every friendship. The office might be waiting for her, it was true, but for right now, she was just a young woman with a good breakfast—and much of her life—spread out before her.

Oren would want her to appreciate that, and Emma pictured his dancing blue eyes as she took a bite of her bagel, relishing the delicious cream cheese and the blueberries she'd sprinkled on top.

That bakery across the street can suck it. Nothing beats fresh berries after a morning run.

"Well, you enjoy your breakfast, Emma dear." Mrs. Kellerly passed by her, floating a little straighter than she had some weeks back, when Emma had mostly ignored her. "And I'll see you tomorrow. Focus on the living. I've got plenty to occupy me, don't you worry."

Emma gave the ghostly neighbor a wave as she sipped her coffee, smiling at the woman's back. She hadn't been as gossipy lately, as if she only needed to check in and see that Emma's optimism had returned. Just long enough to offer a, "How are you, dear?" and make sure she was eating.

And it was almost nice having the old woman greet her after a run. Not normal…but nice.

Maybe that's a sign you're ready to really deal with this Other business, Emma girl.

Taking an extra big bite of her bagel to chew on while she tackled her next chore, Emma grabbed her cell phone off the island. She scrolled down to Marigold's name and dashed off a quick text to the psychic.

Any chance you're free to meet this evening? I'll spring for dinner if you're willing to chat about the Other.

She put her phone down and picked her fork back up, and she could almost hear Oren's voice echoing around her as she did. He'd told her she was incredible, and that what she had to do would be incredible, too, if she'd only stop pushing her talents away.

It was damn well time to listen to the man.

And now that she was back to feeling good, running and yoga-posing her body back into shape, she'd become more eager than ever to figure out the identities of those women in the photo she'd found in her father's storage unit, tucked away in his old desk with a collection of pictures from Emma's childhood.

The very fact that she'd found it among her dad's things suggested there was some importance to the relationships it commemorated. Those women had been hugging up on her mom like they were all sisters, but Emma had never seen them before. Wouldn't women who'd been that close have stuck around to check in on her, like aunts or godmothers?

And beyond that, more importantly, she'd realized as she began coming out of her grieving stupor that her damn fingers turned to icicles when she touched the picture.

It was time to figure out this whole *Other* part of her life.

Emma took the final bite of her eggs just as her phone buzzed with a message from Marigold.

Absolutely! I'll come to your place. We can head out from there. Just text me once you know what time you'll be off work.

"Perfect." Emma plucked up the last fresh berries from her plate and popped them into her mouth. After putting her dish in the sink, she sat down at the island to enjoy her coffee. Gazing around the apartment, she decided it looked brighter than it had in days.

It was cleaner than she'd been keeping it while wallowing in grief, definitely, but either the spring air or her own new outlook seemed to change everything. The cream-colored walls were more welcoming, her couch and chairs cozier, the wood grains of the entryway flooring a touch more luxurious and natural.

I don't know if Oren's watching me, but if he is, he's proud of the progress he inspired. At least, he better be. No other ghost could've turned me around like this.

Emma nearly snorted coffee out her nose at that thought but recovered and went back to smiling like a lunatic as she enjoyed her space. She'd come a long way in the last week, and she could understand if Oren's ghost wanted to keep his distance and let her continue on her own for a bit, proving she could, as that was kind of the point.

The switch had flipped for her, and she *could* continue on her own. Her friends and her team were backing her up, but she was standing up again. Facing the world.

Facing both worlds. On her own.

Her phone buzzed. Stopping the coffee cup halfway to her mouth, she glanced down to read a message from Jacinda.

Powders and Drivers are making moves. Our unit's assisting the Bureau's Safe Streets Task Force. Meeting this morning. Be on time.

Jacinda might not have elaborated, but if D.C.'s two most prominent gangs were finally getting into it, there'd be no rest on the horizon for the wicked or the good.

3
———

Leo pulled his truck to a stop in the garage, a few spaces down from where Emma's Prius had just turned into a spot. Denae reached over and gave his thigh a little squeeze above the knee brace he still wore. The perpetrator on their last case put his leg out of joint with a well-placed kick and nearly stabbed Leo with a shard of glass right before Emma shot the attacker dead.

That was then, and this is a new day and a new case.

"Ready to see what this is all about?"

Denae's hand went still on his leg, but now she stared out the window with a faraway look on her face. Leo knew that look because he'd been wearing it himself most of the morning.

"Not ready to leave the weekend behind yet, either, are you?"

"Oh, you have no idea." She leaned forward without unbuckling her belt and trailed her lips from his chin to his mouth, probably leaving a glaze of her lip gloss to tell the world what they'd been doing.

When her lips found his, he didn't particularly care who

knew what. He tangled one hand in her curls and pulled her a touch closer and tighter, relishing the warmth of her mouth on his. She smelled of his favorite coffee creamer, all buttery sweetness.

He'd drizzled it into the batter for their morning's French toast and then topped their coffee with it to match, over her protests. The woman had stopped complaining altogether once she'd tasted it, though.

She drew back and tapped his nose playfully, then brought one perfect finger up to smudge away whatever residual gloss must've been left on his mouth.

He made a face at her, holding her dark-brown eyes for an instant more. "I can't have shiny lips too?"

Laughing, she finally unbuckled her seat belt. "Not today, Ambrose."

He followed her lead and unbuckled as she let herself out the door, even though he could've spent another few minutes in the truck, if it had been left to him. The glow of their romantic weekend remained, and with how well things had been going, this bit of lingering time prior to another workweek was worth treasuring.

Opening up the back door, he grabbed his bag and caught Denae's eye just as she did the same across from him. "I was serious earlier, you know. I really do want to meet your family soon." He hefted his bag over his shoulder. "Maybe next weekend?"

She blew some curls away from her face, eyes getting that same squinty look that they'd gotten when he'd brought it up earlier…and she'd promptly changed the subject. "Maybe next weekend. Focus on work until then, yeah?"

Without another word, she backed up and slammed the door shut, and he was left staring at his empty back seat. That hadn't exactly been a brush-off, but it sure felt like one.

As he shut the door and observed Denae greeting Emma,

who'd stopped halfway to the garage exit to meet them, he forced himself to lighten up. The so-called brush-off might just be a symptom of the weekend ending. Denae had seemed a little uncomfortable ever since Jacinda's message had come through that morning while they'd been sitting in his kitchen.

He felt the workweek closing in too. Maybe that was it. Not that he didn't love his job, but walking away from a weekend of romance and into a potential gang war wasn't anybody's idea of a smooth transition.

And besides, he'd asked her what was wrong, and she'd said it was nothing. Just a bad feeling.

Gangs in D.C. streets certainly warranted that much.

"Morning, Leo!" Emma jerked her head back toward the garage exit. "How's the knee?"

He grinned, speeding up as best he could to catch up to the two women. "Knee's mostly healed. Doctor said I shouldn't do any marathons for a while. Gotta say, it's nice to see you with a spark in your step. Good weekend?"

"Great weekend," she corrected him, "and a great morning. Yoga in the park as the sun comes up? You should try it."

When Leo raised an eyebrow at Denae, she shook her head. "Forget it, Ambrose. I want all the shut-eye I can get."

"We should spar again sometime soon," Emma grinned, focusing on Denae, "and get us both back in fighting shape."

Denae's eyes widened a touch, and Leo could imagine why. Emma had blown off every suggestion that she join Denae at the gym, even before Oren was killed. Then, with grief devouring Emma's life, she'd ignored suggestions to do just about anything at all.

She's found her feet again. The grief's probably still there, but it looks like she's come through the worst of it.

Once through the parking garage entrance, Emma

flounced her hair and began taking the stairs two at a time. Denae bounded up behind her.

Mia and Vance met Leo at the bottom of the stairs. He let them lead the way up behind their racing colleagues. "You can both walk just fine, and they have more energy than I do."

Vance grunted his agreement. "Hey, at least you're mobile. A knee dislocation could've been a lot worse."

"Fair point. Any idea what happened with the gangs overnight?"

"We all got the same text, and I haven't seen the news this morning."

"Been preoccupied with more important things? I know how that is."

The three of them shared a brief moment of laughter as Mia swatted Vance on the arm.

Leo turned his head so they wouldn't see his face fall into a frown. Much as he'd brushed off Denae's mood going sour earlier, it still bothered him. "If we're working alongside that task force, whoever's meeting us here should know more."

A giggle rang out above them, and Denae flashed a flirtatious grin over her shoulder, which wasn't something she did around their teammates.

He found that odd. That really wasn't quite the Denae he knew and, he had to admit, was coming to love.

I'm just imagining things. Stop looking for trouble, and it'll stop looking for me.

As if that were an option for an FBI agent. He tightened his grip on his bag strap and nearly laughed out loud at the thought.

But no matter. Denae was a badass. Whatever came their way, they'd face it together.

4

Denae followed Emma's lead in lowering her voice as their team headed straight into the conference room. Joking and racing up the stairs had been a nice distraction, but the look on SSA Jacinda Hollingsworth's face pulled a dark cloud over the otherwise light-as-air morning. With her long hair already pulled into a tight bun, Jacinda could've passed for a stern schoolmarm.

A white man Denae recognized from the gang task force stood at the wall, focused on his phone.

Jacinda nodded at the agents as they came in, a sly question in her eye. Denae hoped her face didn't betray her as she nodded back. The SSA made no sign of having picked up on her mood.

As Denae took her seat, Jacinda was already refocusing on the newcomer in their midst.

"First things first. This is Max Stillwell, the longest-running member of the Bureau's Safe Streets Task Force. We're teaming up to solve this crime. Max's connections at MPD will make sure we have access to everything the cops have on these two gangs."

Stillwell nodded at her, then glanced around to meet every team member's gaze. He was older than when they'd last seen each other, with more salt in his salt-and-pepper, close-cut hair and neatly trimmed beard. The man radiated confidence, and she imagined he might've fit in well as an undercover operative in his younger days. She was both glad and worried to have him on their side.

He's good at his job. That's the kind of person we want working this case.

At the front of the room, Jacinda cleared her throat. "Eyes up, everyone, and I'll send these images to your tablets as well." The screen flickered and lit up as Jacinda tapped at her keyboard. She stepped back, giving everyone a view as two images appeared, side-by-side bodies on the screen.

Both men had been killed in an alleyway. Close-up images of the collars and faces showed a number of small tattoos as well as trailing lines of ink present on almost every bit of exposed flesh. Denae bit back a curse. She recognized the Drivers tattoo on the neck of the younger, Hispanic victim. The blue triangle with the red *D* above it stood out bright on his neck.

Blood was splattered all over everything, though. Her stomach gurgled in response. Neither of the murdered men were people she knew. That much, at least, was a relief, and Denae's heart settled. She sat forward, tablet open, as Jacinda continued the briefing.

"We have two murder victims. One is a Hispanic male, twenty, tattoos consistent with the Drivers gang." Jacinda pointed needlessly at the bright-red *D* peeking out from above his coat collar. "And our other victim, a Black man, twenty-four, was a known associate of the Drivers' leader Marcus 'Rails' Foster. Blood spatter analysis confirms neither victim's pockets were disturbed postmortem. Both had small amounts of cash, as well as firearms, in their possession."

Denae frowned just a tiny bit. That didn't sound like typical gang violence.

Jacinda stepped closer to the screen, regarding the images as if they were paintings hanging in a gallery. "The Black man, Charlie 'Rux' Rucker, fired his weapon six times, likely while fleeing his attacker, based on initial ballistics analysis conducted at the scene. Bullets impacted the alleyway in a wide pattern."

Leo tapped out some notes on his tablet. "Mugging gone wrong?"

The SSA turned to face the table. "We're ruling that out. This, according to Max, has all the hallmarks of the first salvo in a gang war."

Emma raised a hand. "Cause of death? That's a lot of blood."

Denae expected Max to answer, but he motioned for Jacinda to reply, apparently happy to wait his turn to speak.

Or he's waiting to drop a bomb on all of us.

"Multiple puncture wounds of a suspicious nature. These men were stabbed three times, simultaneously, likely by a weapon with three blades. In the case of the Hispanic man, Juan Carlos 'Jax' Duran, we have repeated stab wounds," she turned back to the screen and tapped it, "four sets in fact, to his abdomen and chest. Charlie Rucker, also dead on scene, was stabbed in the neck."

Denae squinted at the screen, seeing nothing but a blanketing of blood over each victim, centered on the chest of one and the neck of the other. The man who'd stood silent until now stepped up beside Jacinda, who extended a hand, welcoming him to the head of the room.

Max gave her a nod of thanks before addressing the agents. "The Drivers are originally from Baltimore, where they're known as the B-more Drivers. Founding members started out selling dope from yellow cabs back in the day.

Since developing a presence here in D.C., the Drivers have recently butted heads with the local Powders gang. Nothing we would call gang warfare, though, until now."

Across the table from Denae, Leo jotted another note, seemingly oblivious to the heat and anxiety washing off her. He popped his head up from his tablet, turning to Max. "No deaths before this?"

"Only one that we can attribute, with certainty, to intergang activity or violence. Otherwise, it's been bar fights, some tagging, and street brawls. We'd hoped for the best." The man shifted on his feet, appearing almost uncomfortable.

Mia frowned at the bodies on screen. "And they gave us the worst, didn't they?"

Jacinda hit a button on her laptop, and a new photo confronted them. Written in blood on a dumpster, with one body's expensive sneaker visible from just the corner of the frame, was a telling statement that put Denae's heart back into her throat.

Death by Powder.

"They wanted everyone to know who did this." Jacinda folded her arms. Max, are we certain this is how the Powders communicate a threat? They publicly take responsibility like this?"

"We've seen tags at other scenes, mostly when there's been a burglary. They're a proud gang, and don't shy from claiming turf. Unlike the smaller D.C. outfits, of which there are many, I assure you, the Powders and Drivers explicitly seek to dominate the landscape."

Denae wrote down the phrase in her tablet, even though she knew she wouldn't forget it. "And it's confirmed to have been written in blood?"

He nodded. "Nothing from either crew, until now, has reached such a level of brutality. Like I said, these two gangs have been bumping heads, but it was only black eyes, bloody noses, and wounded pride. Nothing that couldn't heal."

Leaning forward, Emma lifted a hand and caught Max's attention. "Do we know if the victims were involved in any of that? Anything in their records that could indicate a grudge that would lead to something like…" She trailed off and gestured to the screen, but lowered her hand as Max shook his head.

"Not that we can point to exactly. Jax and Rux are known distributors, running corner crews or handling the cash-and-stash part of the Drivers' meth operation in their respective neighborhoods. Neither of them has anything more than possession on their records. They've been careful."

Clicking at her laptop, Jacinda brought up the original image of the two dead men. "The Powders, it seems, are sending a message that they won't tolerate encroachment. The alley borders a known Powders neighborhood. Why they were there is unknown. That they were armed indicates they had hostile intent, but they could've been carrying with only self-defense in mind."

Vance tapped his pen on the table. "Gangbangers carrying in enemy territory looks like a no-brainer. What do we know about time of death? Maybe these guys were there to pop off at a crowd of Powders and ended up wishing they'd brought more guns."

Max stepped forward and lifted his eyebrows at Jacinda, as if asking permission. She waved him on.

"Those and other questions are being considered as we pursue this investigation. I want to encourage you all to remember we're talking about people first. They may have belonged to criminal organizations, but each of these dead men also had a family, friends, a life they wanted to live."

"Understood," Vance nodded, "I just meant to point out possible explanations."

"Of course, and that's appreciated, Agent Jessup. There's another strange thing about all this, however." Max frowned, an edge of frustration leaking into his words. "We have an informant in the Powders, and word is, nobody knows who did this or why."

Denae sat back from the table. "Are we sure the informant is still safe? If they've been tumbled, the Powders could be keeping them in the dark, or feeding them false intel to put us off track."

"We considered that angle. Based on what we've received related to other Powders activity, we're confident our asset is safe."

Vance tapped his pen on his knee. "Well, that's one piece of good news."

Considering the multiple ways this conflict could escalate, and the people it might affect, Denae had to agree.

The task force liaison paced like a pastor about to present a rousing sermon. "Something to keep in mind here is that the Drivers have the market on meth cornered right now. Currently, their product is quite distinctive. It's crystal clear, like glass, and it's driving the market prices in these neighborhoods. The Powders have been trying to figure out how to edge in since the Drivers arrived in D.C. If they wanted a war, they've had time to start one. The timing here doesn't make sense to me."

Vance lifted a hand. "Maybe they weren't prepared for the competition to be so fierce and so fast. This could be their first move after a few months of preparation."

"That's another possibility we're considering, though I'm reluctant to give it much credit. Powders activity has followed a predictable pattern of small-scale burglaries, vandalism, some drug trade, sex trafficking, and catalytic converter thefts."

"Murder isn't in their wheelhouse?"

Max shook his head, but Denae wasn't ready to let the issue drop.

"Couldn't they just be claiming ignorance because they want to protect their own? Your informant might not be at a level that grants access to the gang leader's explicit intentions. They and other low-level members could be operating on limited intel."

"I don't think so." Deeper frown lines appeared around Max's lips. "I trust my informant, and he's on top of things. If he says the Powders don't know who did this," he motioned to the screen, "then they don't know. And to make that clearer, he tells me the Powders have been trying to avoid a war with the Drivers."

"But," Jacinda stepped forward, her fists on her hips, "these men were killed on Powders turf. Whether they've been planning for a gang war or not, that's shaping up to be exactly what both gangs are going to get."

"Could it be an outside player pulling strings?" Emma leaned forward over the table. "Are we just talking about street cred and turf?"

Max shook his head. "First, I don't know if there's an outside player or who it would be. I'm simply saying that the Powders, as a group, don't know who did this. An individual member might, and that puts an even more troubling piece onto the board. If someone inside the gang is vying for control, that person could be stirring up a war with the hope that it creates a power vacuum."

"But you don't believe that?" Emma's eyebrows rose a fraction.

He turned to the screen. "Correct. I don't see that being the case. An attack like this, and with where these men were...on Powders turf...why would they have been there if not to push the boundaries? Like Agent Jessup suggests, it looks like a no-brainer. And yet, we've seen no sign that the Drivers want to start a war any more than the Powders do."

Leo raised his tablet stylus. "What about other competition?"

Max faced the agents again. "It's bigger than turf. Both gangs have hands in the heroin trade, importing from somewhere along the coast. We assume overlap in their suppliers, but that hasn't been confirmed yet."

Denae lifted a hand. "If it were confirmed, would that be enough to trigger a war? Is heroin that big?"

The man actually chuckled. "Heroin is heroin. The drug trade is just another type of pie for gangs to make money from, and every gang wants to be the only one at the table when the proceeds are served." He coughed into his fist. "The Drivers have the upper hand in meth, specifically, because they have a supplier of crystal clear, which is what buyers prefer. But it's a fight for the title with heroin."

At that, Jacinda pulled up a map of Baltimore and D.C., pointing out the two gangs' territories marked respectively by gray and pink shading. "The Drivers were top dog in Baltimore and simply outgrew the terrain. They started edging into D.C., which has traditionally been Powders territory, along with over a hundred and forty smaller gangs in various neighborhoods."

"When did they start edging in?" Emma didn't look up from the notes she was taking.

"Approximately six months ago." Jacinda pointed to the pink shaded area. "The Powders have had free run of D.C. for years. Nobody challenged them, and smaller gangs quickly moved aside or merged with them. That changed when the Drivers came to town."

Max sighed, glancing down at his phone before refocusing on the group. "Violence was probably inevitable, but this seems oddly personal." He waved his phone. "My people on the scene tell me these guys spent their evening at a nearby strip club called Night Trips, which is a known Drivers hangout. Glitter on Jax Duran's jeans tipped off our techs, and now it's been confirmed."

Jacinda gazed around the room. "Any more questions?"

Denae remained as silent as the others, even as she felt a scream building in her throat. But that could wait. It would have to.

Jacinda shut down her laptop and began doling out assignments. "All right, then. Denae and Emma, check out the crime scene and surrounding areas, including the club. Leo and Vance, find whatever friends and family of the victims are willing to talk. Assuming you're up to fieldwork, Leo?"

When Leo nodded, Jacinda continued. "We're expecting an expedited warrant to search the victims' properties, in the event they are no longer occupied."

She traded glances with Max, who gave a pinch-faced nod. "Mia, you and Max will be doing what research you can and checking in again with Max's informant in the Powders, now that he's had more time to put his ear to the ground. Get going."

Denae put up a hand. "Jacinda, Max, if you'd both be okay with it, I'd rather be on the research side of things here."

The SSA's eyebrows shot up. "Explain."

"Just…I grew up around gang activity. Lost friends to it. I think I'd be a better asset to the investigation behind the scenes."

Max regarded her. "You don't think your firsthand experience might be of value in the field?"

"I think it might make me a liability, sir."

The room was quiet for a beat or two before Jacinda spoke. "Fair enough, Agent Monroe, and I applaud your clear thinking. You and Max can head up the work here. Mia, you'll partner with Emma this morning. Let's go, everyone."

Denae excused herself to use the restroom. She sped toward the door, phone in hand and hoping with everything she had that her call wouldn't go straight to voicemail.

5

Mia and Emma sat in folding metal chairs in the cramped back office at Night Trips. Video monitors in front of them replayed the previous night's activities, including Juan Carlos "Jax" Duran and Charlie "Rux" Rucker's final appearance at the club.

Mia rolled her eyes at Jax's antics.

He shimmied in place, belly against the stage and waving his hands at strippers who were happy to take his money. Mia shook her head as the twenty-year-old tucked yet another bill into a G-string that was already crowded with them.

"I guess they enjoyed their last night out."

On the other monitor, the one Emma had said she'd watch so they could divide and conquer, Mia glanced over to see Rux getting a lap dance in a private room. None of his clothes had come off, even if the dancer in front of him was two spaghetti straps shy of being completely nude.

Rux couldn't have been more different from Jax, the way he sat back in an easy chair, sipping on a drink while the dancer swayed over him.

Mia stretched in her chair, arching backward far enough that her hands touched the door of the tiny security office. "I'm not seeing anything suspicious, just a couple guys buying some sex work, and it's even the legal kind."

"So far, anyway, but we know that guy is only twenty years old." Emma stabbed a finger at Jax's dancing image. A dark beer bottle was clearly visible in his left hand, and he took a pull from it before stuffing more money in the nearest G-string.

A knock sounded at the door, and the manager they'd spoken to earlier, a guy who called himself Veevee, popped his head in. He met Mia's gaze before nodding at the monitors. "What I told you. Just a normal night for these guys."

Mia paused the feed just as Jax leaned in to whisper some sweet nothing in a stripper's ear. "They come here a lot?"

Veevee leaned on the doorframe and crossed his arms, but more in the way of boredom than a defensive stance. He couldn't be older than his mid-thirties, but reeked of stale sweat and had the jaded expression of someone twice his age. "I mean, yeah, sure. Not every night, but they were regulars. Knew the girls' names, had their favorite bartenders and all that."

Mia stood, put on her best dimpled smile, and took a step toward him, forcing him to back up out of the cramped office space. "And your bartenders are all certified or have taken approved training to be responsible servers of alcohol, correct?"

The manager straightened and met her gaze. "If these guys were underage...look, they're Drivers. This place is basically their bar, and they just let me run it."

"And knowingly serving alcohol to someone not of legal age will let you pay a fine and have your license to sell suspended."

He actually laughed. "Well, that's where this goes sideways on you. I'm not the licensee, am I? I don't even pour the drinks."

Mia let the issue go, but she'd be putting in a call to MPD when they were done. Veevee might've wanted to dodge a charge, but as the acting manager of the establishment, he'd be on the hook for anything illegal that occurred under the roof.

His days of avoiding responsibility for what went on inside the bar were over.

Mia turned back to the screens. On the one in front of Emma, the dancer backed off Rux. He grinned and picked up his drink after handing her a bill.

Veevee inched his way into the office and pointed at him. "You see that? These guys always opened their wallets for my girls. Tipped well and didn't disrespect 'em or try to cop a feel. Rux there, he even helped us out when a customer went for Celine, like," he lifted his hands in front of his chest, "well, you get the idea."

Mia managed to keep her smile in place and her sarcastic response to herself…barely.

Emma jumped in. "Is what we're seeing here representative of both men when they visited this establishment?"

"Oh, yeah. The young one, though," he gestured at Jax, still frozen mid-whisper, "he never stopped hitting on my girl Amber."

"Your girl, as in girlfriend?" Mia raised an eyebrow." Or employee?"

"The second one. You askin' if I sliced these dudes? That'd be a hell to the no, Little Miss Federella."

Mia's smile fell, to be replaced with a stern glare. "I wasn't aware that the cause of death had been made public, Veevee. Care to tell us how you know they were 'sliced'?"

"Pretty hard to miss all the talk on the street. Especially when it happened in Powders town. Word gets around if something like that goes down, ya know?"

Mia knew, but she wasn't about to let him go that easily. "You've no doubt provided an alibi to MPD. Care to share that with me and Agent Last?"

He put his hands on his hips and shook his head. "Damn Feds. Yeah, I'll share. I was here until closing, which was right about the time Rux and Jax took off. They left, Amber and the other girls tried to get a few more customers in from across the street. One guy bit and dropped a whole five dollars for the girl on the pole. Didn't even buy a drink before he left."

"And you have no reason to believe he or any of your other customers might've followed Jax and Rux on their way home? Maybe on a tip from you that they'd just left?"

Veevee apparently knew when it was time to put his tail between his legs. He lowered his voice, but he still had some bark left to share. "Why the fuck would I want them dead? These guys were good to me and this bar. Always tipped, always looked out for all my girls."

"I'll need your name and a contact number, Mr…?"

With a defeated slump to his shoulders, he dropped his hands off his hips and gave his name. "Hanson. Vincent Victor Hanson. I'll get you that number before you go."

Emma's video was still playing. Mia watched from behind her as Rux disappeared from the little back room and Jax arrived to take his place. The twenty-year-old gazed at the stripper with puppy-dog eyes as she stripped for him, swaying lazily around his chair.

Emma pointed at her. "This woman who gave both of them dances is…?"

"That's Amber. She was sad to hear about them getting killed. The tips they gave her were something else."

Mia sighed, watching the same dance play out once more. Jax looked more like a teenager than a man, he was so entranced with the woman. "I don't guess she's here today?"

"After getting off at two last night and then hearing about Jax and Rux?" Veevee snorted, rubbing at his lined forehead. "I'll try to get her on the phone, and I'll get you my number. Gimme a minute."

As he disappeared into the hall, Emma paused her video feed. "He's running a strip bar and serving to a twenty-year-old, and he talks about the dancers like he owns them. 'My girl Amber' and 'all my girls.' This place is going down."

Those same suspicions had been prickling along Mia's scalp as well. If his involvement in sex-trafficking proved accurate, he'd be looking at jail time, possibly twenty years if any of the club's dancers were underage when they'd been "hired."

"Can't argue with you there." She pushed play on her monitor again, and Emma did the same on the one she'd been watching.

On the backroom feed, Amber perched up on the arms of the chair that Jax occupied. The stripper swayed her hips and shook her blond hair in front of her breasts so that the strands nearly tickled the young man's nose.

"She actually looks like she's having fun," Mia pursed her lips, "but I don't know how she's staying balanced on those heels."

Emma chuckled. "Part of the job, I guess."

Another quick knock on the door signaled Veevee's return. He passed in a sticky note with a number on it, along with a cell phone, mouthing Amber's name as he did.

Emma took the phone with a nod and hit speaker. "Amber? This is Special Agent Emma Last. I have Special Agent Mia Logan with me. Can I get your last name?"

"It's Wilson." The breathy voice sighed, and there was the

sound of liquid pouring into a glass. "I don't know what I can tell you."

Mia reached out and paused the feed in front of her. "We understand you provided dances to Juan Carlos Duran and Charlie Rucker last night, and that they were regulars of yours."

"If you say so, sure."

"Excuse me?" Emma raised an eyebrow. "You're saying you weren't with them last night?"

"No," the woman paused to take a drink of something, "I'm saying I'll have to take your word for it that those are their names. I danced for a lotta dudes last night, but I think I know who you mean. Jax and Ruxie, right? Yes, I knew them, and yes, they were regulars."

"Fair enough." Emma's shoulders relaxed a touch as she sat back in her seat so that the plastic creaked beneath her. "What can you tell us about how they were acting last night? You notice anything out of the ordinary?"

"Them two are about as ordinary as it gets. Ruxie sips his gin and sits back like he's the king of the world just watching it go by. Jax's more like a little schoolboy than a man, and I swear..." she sighed, her voice going quieter, "he kept trying to get me to go home with him last night, before he and Ruxie took off."

"Did you see what kind of car they got into? What color, make, or model?"

The line was silent for a moment. "They were just walking. Mighta had a car down the street, or somebody picked 'em up, I don't know."

"And how would you say they behaved last night, in the club? Were they more excited than normal, quieter? Reserved or angry?"

"No, nothing like that. They were just...Ruxie and Jax, ya know? Like always."

Emma waited, hoping Amber would offer more details, anything that might help explain why the two gang members had wandered into enemy territory.

"Amber, did you know they were Drivers?"

Silence held the line for a minute before Amber replied. "They were good to me. Never got violent in the club and looked out for all the dancers. I hope you figure out who killed 'em."

Emma's eyes went hooded, and Mia understood why. The stripper sounded sad and truthful. And the men on the video feed had been young, just having a night out. Gang members or not, they hadn't deserved what had come for them in that alleyway.

Mia saved Amber's number to her phone, then read out her number, making the dancer promise to call if she thought of anything. When she hung up, she set the phone aside and frowned. "Shall we go outside and retrace their steps? I don't know about you, but I am not a fan of the smell of a strip club in the morning."

6

Emma let Mia lead the way down the cramped hallway from the strip club's back offices. She stayed close behind her colleague, happy for a chance to exit the dark, claustrophobic conditions.

As they emerged into the lounge area, Emma waved to get Veevee's attention. He was nursing a mug of steaming coffee and inhaling a croissant at the bar.

"You ladies all done?"

Mia extended a hand, holding her and Emma's business cards. "We left your phone by the monitors. Thanks for your time and your number."

Emma flapped the sticky note he'd given them. "I'll be double-checking with MPD about that alibi. I'm guessing they already told you, but don't leave the area."

He stared at them and silently sipped his coffee, not saying another word as they turned to exit the club.

Emma waited until they were several steps out the door before calling Jacinda with an update.

"We have contact information for the dancer who interacted with the two victims last night. Amber Wilson is her name. We spoke to her, and she claims to have known the victims by their street names only, Jax and Rux. We should probably get a tox screen on the victims as well. They were drinking pretty heavily last night. That might have figured into Jax and Rux's decision to end up in enemy territory."

Mia bumped her on the shoulder. "He was Ruxie for most of that phone call. That could indicate a relationship beyond him being a regular."

Emma passed that along to Jacinda as well.

"Good work, both of you. I'll get this to Max's task force. But I imagine they're well acquainted with Ms. Wilson if her regulars are Drivers. And we have tox back already. BAC levels for both men were over the limit."

"One other thing on that, Jacinda. Let Max know this bar should be under surveillance if it isn't already. The manager, a guy named Veevee Hanson, confirmed the Drivers effectively own the establishment." Emma read off the phone number he'd given them and said she'd follow up with MPD about his alibi.

"Don't bother. Max has his people collecting everything the police have obtained so far. For now, head over to the crime scene. MPD are still examining every stretch of pavement between the two locations. You might spot their techs on your way. Anything else?"

"Only that Veevee claims he's not the licensee for the club's alcohol service, and he admitted to knowingly allowing his bartenders to serve Jax Duran, who was underage."

Jacinda explained that Max was already working with MPD and ABCA to revoke the club's liquor license. "He's not optimistic, though. Short of condemning the building, it'll be hard to keep the place from operating. Another licensee will pop up, and it'll be business as usual within a month."

The SSA ended the call, leaving Emma and Mia standing in front of the strip club, where the club's parking area sat on one side of the building, entered by a gate that faced the street. An alleyway ran along the other side. Emma assessed both avenues of approach to the club.

"They were on foot, which seems odd, doesn't it? There's a parking lot right there."

"Could be Amber was right. Somebody picked them up. If they were intentionally moving into Powders territory, they'd have wanted a quick getaway and would want the car out of sight for any potential witnesses."

"But this is a Drivers bar, right? Their home turf. Should we walk the area?"

They both looked at the Bureau vehicle parked on the street. Mia shook her head. "It's alarmed and locked, and it's only ten in the morning. But Jacinda'll have an aneurysm if it gets boosted while we're investigating an alleyway. I'll drive?"

Emma agreed and waited while her colleague crossed the street and got the SUV started.

Mia nosed into the alleyway, and Emma stepped up to open the door. She paused with her fingers just touching the handle.

A deep, almost suffocating cold descended around her, pressing in from all sides and rooting her to the sidewalk. Mia's eyes rounded in surprise, and she mouthed, *Are you okay?*

Emma nodded and pulled the door open. "Just got a blast of Other cold. There's a ghost around here somewhere."

She climbed into the SUV and shut the door, halting with one hand raised to pull on her seat belt. Charlie Rucker's ghost lurked up ahead beside a restaurant dumpster. He stood in a puddle of greasy water and what was probably vomit.

His neck was a mass of bloody tissue, and his shaved head

tilted to one side, away from the wound that had taken his life. But his white eyes were on Emma as Mia rolled them deeper into the alley.

Emma caught Mia's shoulder to stop her. "I have someone to talk to out there. Do me a favor and pull up next to that dumpster."

"Who is it?" Mia asked as she brought them alongside the restaurant's back entrance where the dumpster sat.

"Looks like Rux. Black, bald, approximately six feet tall. Major trauma to the left side of his neck."

Mia's lips thinned into a nervous line. "Even though I believe you, this is still the weirdest thing I never thought I'd be doing as an agent. Can we make this quick?"

"That depends on him, I guess."

Emma lowered the window and had already formed the question she intended to ask. Drawing breath was getting difficult with the pervasive cold surrounding her.

"Rux?" Her whisper had no effect, and she tried again a touch louder. "Rux, I can see you. Can you tell me who did this to you?"

He wavered, shifting his weight side to side. His hands bunched and un-bunched in his pockets in rhythm with his stepping. The ghost was anxious, maybe flat-out traumatized and in shock, if that was possible for ghosts.

"Jax and me's gone. Black cat scratched us good." He flickered out of view to reappear up ahead.

"Mia, he moved to that next dumpster. Let's keep going down this alley. If Rux takes a detour, I'll let you know."

They pulled alongside the ghost's new position, and Mia idled the vehicle while Emma lowered her window. She called to him again, but he didn't reply.

One hand darted up to swipe over his shaved head, leaving a trail of blood where it ran. "Claws in the dark. Jax and me's gone." He vanished again, going out of sight with trails of his ghostly figure spraying out in every direction.

Emma relayed his message to Mia and looked for him to appear again, and he did. But farther along, near an intersecting alley.

"He's on the move again."

Mia got the SUV in motion, and Emma updated her on Rux's position as the ghost continued his pattern of popping in and out of view. He was getting farther away each time.

Finally, they reached a cross street at the end of the alley. Rux's ghost hovered there briefly, then winked out of view. The deep Other cold that clutched at Emma evaporated, leaving her free to breathe fully without feeling like her lungs might freeze.

She checked their GPS. The crime scene was a few streets over, on the other side of a narrow greenbelt that ran between apartment blocks.

"That's Powders town over there. If his ghost is trying to lead us there, I'd say he and Jax walked this alley on their way."

Mia slapped the steering wheel. "But why? The videos we saw didn't give me the impression they were on the prowl or getting ready to hit the competition. Amber said they were just their normal money-stuffing, boozy selves."

"Maybe they were waiting for a predetermined time to make a hit."

"But with no sign of being anxious or stressed? How many hits could Jax have under his belt? The way Amber talked about him, it sounds like he was just a goofy kid."

And when it went down, only Rux fired his gun. Jax didn't even get a single shot off.

"Let's see what the techs have at the scene. Maybe something there will help us make sense of a ghost who's afraid of cats."

Mia drove the few blocks to the crime scene at a cautious pace. "Let me know if he shows up again?"

Emma said she would, but all signs of the Other had faded.

Back to nothing but boring, real-world crime scene details and city streets that could stand to be improved.

The SUV shuddered as Mia took them over a series of potholes and a deep gutter.

After they pulled in and parked at the crime scene, another nearby alley, Emma sidestepped a tech and walked closer to the building where the bloody *Death by Powder* message had been painted in six-inch-high letters.

Close up, an unevenness in the writing became clear, with some circles at the joints of letters suggesting the words had been written by a finger. Emma caught the tech's eye and pointed at one of the dots. "Any chance we're gonna have fingerprints here?"

"Doubtful." The man shrugged. "Based on the stroke pattern and texture, we're probably looking at a gloved finger."

Emma sighed and turned back to Mia, who stood over the body of Juan Carlos "Jax" Duran. His young face was set in a grimace of shock. A tech knelt beside him, collecting fibers from the asphalt, but Emma guessed they'd come from his clothes.

Given the narrow alley, another tech stepped along behind his colleague with his back to the wall, sidestepping in order to get by. Which brought up another question…

Emma glanced up and down the alley, eyes narrowed. "How did someone sneak up on these guys?"

Mia gestured to the dumpster. "Came out from behind it?"

"Or on top of it." Emma went to her toes but couldn't quite see over the bulky metal container. Above it, though, a fire escape ladder ran up the side of the building. She eyed the ladder, wondering, and then flagged the tech's attention. "You guys make sure to check the top of the dumpster, that fire escape, and the roof it leads to, okay? See if our killer came or went that way."

He nodded, jotting himself a note.

Pacing over to Charlie Rucker's body, Mia sighed. "What do you think, Emma? Could somebody be setting the gangs against each other from the outside?"

"I just can't figure out why." Emma knelt by the corpse, noting that Rux's eyes had been a striking deep brown before the Other had turned them white. "I mean, if these gangs are both vying to be top dog around here, we'd...what? Be looking at a totally unknown party trying to move in and divide and conquer? That would have to be a big organization. We should check with the National Gang Intelligence Center, see if they have any leads."

"I've never hoped you were more wrong, but yeah, we should check just in case." Mia shook her head and adjusted her coat. Then, catching Emma's eye, she nodded toward the SUV. "Shall we?"

Emma opened her mouth to reply but stopped short. The dumpster beside Rux's body was the same dirty green as all the others in the alley, but three strange streaks, which appeared to be gouged into the metal, caught her eye. She waved Mia over. "Look at this."

Mia whistled. "They look like claw marks. I guess we should be on the lookout for Wolverine, huh?"

"Or a Clifford-sized black cat, like Rux said." Signaling for a tech to come over when he got a chance, Emma couldn't do much more than shake her head. "I mean, we can't be sure these marks are fresh, but I'd wager they're related."

She pulled out her phone and took a close-up shot from multiple angles. Whatever made them, it scraped the dumpster's paint away and left a distinctly clawlike signature. The morning sun glinted off the exposed bare metal.

On top of the bloody writing just steps away, the marks made her feel as if they'd stepped inside a slasher film.

Emma sent the photo off to Jacinda and the rest of the team, hoping Max's informant might have some enlightening information. "I'm thinking this wasn't Wolverine. More like Freddy Krueger."

Mia gave an exaggerated shiver that didn't look entirely forced. "Perish the thought. Perish the damn thought before it takes shape. Can we get out of here now?"

Emma waited for the tech to come over and get a glimpse of the claw marks, and then she nodded. She gave one last look around the alley in case Rux's or Jax's ghosts might make another appearance, but no luck.

I don't know how they could help, though. It wasn't a ghost who left that message in blood.

7

Leo parked the Bureau SUV against the curb in front of Charlie Rucker's address and left the engine idling. Vance tapped his shoulder.

"We getting out?" His partner gave him a nudge this time. "Hey, Ambrose. You in there?"

"Yeah, sorry. Just thinking about Denae. What she said about growing up around gang activity. She could've been a statistic like these two guys, you know?"

Vance met his gaze. "But she wasn't. C'mon." He climbed out and shut his door, standing with his back to the window. Fresh, deep-green paint covered the shotgun row house, and there was a new iron grating across the screen door. The place looked small but well-kept, and the bright-white shutters hung straighter than just about any other door or window on the block.

It stood out because the houses on either side of it could've used a new coat of paint and some carpentry work to look half as nice.

Stepping out of the SUV, Leo noticed a curtain being

pulled sideways just enough to peer out. He motioned with a hand for Vance's attention. "Someone's inside."

When they reached the porch, Leo raised his fist to knock, but the door opened first. A heavyset woman with dark skin and curly hair working to escape a bun stood in front of them. She could've been in her thirties or forties if Leo had to guess.

The woman swiped tears from both cheeks. "You must be here about Charlie."

Leo flashed his badge. "Special Agents Leo Ambrose and Vance Jessup, ma'am. Are you Mr. Rucker's…?"

"I'm Charlie's mother, Jenna Rucker. Come on in." The woman backed up a step and opened the door wide. Leo led the way into a small entryway with warm, wood-grain floors. To the right, a fireplace framed in white marble filled the far wall of a cozy seating area. The narrow home had been completely redone, and the living area opened into a neat, bright kitchen.

Vance stepped in behind him. "Holy cow."

Leo just stopped, fighting not to show his surprise, but the woman *tsk*ed, and wiped at her face again.

"My Charlie had good taste and redid a lot of this himself. Was gonna sell it for a profit and make over another property next year. Only had the tile left to do in the second bathroom."

Leo followed the woman over to a low-slung couch and took a seat across from her in a cowhide armchair. "He was a house flipper?"

"He was. Charlie had ambition. Was putting that money to good use." Jenna Rucker leaned back in the couch. "He wasn't gonna be a Driver forever. He had plans."

Doesn't sound like someone who would walk into Powders territory looking for a fight.

Vance settled into the seat beside Leo after examining a high-end mirror. "But he was a Driver, Mrs. Rucker, if you'll forgive us for saying so. Did he have enemies you could name or describe for us?"

She frowned. "If you wear that tattoo, you got enemies. Just how it is, but Charlie wasn't bad. He got jumped into the gang when he was eleven…maybe it was ten. I forget. He was a good kid. He didn't deserve this."

"Had he said anything about the Powders?" Leo leaned forward, holding her gaze. "Anything about recent trouble?"

"Just that there was peace for now, and I should stop worrying." She shrugged and wiped away another tear. "Same thing he always said. He moved out when he was sixteen."

"And his part in the gang…?"

"He ran distributors. Was going to come to an end eventually." Jenna spoke firmly, though Leo saw a shade of doubt in her eyes. "He was doing well for himself. Working more on flips than on Drivers business. He just…couldn't leave his friends behind."

"And had he been in any fights recently?" Vance had his tablet out, ready to take down anything the woman might offer, but she only shook her head.

"Charlie didn't fight. He had enemies like anybody in a gang will, but I'd never seen him bloody or with his knuckles all scraped up like he'd been fighting. He considered the other Drivers family. Tried to encourage them to think about their futures, like I did with him."

One more notch in the they didn't go there looking for trouble *column. Unless Charlie Rucker wore one face to talk to his mother and another when he was out on the streets.*

Leo stood up with a sigh. If the killer hadn't been targeting Charlie or Jax as payback for a slight, then maybe they'd gone down that alley to start something. As worrying as it was to consider, a large-scale gang war seemed to be brewing. "Mrs. Rucker, I am sorry for your loss. We're going to—"

She held up a hand to stop him, even as she rose from her seat. "Don't make promises you can't keep. Just stop any further violence, please. It's hard enough to survive around here without our boys dying on us even when they're trying to make a good way out."

With a nod, Leo passed over his card and then followed Vance to the door.

Outside, he listened as the door locked behind them, then glanced up and down the street as he headed to the SUV. On second inspection, he could see that although the neighborhood at large was somewhat run-down, a lot of the houses on this block showed signs of newish landscaping and other improvements. Renovation was going around, it seemed.

"Putting gang money to good use?"

Vance scoffed. "Maybe Rux was. But notice that she didn't deny he was in the gang. This money didn't come from nowhere."

That's as true as it is sad.

Fighting off the sight of the grieving mother, Leo programmed the GPS for Jax's duplex, which was twenty minutes away without traffic.

The traffic gods were good to them. They arrived in fifteen.

Juan Carlos Duran's duplex was one of four that stood in a row along the street behind a patch of dead grass. Each of them featured a porch leaning at a sharp angle, making the whole row look like a jack-o'-lantern's teeth. Leo imagined the dwellings were cramped and dimly lit inside. Their exteriors showed more wood than paint.

Vance tucked his bag deeper into the floorboard area of the SUV, hiding it from view. "And these guys hung together?"

Leo was already out of the SUV, just in time to see a petite, light-skinned blond come around the side of the first duplex, which was the one they had on file as belonging to Jax. He flagged her down before she got a chance to pretend she hadn't seen them. "You a friend of Jax Duran?"

She frowned, fidgeting her hands into the pockets of her oversize hoodie. Beneath it, her legs were bare and as fit as an athlete's. He couldn't help wondering if she wore shorts or even anything under the hoodie, and whether she had a mother worrying about the same thing at home. She looked that young.

Vance coughed, fighting for her attention as he held up his badge. "My partner asked you a question."

"Fine, okay. Yeah, we're friends. You could say that, I guess."

Flashing his badge, Leo nodded around the side of the house. "I'm Special Agent Leo Ambrose. You know what happened to Jax last night?"

"I heard." She shook her long blond hair away from her face, and Leo noticed glitter clinging to the edges of her cheeks. Leftover from makeup, maybe.

"Mind telling us your name?"

Her eyes narrowed, and she gnawed at her lower lip. Vance opened his jacket to reveal the handcuffs on his left hip as he put his badge away.

The young woman huffed and swiped at her hair again. "Whatever. I'm Amber Wilson, okay? I work at Night Trips, where Jax was at last night."

"What are you doing here this morning?" Leo gestured to the side of the house. "We gonna find out you broke in if we go around that way?"

"No!" Her cheeks went red, eyes a little wider. "He stole something that's mine when I was giving him a dance last week. Distracted me with money and took it from my clothes."

Leo waited for her to elaborate, but she looked like she might just flee instead, so he prodded her. "Stole what, Amber?"

"A necklace." Her hand moved from her pocket to her neck, as if to touch something that wasn't there. She fluttered her fingers against her skin, an expensive manicure glinting in the sunlight as she did. "It was an antique that belonged to my great-aunt, and this seemed like my one chance to get it back. I talked to him about it last night, but he said he didn't have it, so I figure it's here."

"He said he didn't have it on him or didn't have it at all?"

"Both. Neither. I don't know." She blew air out of her mouth, fluttering her long bangs and rolling her eyes like a teenager. "He kept trying to get me to go home with him, and I'd already told him no, like, a million times. I just want my necklace."

Vance caught her eye again. "And what can you tell us about Jax and his Drivers buddies?"

She scowled, aging a decade with the expression. "Nothing I haven't already said to the women who called me earlier. They said they were Feds. You guys do talk, right? Can I go now?"

Vance glanced at Leo for an argument, but he only shrugged. It seemed she'd already spoken with Emma and Mia, so they could compare notes about her later.

Leo took down her contact information as she tapped her sneaker in the dead grass. He and Vance both handed over their business cards. "Call if you think of anything. And we'll be checking on the address and phone number you've provided."

"I'll add these to my collection." She shrugged and walked away, making a show of dropping their business cards in the gutter.

Shaking his head, Leo turned and headed toward Jax's front porch.

The old wood slats creaked beneath his boots but held his weight. A knock garnered no response. "If anyone's inside, this is the FBI executing a warrant to search the premises." He and Vance put on gloves and shoe covers, then Leo tried the door.

It creaked open with a little shove.

"Nice security." Leo stepped inside, eyeing the mess of empty pizza boxes and takeout containers that littered secondhand furniture. The one semi-clean area off to one side of the living room boasted a high-end gaming setup and four expensive flat-screen monitors.

Two of them were still on, showing a racing game. Leo took photographs of the screens, making sure the player names were in focus.

"Somebody named 'Snake2121' knows what they're doing. Look at the scores. Poor 'ShortHop' is down by a few million points."

"You'd think Jax'd lock up to protect that rig, at least."

Vance turned and examined the front door latch and strike plates. "Huh, I stand corrected. It looks like he did or would have. This is a new dead bolt, and I'd bet these are three- or four-inch screws going into the studs behind the doorframe."

"You think somebody was here and bugged out when word got around the Feds were coming?"

"Probably. Not much we can do about it now, but MPD should probably have patrol add this address to their regular beat. Who knows? Maybe ShortHop's our unsub."

Leo laughed. "My money's on Snake2121, but no bet, just

in case. I'll search the bedroom while you take the pizzeria out here."

Jax's bedroom was no cleaner than the living room. The most suspicious thing Leo found was a handgun lacking any serial number or manufacturer markings—a ghost gun.

This kid wasn't even twenty-one, and he'd already engaged in a federal crime that could've landed him in jail for a year at least.

Leo took photos of the gun's position, where he'd found it in a bedside table drawer, before placing it in an evidence bag. Expensive clothes hung in the closet, suggesting where Jax Duran's priorities lay, as did jewelry in another nightstand.

He examined each strand of gold and silver chains, including a few pendants with precious stones in them. They all looked like recent designs if Leo had to guess. Nothing looked like it would qualify as vintage, much less antique. And nothing came off dainty or feminine.

Guess Amber's necklace is still unaccounted for, providing she knows the difference between antique and something that happens to be older than she is.

Leo joined Vance in the kitchen. He was busy poking through drawers. From the look on his face, he hadn't had any luck either. Without hesitation, they weaved back through the pizza boxes and out to the front porch.

Leo pulled the front door shut behind them, ensuring it seated in the jamb.

A dark-skinned girl appeared around the hood of their SUV, like she'd been hiding and waiting for them to come outside. "Hey, y'all got the time? I'm late for an appointment."

Leo stepped off the porch and reached for his phone, but Vance put a hand on his arm.

"How about some ID, miss?"

She approached, cautiously glancing around, and raised her hands as if they had their guns on her. She looked even younger than Amber but was taller and wore her hair in a close braid around her head. Her t-shirt and jeans hung loose on her frame.

Leo held up his badge, and Vance did the same.

She simply met Leo's gaze and kept her hands up. A Drivers tattoo showed on her right wrist. She spoke quietly, almost in a whisper. "You two looking for who hit Rux and Jax?"

"We are." Leo handed over his card. "Are you saying you have information that might help us solve the case?"

She shrugged and kept her hands in the air and didn't accept the card. "Ain't saying anything like that, because I don't know it. Jax was a friend, and because of that, I'm telling ya, ya gotta talk to Snake. Him and that girl he brings around here. They know what's up."

Leo blinked. "Snake and which girl?" He moved forward, and Vance stepped to the side to cut off the girl's retreat. But she was fast on her feet and skipped back two steps, putting herself behind the SUV again.

"Anyone knows anything, it's Snake and his girl, but you didn't hear it from me."

"Okay, but who are you?" Vance's question ended in a shout, as the girl had already turned to sprint away. He sighed. "We could follow her."

"Down a one-way street?" Leo pointed in the direction the girl had gone, her tall form already disappearing around a corner. "I doubt she was even carrying ID if she just wanted to pass on that tip. At least we've got something to go on."

Vance cursed under his breath and stalked toward the vehicle, Leo following behind him. They'd have to ask Max if he knew about someone who went by the name "Snake." Whoever that was, he'd probably been inside Jax's duplex just before Leo and Vance arrived.

But if he's involved in Jax's murder, why would he hang out playing video games in the dead guy's filthy house?

Unless this is about territory, and Snake is moving in?

8

With my feet bouncing in the ring, I was featherlight. Despite the anger, despite the humidity in the gym, despite the stink of sweat around me, I was in the zone, and Curtis knew it. He couldn't beat me today if his life depended on it.

"Face it, Curtis. I'm faster than you." I whipped in and hit him with a hard gut punch, doubling him over before he could reply. He spit out his mouth guard in a hiss of pain.

His gloves on his knees, catching his breath, he eyed me as I kept bouncing. "Dammit, slow up already! What's into you today?"

"Just keeping on my toes. You know how it is."

He waved me off and headed to the corner of the ring for his water bottle. I bounced along behind him, knowing it'd annoy him. I was too high on adrenaline to care.

Let him come at me. See what happens.

Curtis unstrapped his sparring gloves and leaned back against the corner post. "I need a breather." He sucked down water like it was his last. "What the hell you so fired up about anyway?"

"Nothing." Before he could see the lie—he damn sure

wasn't gonna hear it in my voice—I went back to my corner to get a rest of my own.

Taking out the two Ds last night was something else. I didn't want to kill them, just talk to them, get something that'd help me find Snake. But they started up on my girl Celine, and you don't fuck with my family like that.

My sister's face flashed in my mind, and I thought about what Celine told me the other day. About how Snake was hanging around Night Trips with those two Ds I smoked. And about how she saw him going into the Starlight Lounge the next day, hanging around the bar where my sister worked.

Chatting with her. Flirting.

I'd warned him. I warned them both, but she was still letting him in, letting him hang around.

My sister had to pay for her betrayal, and she'd damn sure watch that Driver pay for leading her astray.

We both belong here, with the Powders. Like Dad wanted for us. After he died, the Powders did exactly what any family member should've done. They took us in.

I got up and bounced on my toes, then threw a few punches, ducked and dodged like it was prizefighting night and I was up against a worthy opponent.

Curtis and some other dudes in the gym hooted at me, threw some signs, and whistled.

Let 'em watch and shout and call me shawty like I'm any other bitch they know. They'd be calling me something else before I was done.

My biggest fear was that my sister's betrayal was a symptom, a sign that if she could be disloyal, any of them could.

The Drivers were moving in, both in our territory and in our personal worlds.

I leaped sideways and swirled into the corner, kicking out

and following it with an uppercut. A guy who'd been up on the side of the ring fell backward in surprise, and I snarled at him before I kept shadowboxing.

Curtis hooted and laughed behind me, enjoying the show.

All of them were acting the clowns. Unable to see what I was fighting for.

I turned, shadowboxing ahead of Curtis. "You remember my old man?"

Curtis grinned, bobbing his head. "For sure, for sure. Diamond Chip Jackson taught us everything he knew right here in his gym. Man was a legend."

"That's right. Brought me up to step into his shoes, too, just like you and the rest of the Professor's inner circle."

The Professor. That was what we called Tyler, because he was always talking about rules and running our gang like it was some kind of business. The dude couldn't even muster the courage to tell us to knock it off, almost like he was happy we'd come around to the idea instead of throwing that name around like the insult it was.

Curtis was watching me while I shadowboxed around the ring. I could see him in the corner of my eye, wary almost, like he knew I was thinking about the guy who led the Powders like a schoolteacher instead of a warrior.

"My dad was a real one, eh, Curtis? Knew what it took to get the job done right."

"No argument from me. Chip had dudes winning Golden Gloves. Diamond's Gym was the place to be before…"

He didn't say more, which I appreciated. He could've, after all. Could've talked about how the man we'd all looked up to as a righteous fighter had taught them just fine, dominating the ring. Until he went into the bottle and didn't come out.

But I'd learned from that. Hell, we all had.

Curtis stretched off to the side, maybe working up to

another round. "You hear the Feds started looking into those Ds that got smoked? One of the crew saw them poking around."

"I heard. They find anything?" I kept bouncing on my toes, throwing punches into the air between us.

"Don't know. I can't wait to find out what idiot did it. Last thing we need is damn Feds sniffing up our asses."

I wanted to hit Curtis for calling me an idiot. He couldn't see the bigger picture. The Powders needed to reclaim what was stolen from us.

What good was a family if we didn't stand up for what was ours? If we just let somebody else move in and take up our space, what kind of family could we be?

Might as well be like them homeless dudes, carrying everything they own in a damn garbage bag, just moving along whenever somebody says, "Boo!"

"No, the last thing we need is the Drivers in our business."

Who cared if the Feds were involved? I'd wanted to get Snake, but he wasn't there. Instead, the world had two less Ds taking up oxygen. I'd get Snake next time. Celine'd call me again if he showed up at the club.

I had other ways of finding him too. He liked to paint, and that meant all I had to do was follow the trail of fresh Drivers tags.

Curtis casually shadowboxed in his corner, readying himself to come back in. "Writing in blood, man. That's some *Candyman* shit."

Then I'm a freak show with a knife...that's fine by me.

I grinned, facing him and making a game of mirroring his moves, predicting them. He sped up with me, embracing the old game, jab for jab, dodge for dodge.

Curtis, my brother, and the rest of the Powders had no idea what I was doing for them.

My only regret was the Drivers bastard sleeping with my

sister hadn't been with those two jokers at the club. I'd seen him coming out of there with them one night. Figured that was his hangout.

My girl Celine called to tell me Rux and Jax was back last night. I followed them as long as I could risk it, but Snake never showed.

I'd have to find another way to take him out. And maybe this was better. The Drivers were down two men. Snake would get the message.

Jabbing out, I thought about Snake's face again. How much I'd wanted to lay into him that night when I'd found him lounging around at my sister's in his boxer briefs. Like he owned the place. Owned *her*.

As if he could ever claim a member of my family for his own. That dude was a punk, a nobody with nothing but a can of paint in his hand.

I would've killed him on the spot if my sister hadn't started screaming bloody murder, loud enough to wake the neighbors and bring them running.

They got off easy that night, but I'd take care of her man soon.

Curtis shot both of his arms out to each side and stood straight before he kept bouncing—our old signal that it was time to quit gaming and get back to sparring—and I was ready for him.

I shot forward, giving him an uppercut that knocked him back a step. For a moment, I imagined the blades sprouting from my gloves, flaying his face as I jabbed again, but it was Snake's face earning my rage right now.

Picturing my blades cutting through his eyes and carving up that stupid grin that had stolen away my sister, I jabbed harder, then dodged deeper when Curtis came in with a blow.

I wanted to kill that scum my sister was dating.

Along with any members of the Drivers or anyone who stood in the way of us running this city. Anyone who wasn't willing to fight could just bow on down, and I'd do them the favor of opening their veins, because we weren't having that weak-ass, cowardly shit on my watch.

Anyone who didn't see that now would see it soon. The Powders, my family, needed me to help them attain the power and domination they deserved.

I was gonna see to it that I delivered.

9

Leo swallowed down the beginnings of his second chicken taco, waving at a passerby with the other half. The woman scowled at him and sped up, and he sighed. Across from him, Vance wiped spicy salsa from his lips and chuckled.

They'd parked themselves at a picnic table next to a taco truck partly because it was lunchtime, but also hoping they'd be able to cozy up to someone in this run-down neighborhood and get some information.

Instead, the women in the taco truck were eyeing them with annoyance. Leo forced a smile in their direction and reminded himself to tip them—again—before leaving the area. Even with their dressed-down attire, the one thing he and Vance had managed to accomplish so far was to scare off their normal customer base.

"Least we got a decent lunch out of the neighborhood." Vance sucked sauce off his fingers. "Might have to come back here."

Leo tried to slow down to savor the chicken and avocado, one of his favorite combos in tacos. The ingredients were fresh. The salsa wasn't bad. For D.C., a decent taco. He shrugged at his partner but spoke under his breath. "You haven't had Miami tacos, man. Talk to me after you do."

Taking the last bite of his lunch, Leo wiped his hands on a wadded-up napkin before he fished out his phone. No new texts, which meant Max still hadn't dug up anything on who their "Snake" was. They'd been wandering through Drivers territory aiming to learn something but gotten nowhere.

"We don't even know who that girl was who told us to look for him and 'his girl.'" Vance dropped their trash into a nearby bin. "Maybe it's a wild-goose chase. Hell, that wouldn't surprise me. It would make sense. Helping the Feds probably yields a hefty punishment around here."

"You saw her act. Asking us for the time, then putting her hands up while she was talking. Anybody watching would see her complying, not helping." Leo met Vance's gaze and just stopped himself from ribbing him for fiddling with his tie again. Nobody would've noticed the salsa if he hadn't slopped water onto the fabric to wash it off.

Vance waved him off and stalked onto the sidewalk. "Like you said, we'll go a few more blocks. See if we get anywhere. Your idea, remember?"

Dang it, we're so frustrated, we're starting to bicker. Jacinda'd love us to bring that back to the office.

Still, he followed his partner, keeping his eyes peeled for any person—or thing—that might give them a clue or the time of day. But mostly what he saw was art.

Until now, he'd seen scatterings of it—the blue triangle topped with a red *D* that signaled the Drivers' presence—which reminded him of the last time he'd been in an impoverished neighborhood.

At least now we're not looking for a guy who kills children.

Denae had been with him that time, visiting dilapidated apartment blocks and underfunded schools. She'd grown up in similar conditions and gave him a lot to think about when all he'd been ready to do was brush off these streets as "gang-infested" and "run-down."

"It's horrifying when you first see this stuff, so yeah, I get that you're upset. Most families I knew worked hard, did everything they could for their kids."

He kept her words in mind as he and Vance headed down the block. And it was there he saw something that surprised him.

Every wall in sight was covered in graffiti, but here, the tagging gave way to elaborate artistic renderings. People's faces were depicted in clear, vivid color and were free of damage or any tags that might mar the images.

In one mural, a group of children stood solemnly around a grave site, and the headstone was clearly marked with a woman's name above birth and death dates.

They kept going to the next corner, but upon turning it, Leo's face fell. Drivers' tags overwhelmed anything he might have deemed as art.

He bent to examine the symbol painted across an abandoned car. Here, the red-and-blue symbol served as a base for something more. Tiny, sticklike fingers danced around the edges of the triangle with musical notes, and the *D* shined with a careful shading of blue that made it look three-dimensional.

Vance waved him forward to the side of an overpass and pointed at a portrait. "Max told me about this one. It showed up soon after the Drivers got here."

The gang's symbol was at the center of a life-size, bare-chested illustration of a man. The Hispanic man was so detailed in portraiture that his stubble looked real, and his intense brown eyes had enough depth to seem alive.

Leo leaned in and discovered that he could read the name tattooed on the man's arm. "*Gino.* Who is he?"

"First leader of the Drivers, from way back before they came to D.C."

"The artist is talented, whoever they are. They've really been here only six months? The number of murals on these two blocks alone must've taken weeks to complete."

"Maybe it's not just one artist. We'd have to get paint analysis done and run the images through a tracker. I'd bet Max's people are already on that." Vance wandered over to another rendering, this one of a car decorated in the Drivers' insignia speeding down a rotting fence. "You see these lines?" He pointed to black lines along the edges of the car's tires. "They're in the portrait, too, around the line of the man's jeans. Could be our artist's signature."

Leo leaned in, squinting at them. Their artist had used some tool to spiral them out from a spray of paint and effect the look of…

"Serpents." Vance had said it just as Leo thought it, and he nodded, still examining the art.

"Snakes, you got it. So the guy we're supposed to talk to is the Drivers' artist. That should help us find him, if Max's people are looking into it. I hope Snake doesn't turn out to be our unsub, though."

"Why not?"

Leo thought again about Denae's admonishing words. "I can't help but admire all this, illegal or not. And no matter who painted it or why, it's beautiful, in its own way. It's a statement, yeah, but it's also an expression."

He went to another graffitied part of the fence and stood back to gaze at it. Blue clouds with red birds spiraling across them, each bird wearing a blue *D*. The ruffled puffs of clouds swam with serpents now that Leo knew to look for them. He leaned closer to examine one bird that seemed out of place and caught a scrawled word along the edge of a wing. "Look at this. Says *La Serpent*."

Vance stepped in closer, sighted the signature, and fished out his phone for a picture. Then he moved back to the car, leaned in, and called out after a moment that he'd found it there too. Leo was already on to the next picture and found the scrawl in the beard of a Driver.

"Some of this paint looks pretty fresh. It's still bright, not faded by the sunlight or scratched up."

"Is any of it still wet?"

Leo slipped a glove on and ran a finger over the surface of the image he was inspecting. It didn't smudge, and nothing came off on his glove. "Bone dry. But, still, it looks pretty recent."

"Maybe he's nocturnal. Comes out with the other freaks and does his thing."

"Hey, just a thought, but the people who live in these neighborhoods are people, Vance. Like Max said. Calling them freaks doesn't help us find our killer."

"True enough. Not sure what staring at a bunch of graffiti does for us either. I'll call in what we've found. See where Jacinda wants us to go next."

Leo left his partner to it and walked deeper under the underpass, examining La Serpent's work as he went. The colors shined through even in the darkness, more alive than the neighborhood, and he snapped a few more pictures for Denae.

He hoped they'd convey his appreciation for the art and help her see he understood these streets were more than just gang territory. That might get them through to the next weekend, when gang life would hopefully be about as far away as D.C. would allow.

10
___

Denae, Max, and Jacinda were all gathered around the conference table, a mostly empty pizza box between them. Emma and Mia came in, dropping napkins and sandwich wrappers in the trash. Denae hoped their working lunch hour had been more productive than what she, Max, and Jacinda had accomplished.

"Tell us you got something, Emma. Mia?"

Emma shook her head. "We stopped by a sub shop known to be frequented by Powders, on Max's suggestion. Figured we might overhear something."

"And the result?" Jacinda eyed them both.

With a snort, Mia gave a glib but thorough report of their adventure. "The result was that as soon as we were through the door, every customer, whether eating or in line, suddenly remembered other obligations."

"That's it?" Jacinda stood from the table.

"Emma and I also managed polite conversation with the employees. They were happy to talk about anything related to ordering a sandwich."

"Hence our return to the office," Emma slumped into a

seat, "but it looks like you fared as well as we did. Did anything happen before we got in?"

Denae leaned back in her chair with a sigh. "Max talked to his contact, but the Powders are still clueless."

"Dust is starting to settle," Max finished chewing his pizza crust, "but all my guy could tell me is that their leader, a Tyler 'the Professor' Michaels, is furious. He had a plan to deal with the Drivers that went very differently than this but was keeping quiet about the details. He and his captains are working to find out who's responsible ASAP and punish them."

Denae leaned forward and grabbed a water bottle from a stash left in the middle of the table, watching Max idly as she did. "How did you manage to gain an informant in the Powders anyway?"

Max grinned, while his eyes dimmed a bit. "Luck, more than anything, but I promise it's a trustworthy source."

"Come on, Max, enough is enough." Denae slammed the unopened water bottle on the table. "You want us to trust you, you gotta tell us the play. Who's the source?"

"Denae!" Jacinda glared at her, but Max waved off the reprimand.

"I get it." He sighed and met each of their gazes in turn before turning back to face Denae. "You find out my source isn't sitting in prison, waiting on some deal to get finished, you have to wonder."

Denae lifted an eyebrow. "Go on."

Max reached for another crust and examined it before taking a bite. "My son, Harmon, used to be a member of the Powders. He went by the name of Harmony Still, because he was a musician. He played tenor sax in school."

Denae softened a little. "And?"

The liaison's eyes moistened as he spoke. A tear fell, and he wiped it on his sleeve and picked up the conversation.

"And this was before the Drivers really got a foothold here." He gnawed on the pizza crust some more and grabbed a water bottle for himself.

Denae waited until after he'd taken a sip. "Tell us everything you know."

"Once the Drivers started claiming territory and cornering the meth market, the Powders tried to edge their way in. The Professor wanted a share of the money that the crystal clear was bringing in. But the Drivers had the market on lockdown. Still, the Powders tried to claim what they could, sometimes by robbing Drivers distributors. Harmon was sacrificed when his fellow Powders left him behind so they could get away with a few hundred grams of crystal clear, on Professor's orders."

"You mean he ordered them to leave your son behind? Did he know you—?"

"No." Max shook his head. "Professor didn't know about our relationship. The order was to get the money and drugs and run."

Emotion hung on every word of their otherwise taciturn liaison's face.

"One of Harmon's friends in the gang escaped that same night, by the skin of his teeth. He wants revenge for how easily Professor turned a blind eye to Harmon's death. My source's reasoning is that it could've been any gang member to die that night. Professor doesn't care about his people. He's only interested in money and power." Max shrugged.

"Forgive me for pushing, Max." Denae gentled her voice, though she wasn't going to let him off easy. "I know this must be hard to talk about. But you told us the gangs didn't engage in this level of violence. Was this a one-time thing? An anomaly?"

He shrugged, examining the crust as if it were a masterpiece. "Could be. I'm really not sure why it didn't result in open warfare between the gangs. My source speculated that Professor knew he was outmatched and decided to try a different approach."

Denae wondered if Max Stillwell was turning a blind eye to other eventualities, based on the recent murders. "Max, I hate to ask, but have you considered your source might be the, well…source? For the murders, I mean."

"Highly unlikely. So much so that I'm almost disgusted you'd ask it, but…you're new to the story still. I get it. My source…shit." His nostrils flared.

Emma leaned forward. "Your source what?"

Max blew out a long breath. "My source is a young woman named Tamila Brown. She's run with the Powders since she was forced in at the age of ten."

Denae pressed her hand to her stomach. The plight of the young girl, and countless others in her situation, weighed heavily on her. "Forced in" was too mild a term, too superficial to describe the harrowing reality these children faced. It went far beyond that. The whole process was about systematic grooming, a deceptive web woven to ensnare those who fell through society's cracks.

It could start with an older youth offering a shield against bullies, slowly cultivating a relationship grounded in trust, which gradually transformed into unwavering loyalty and obedience. Then came the subtle demands, the exchange of favors for a semblance of family, each one pulling the noose tighter around their necks. Or it might be the exploitation of vulnerability, a fabricated tale of hardship used to lure them into committing petty crimes, with each wrongful act dragging them deeper into a mire of debt and fear, making the gang seem like the only refuge.

The notion of choice in such circumstances was a cruel illusion, akin to choosing between removing splinters from one's eye or facing the threat of a hammer. Every attempt to break free was met with a stark, chilling reminder that they were owned, body and soul, by the gang. To call it merely being "forced in" was to trivialize a reality far more devastating than most people could ever understand.

Emma scrubbed her hands with her face. "Ten years old? That's soul crushing."

Max nodded. "Tamila and Harmon were classmates, and she'd had a crush on him since the fifth grade. She came to me with information the day after he was killed. Since then, we've been working together to undermine the Powders, with the plan of eventually bringing them down. Or at least getting them out of our city."

"I'm sorry." Denae's whisper was heavy, dragged down by the weight of what was happening to these kids.

Max shrugged. "All good. Like I said, I get it. You needed to know."

Denae opened her water and took a sip, letting the cool liquid chase away the anxious heat building up in her chest. "Any word from Vance and Leo?"

Mia flipped her tablet open. "Yeah, did they find their Snake?"

The water bottle slipped from Denae's hands, bouncing off the table and splashing her shirt. She caught it before it toppled over. Beside her, Mia was holding her tablet up from the table.

"You okay, Denae?"

"Yeah. It...just slipped. My fingers were wet."

Jacinda cleared her throat and rejoined them, taking her seat across the table beside Max. She opened her tablet and read from a message.

"Vance and Leo found a collection of graffiti and street art, but the artist wasn't there to discuss it. They did, however, run into Amber Wilson, the stripper Agents Last and Logan spoke to by phone. She was outside Jax Duran's place. Claims he had stolen a necklace that once belonged to her great-aunt."

Why are we still talking about these two guys? They're already dead, and there's plenty more Drivers who could end up being targeted next.

"Jacinda, Max, I know we didn't find anything to indicate an outsider might be targeting both gangs." Emma rested her chin in her palm, tapping her cheek with one finger. "So this is looking more like Powders and Drivers building up to something. But why this way? Why so personal? Is there some individual with a potential grudge against these two guys? Not gang-related? Maybe a revenge thing?"

"If it was revenge, it would almost have to be somebody in the gang, though, right?" Denae gestured a thumb toward the message scrawled at the crime scene. "Grieving family members, like Max here, don't tend to get violent themselves. Frustrated community members aren't likely to leave messages in blood. It takes some real hate for that, and gangs can generate that kind of hate toward an enemy." She felt her expression go a little sour as she spoke.

Jacinda leaned forward. "I think Denae's hit the nail on the head."

"Plus, the weapon is so bizarre." No gang member Denae had ever met, and she'd met a few over the years, used such a strange, intimate item. "It means getting up close and personal, not like a gun."

Emma drummed the rest of her fingers against her cheek. "The weapon bothers me the most too. Why use something so unique, like a signature? Gangs generally use guns with no distinguishing features. Serial numbers filed off. They don't want to get caught."

Max met her gaze. "They can also have such a dispassionate attitude that getting caught isn't even part of their decision process."

"That may be true, but using a weapon like this makes me think the unsub is either so checked out of society they think themselves above it, or they just don't give a damn about anything."

"It doesn't surprise me that a gang member would get so up close and personal." Denae needed her team to understand the nuances. "Some of them have to choose food over clothing, clothing over rent. Water over electricity or heat. They see their rivals as threats to their survival. It still tracks that they'd use a weapon like we see here."

Max nodded along as Denae spoke. "They're on the wrong side of the law, and they're often violent, but the gang is more than a job for a lot of them. For many, it's a family. Protecting each other and their money and their territory? Those are the priorities."

Denae sat forward. "That's my point exactly. This unsub wants to be noticed. They want to make a statement with what they're doing."

"Blaming it on the Powders," Jacinda kept writing, keeping note of everything being said, "means the Drivers' deaths are bound to come back on the Powders. They're just asking for someone to retaliate, which was a very specific choice. Regardless of weapon."

"Maybe that's it, Jacinda. Maybe they're looking for retaliation." Mia leaned in, writing on her tablet as she did. "Even trying to start a gang war if it comes to it…like we discussed before. This could be someone seeking to create a power vacuum they hope to fill."

Max nodded. "I know some Powders haven't been happy with how slowly Professor's been making moves. The Drivers've been raking in money with their meth deals, and there are plenty of Powders who want some of the pie sooner than later. One of them starting a gang war to get things moving feels extreme…but if we think of our guy as someone at the end of his rope, losing his grip and writing messages, we're not talking about a non-extreme viewpoint anyway."

Lifting a hand, Mia glanced around at everyone else. "Can we go over it from the top, and make sure we all have the same notes?"

Jacinda nodded at her to lead them in a recap. "Good idea."

"We have an unsub with a presumed connection to the gang, who may or may not be seeking revenge, but who's aiming for violence. They have a deep, personal connection to that violence and are willing to get their hands dirty in doling it out. And they want to make a statement, hence the weapon and the message in blood."

Emma picked up the thread. "All of which indicates a premeditated attack, not one made in response to the victims being in enemy territory. If this was planned, our perpetrator knew those guys were going to be walking those alleys after their night at the club. Or they followed them from the club."

"And that means they have some way of knowing where Drivers are going to be." With her heart in her throat, Denae reached for her water bottle. She took a slow sip, forcing her jaw to remain steady.

Emma was already standing up. "We'll go talk to the girls at the club again. Maybe Jax and Rux normally brought friends. If so, and if those friends are still alive, we need to have a conversation with them."

Mia waved her phone at Emma, mouthing that she was already dialing Veevee's number.

Max and Jacinda conferred on their next steps as Emma and Mia gathered their things. Denae watched them all in her peripheral vision, doing her best to keep her face neutral.

Death by Powder.

The message seemed to be mocking her.

11

Emma tried the number Veevee had given them while Mia drove through some of the worst downtown traffic she'd ever seen. After three tries, she gave up. "No answer, and the call keeps dropping."

"That number he gave us was probably crap." Mia had to slam on the brakes to avoid rear-ending someone who cut in front of them. "What is up with the roads? It's Monday, not Friday."

Emma tapped at her phone and groaned. "Big accident up ahead has an intersection closed down. We're looking at red for the next eight blocks, and even the alternate routes are jammed up."

"I just want to get to the club before Amber starts dancing. Is that too much to ask?"

"Should I lower the window and let the nice people know two federal agents have to talk to a stripper and could they please get out of our way?"

Mia laughed. "If I thought it would help, I'd say yes. But maybe just try the club's direct line and see if Veevee's still there?"

She did and got to the point as soon as her call was answered. "This is Special Agent Emma Last. My colleague and I spoke with Veevee earlier. Is he there?"

After a few seconds of garbled background chatter that Emma could only barely hear, the speaker replied, and it wasn't with good news. "Nope. Already skated to do some errand."

Emma rolled her eyes. "Will Amber Wilson be in tonight?"

That earned her more background chatter that lasted so long that she gritted her teeth. Finally, a response. "Yeah, she'll be in at five."

She ended the call, checking the time. It was already four. "The good news is Amber will be in at five, and I think we ought to talk to her in person this time."

Mia took them around a corner. "I hate to ask what the bad news might be."

"The illustrious Vincent Victor 'Veevee' Hanson has apparently gone incommunicado. That was his head bartender I just talked to. Veevee headed out on an 'errand' shortly after we left this morning. He was supposed to be back after lunch and isn't answering his phone."

Mia groaned. "We should let Jacinda know. They can get out an APB for him, at least."

Emma tapped out a quick text to the SSA, who replied promptly that Max would, indeed, be alerting all agencies in the area to Veevee's connection to their case as a person of interest.

"Do you think he's missing, or are we going to find him with signs of Freddy Krueger's attempts at reconstructive surgery?"

Mia *grr*ed at her. "I really wish you'd quit with the Freddy jokes."

Emma led the way into the strip club, pausing just inside the door. Pop music provided a low-level buzz to the atmosphere, and the lights were brighter than when they'd come before. The wooden floors gleamed, but a good number of the tables had men waiting for the show to start.

A couple of young guys occupied seats by the stage. They looked like college students, with book bags and sweatshirts on. One of them sipped from a drink while the other counted out dollar bills into two stacks. Across the room, a man sat alone at a table in the corner. He wore sweatpants and a long-sleeved t-shirt. The table held two empty beer bottles, and he was working on a third.

At a table closer to the door, a man sat with a bottle of beer while he did a crossword puzzle.

She wasn't sure which was more surprising, that he was doing that, or that he could concentrate over the noise made by the patrons who were already on their second or third drinks.

What she'd expected of a late-afternoon strip club crowd, she wasn't sure, but it hadn't been this atmosphere, topped off by visibly drunk patrons yelling at the stage, announcing the time, and demanding that the show start.

"I paid for entertainment!" The man in the corner waved his beer at the bartender, showing off a hole in his t-shirt's armpit. "Where the hell is Kimmie?"

"Hold your horses." The bartender, a different man than the one she'd spoken to on the phone, barely glanced at the loud drunk.

Squinting past the bar, Emma saw another group of men playing a round of poker while they waited for the show. One of them had his phone open to a dating app as evidenced by his constant, indiscriminate right swiping.

Mia stepped closer to Emma's side as a server hurried by with a fresh tray of beers, managing to speed by even on four-inch heels. The girl wore a bikini top and a slip of fabric that might have been long enough to qualify as a skirt. It flipped up as she moved to reveal a thong. "This is…something."

"Sad, ain't it?" A bartender they'd seen that morning when they'd come into view the surveillance footage had approached from behind, shaking his head. "This is the worst time of day. Guys get here around four and start pregaming for the dancers to come on at five to get the night started. These sad sacks think they have a chance with any of the girls in here. In their dreams, right? I hate the day shift."

Emma tilted her head. "There are other jobs in the city, but I guess the money's better than what you'd get waiting tables or driving a cab."

He sniffed and took it in stride. "Then you've got the weirdos like the nerd over there. He comes in every Monday like clockwork and does a crossword puzzle, then leaves. Never watches the show or tips the girls."

Mia coughed to steal back his attention. "You and Emma talked on the phone a bit ago. You said Amber would be in?"

"Yeah." He headed toward the back hallway, waving at them to follow. "I told her you were coming."

Mia and Emma found themselves taking a left to pass behind the stage area, down a red-lit hallway that reeked of deodorant, sweat, and beer.

They found Amber sitting and staring blankly at her phone, parked on a bench in a small greenroom ringed by makeup desks. The smell of overly floral perfume formed a wall as they entered, and Emma had to fight the urge to ask for a gas mask.

Another stripper wearing a loosely tied robe was

finishing off her makeup, but a loud *ahem* from the bartender made her pause in the middle of brushing an eyelash.

"Celine, these nice federal agents need to talk to Amber, so…"

With eyes wide in disbelief, the woman gathered her makeup and quickly exited the room.

The bartender met Emma's eyes and nodded at Amber. "Try not to keep her too long, all right? Running a business here and all. And since Veevee bailed on us, I'm where the buck stops until…"

Emma prompted him with a flick of her fingers. "Go on. You were saying."

He did a little back-and-forth dance. "Until we get a new manager."

"We'll let that go for now, but just the same, we'd appreciate your name and a phone number before we go. Preferably a phone you plan on answering that's still in service."

"Sure, yeah, I can give it to you right now." He carefully reached a hand to his back pocket and drew out a phone with two fingers. Mia had him text his information to her.

"Back to Veevee, and Amber, this is a question for you as well. He didn't leave any indication of where he might go?"

The bartender answered first. "Not a peep. I honestly expected him to come back like he usually does. You must've spooked him. Can I get back out front now? I can hear things getting crazy out there."

He was right. Shouts and laughter came down the tight hallway, the noise finding its way into the dressing room, bouncing around to put Emma's teeth on edge.

I'd honestly take a graveyard full of ghosts over this any day of the week.

She waved the bartender off and turned her attention to Amber. "Any idea where Veevee went, or why he took off?"

The petite blond dancer shrugged and lifted a hand to point out the door at the retreating bartender. "What he said. I haven't seen Veevee since last night." As she straightened up a touch and tucked her phone beneath her thigh, her silk robe twisted around and molded to her pale figure. Amber's makeup glittered gold around her eyes and red around her lips.

As if uninterested, Mia sorted through some of the jewelry scattered over the makeup table with a fingertip. "You spoke with some of our colleagues earlier?"

"Wish you'd all leave me alone. I haven't done anything wrong. It's not my fault I was the last one who saw Jax and Ruxie alive." The girl's voice broke on a little whimper of annoyance, reminding Emma of a teenager protesting her innocence. She rocked on her ass in the robe, which gaped apart to show a good bit of chest and thigh.

Taking Mia's cue, Emma watched Amber's face. "Amber, we understand you were outside Jax's duplex looking for…a necklace? Did you find it?"

She didn't meet Emma's gaze at first, then turned her head to the side and talked at the mirror in front of her. "Didn't have a necklace or nothing. I was just…I wanted to see if maybe whoever killed Jax was trying to rip him off too. Take all his stuff, ya know?"

"And if you'd found them, what were you planning to do?"

The stripper swiveled her head and stared at Emma, then at Mia. "Call you? Call the cops? Somebody's gotta do what's right for people like me and Jax. He was a kid. Wasn't even supposed to be drinking, but they served him anyway because he ran with the Ds."

"Do you think he was killed because of his gang affiliation?"

"Kinda has to be, doesn't it? Shit, I don't know."

Emma stood beside Mia but leaned against the makeup counter behind them in a casual posture. She waited for Amber to calm herself before continuing. "Amber, we don't like having to bother you any more than you want us here. We just have a few more questions." She waited for some sign the girl heard her but went on anyway as the silence stretched. "Did Jax and Rux come in here often? Was it always just the two of them?"

"Like I told you, Jax was super into me. A little more pushy than I would've liked, sometimes a lot, but he was cute about it. Just a kid with a crush, ya know? He was sweet."

Emma nodded, thinking again how weird it was that the stripper called Jax a "kid" when he'd been just two years younger than her.

"And he and Rux were your most regular customers? Easiest to get along with? Help us understand why you care this much about them, Amber. Were you dating either of them?"

She flapped a hand at the air and laughed. "Hell to the no, on that. They were just sweet, like I said, and they tipped so well."

"And it was always just the two of them? No friends or other members of the Drivers came in with them?"

"They brought friends before, other Ds, yeah. But it wasn't weird for them to be here on their own, if that's what you mean."

Mia pressed before she could change the subject again. "Any friends that stand out? Came along more often than usual?"

The air went thicker, colder, and Emma stretched her arms and shoulders in order to hide the fact that she was glancing around the room.

Sure enough, back near the doorway, Jax's ghost lurked by a row of coatracks littered with hoodies and purses. Blood covered the front of his shirt, and his hands were stuffed into his jeans, but his white-eyed gaze focused on the stripper.

Amber reached up and dabbed at some cakey eye makeup with a brightly painted red fingernail. "I guess, yeah. One guy I remember, he came in with them more than anybody else."

"Did he have a name?"

The stripper gave Emma a look that could have spoiled milk. "I imagine he did. He never talked much. Didn't want extra attention or anything. I always got the impression they kind of dragged him along."

Figuring it was too much to hope for, Emma asked her question again anyway. "What about this name you imagine he has?"

Sure enough, Amber rolled her eyes as if they should've known better. "I didn't answer that question the first time, did I?"

"No, you didn't. But that doesn't mean you don't know his name. In fact, it makes it more likely that you do. I'll give you a tip. Next time you want to lie to the Feds, plan your story out and practice it."

Mia adjusted her position to block the door, in case Amber bolted. "Amber, even if you'd practiced a story, we'd probably still catch your lie, because we're trained to do that."

"Fine. Fuck, you got me. I never talked to the dude, but I heard Ruxie calling him Snake."

Emma glanced to Mia, seeing recognition in her eyes as well. That was twice now that this artist had come up. "Any description?"

"He's a Black guy. He had a hat on, so I don't know what his hair looks like. I figure it was like Ruxie's. And he's about halfway between him and Jax, height-wise."

"Any distinguishing marks? Tattoos, scars, maybe eye color? Anything you can give us would be helpful." Mia cradled her iPad in one hand, ready to take down whatever Amber might offer.

The dancer shrugged. "Some tattoos on his forearms and neck maybe, but I couldn't say for sure. Hard to see 'em on dark skin in here. Eye color, I don't know. They're never looking at my eyes, so I don't bother looking at theirs."

Emma doubted Amber's insistence on having little to share. She was likely covering for Drivers members and making sure she had a firm story to tell any other members who might ask what she'd told the Feds.

"And Jax and Rux never came in with anybody else."

"Not in months." Amber frowned, as if trying to remember, and dabbed at her eye makeup again. Emma only just refrained from grabbing the girl's wrist. *How the hell does she not poke her eye out with those nails?* "We get people coming and going all night long, so most people don't stand out. I just remember that guy because he was clearly not into being here. Like, total one-eighty from Jax."

Emma snuck a glance back toward the ghost as he dropped to his knees, shaking his head with a grimace. "We was gonna be a thing. Just had to get her number."

A ghost with puppy love. Wonderful.

His gaze came to Emma's. "Girl really knows how to stab a guy through the heart."

Well, there's a choice of words.

Biting back a sigh, Emma focused on Amber, who seemed even younger to her with Jax's ghost crushing so hard five feet away. And just when she thought the strip club couldn't get any more depressing.

"Do you remember anything else about this Snake?"

"No. He just...oh." Amber's eyes widened, like she'd surprised herself. "I heard him talking about Starlight once."

"Starlight? As in, from the night sky?"

The question earned Emma another disgusted eye roll.

"As in, the Starlight Lounge. He wanted Jax and Ruxie to go over there with him. That was the last time he came in."

Emma jotted down the name. "Starlight's another strip club?"

"Just a bar. Or maybe a restaurant. I ain't been inside, so they could have strippers, I guess. But it's fancy. Forty-dollar appetizers, ya know?"

Jax's ghost grunted behind her. "Lame and expensive."

Emma traded a look with Mia, and the other agent closed the cover on her tablet. "We have your contact information from earlier, so just keep your phone around in case we need to call, okay? Thanks for your time."

The young woman pushed to her feet and, in one move, dropped her robe on the floor, revealing an almost nonexistent red, white, and blue corset and shiny blue short shorts. She swept between them and was gone a second later, the cold of the Other following her as Jax's ghost flowed out of the room in her wake.

Emma sighed. She could've guessed he'd follow the woman, and there'd be no questioning him now anyway.

Mia stood and glanced around. "Any visitors?"

"Not anymore. Jax was here, but he left to catch the all-American show." Emma shook her head, stowing away her iPad in her bag. "Ready to head to this Starlight Lounge?"

"Lead the way." Mia gestured toward the door, side-eyeing rows upon rows of makeup lined along the green table stalls. "This is another life, I guess, huh?"

As they passed the stage, the drunks from before were lulled into what passed for contentment in a place like this. And Celine, the stripper who'd been in the room with Amber, was now on stage, mostly nude in go-go boots, a thong, and a cowboy hat. She spun away from Emma and Mia as they moved through the room.

In the car, Emma pulled up the Starlight Lounge on GPS while Mia updated Jacinda.

When Mia put the phone down, though, she wore a thoughtful frown. "I wanted to think Amber had nothing to do with this, but now I'm not sure."

Emma thought back to the sizes of their victims and the petite stripper. "Only if she had help. She must've known the guys carried a lot of cash and knew she could play it off as a gang killing…"

"But they weren't robbed. Even their guns were left behind."

Emma's foot came off the gas for a second. "So we're back to it being revenge-motivated or the first salvo in a war. Dammit."

"You said Jax's ghost was in the room?"

"Yeah, he mostly hung around making puppy-dog eyes at her. Well, dead—"

"Don't say it. Please. You've given me enough nightmare fuel already."

"You do know this case is probably going to get worse before it gets better, right?"

Mia stared out the window. "That's why I need you to stop making it harder than it already is."

Emma let the silence stretch until Mia looked her way.

"Hey, Emma. I'm sorry. This is just not feeling like a case we're gonna win, you know? We're on the ropes, and so far, nothing we've tried has really paid off." She put out a fist for a pound.

Emma dropped hers on it. "We're good, Mia. And you're right. I wish you weren't, but…"

"So Jax. What'd he do other than ogle a woman he never touched and never will?"

Emma relayed what Jax had said back in the dressing

room. When she finished, she and Mia were both stewing over his phrasing.

Mia pursed her lips. "He said she knew how to 'stab a guy through the heart?' Those words?"

"Yeah…but if you'd heard him, you'd wonder too. He seemed more embarrassed than angry. Not how I'd expect him to act if she literally stabbed him or knew who did."

Mia jotted down the words in her notes. "Do we want to ignore it though? You've said ghosts tend to be less than clear about what they mean."

"I don't know if we can ignore anybody at this point. Let's head to the Starlight and see what the stars can tell us."

12

I rocked side to side in my chair and bounced my foot on the stained carpet in the Powders HQ. We were upstairs in an old office space the Professor found for us and having a meeting to talk about "all the shit that's been happening." Part of me wanted to leave, take off back to the gym and find somebody to spar with. My hands itched to be boxing.

Dad would've reminded me to focus on my family, the people who are around you all the time, seeing to it that you don't get forgotten. Curtis and them, even Prof, lame as he was, they were my family now. So focusing on them was all I'd be doing.

Curtis had the same tired look on his face as I felt pulling on mine. I lifted my elbow to him as he sat down next to me. He raised his up to meet mine in a bump, and we traded a laugh.

For that moment, I remembered what the Powders meant to me.

Family, backup, support.

Always knowing where you belonged and who you belonged with. That was what the Powders used to be. Until

Prof started running things into the ground, treating our gang like some kind of office club. He even had dudes assigned to make sure the fridge at the gym was always stocked with energy drinks.

What kind of gang leader makes sure the damn fridge don't run out of PowerBlast but lets the enemy walk all over our territory?

Drivers took our streets first, and now one of them had his hands on my sister.

Across the room, Prof sat up on a desk with one leg crossed over the other like he was about to lead some kind of prayer group. This old office building had gotten to him, made it too easy for him to think of himself as a manager instead of a warrior.

Prof used to be someone I respected. The night my dad died, he brought hot chocolate and stood in the prison waiting room with me and my sister. He'd talked about how we didn't have to worry about a thing, not one thing. He'd take care of us. I believed him.

But now he was weak.

I didn't care how tough he looked, how cut and hard he tried to be. Squinting at us like some old-ass schoolteacher instead of a father figure, leaning on his desk while the rest of his inner circle stood around like kids called into the principal's office.

This poser shit here was why my sister had been tempted by that Drivers asshole. It had to be. Prof's lame ass didn't know how to take care of a family.

Compared to our dad, Prof was about as tough as a beanbag chair with half the stuffing falling out. "Y'all, come together now." He put both legs down and slid off the desk a little. Curtis and me shifted our chairs to make room for some of the other dudes who'd been hanging around in the corners.

Probably talking shit about Prof, just like I'm thinking shit.

When we all got settled, our glorious leader started up his bullshit.

First, he stared around the room, tension growing in the silence.

Like that man knows a damn thing about tension.

"Y'all know why I called y'all in here, yeah?"

Muttering sounded behind me. Curtis nodded, but I just sat. Waiting.

"The plan's gone to shit." Prof banged his hand on the metal desk beneath him, as if daring any of us to disagree. Fool hadn't given us enough information for me to even be sure what he was talking about. And I doubted the others knew any more than I did.

"I'll ask if nobody else will." I leaned forward, focused on him. "What plan is that, exactly?"

More muttering behind me. Curtis cursed under his breath. Did he know more than I did?

Prof stretched his fingers and curled his hands into fists, but his eyes didn't flinch away from mine. "Ain't nobody told Li'l Chip, huh? All right. I've been talking with Rails. We were talking truce."

A truce.

"You mean," I spoke quietly, clutching my own thighs like they might slap me around and wake me up, "Rails Foster, leader of the Drivers? That the Rails you mean?"

Prof lurched off the desk and began pacing in front of it. He wove around in a figure eight, landing in front of the window that looked out on Queen Street and the center of our territory. "Y'all know we're moving plenty of H around here. Good business."

Murmurs of agreement from all of us. No argument there.

"But the Drivers are running some crystal-clear methamphetamine. Fine product. We'll never touch it, let's be straight. But me and Rails cut a deal where we can all get paid, us and Drivers both. Said the Drivers would stop pushing H so we could own that whole pie. But we gotta stay out of the meth deals. We run the H, they run the meth. That's the truce."

"What about when they decide they want more? Like when they moved here from B-more in the first place?"

"Rails gave me his word."

I was not the only one who grumbled.

Prof raised his hands, like some kind of preacher. "Before anybody starts some shit, I'll tell you. He might be a Driver, but Rails is no bitch. He talks straight, doesn't play games." He turned from the window and went over to lean on his desk, from Tyler the Preacher to Tyler the Professor again.

"Drivers cut down Harmony Still and three others. You going to deal with Rails, the man that made that happen?"

"Drivers just lost two Ds. We're square."

Square.

With Rails Foster.

The enemy.

My blood boiled, but I kept my hands flat on my legs, just like Dad taught me to do in the presence of authority, especially when it was an authority I didn't trust or believe in.

Prof, of course, was still crowing about his grand plan.

"Real problem is the cops and the Feds. We pull together, Drivers and Powders, we're in a better position to keep clear of all that. We can make money where we want to instead of stepping on each other's toes and shit. Or fighting about who owns what street corner."

Curtis grunted at that. "So we just selling Aunt Hazel and that's it? Why we not try to cut in on the crystal clear, man?"

"Because their supplier, whoever it is, doesn't want to deal with anyone but Rails. We could keep fighting, but working with the Drivers is the better play. It's the only way we get anywhere, and you know it."

I should stalk over there and throw Prof headfirst through that window. Wouldn't take me but a second, and he wouldn't see it coming, because what the hell did he have to fear from little old me?

But if I did that, the guys behind me, even Curtis...they'd be on me in a second, and I'd be done.

"The *Drivers* cut up our territory and took what was ours. They split up our family, and that makes them our *enemies*. They've killed our family."

"Listen to—"

I put a hand up. He didn't need to be no damn peacekeeper right now, not if he was just gonna be bending over to take this bullshit plan Prof was trying to sell. "If their meth supplier only wants to deal with Rails, that just means we need to own him, instead of being a pansy-ass—"

"That's enough!" Curtis slammed to his feet and landed in front of me, aiming a finger in my face. "You may be up here with us, but that don't mean you get to fly with disrespect."

Prof stalked across the room and pulled Curtis away with a hand on his shoulder so he could look me in the eye.

I heard more shuffling behind us, but so far, it was just me and him and Curtis having a staring contest, and I was just fine keeping it that way.

"We should be out there." I stood up, facing him nearly nose to nose, 'cept I was a touch shorter. "Killing them, not making deals. How do you not see that?"

For a second, I thought he'd agree, but then he sighed. Without a word, the idiot went back to his desk. Beside me, Curtis grunted and slammed back into his seat. Reading the room, hoping it would make a difference in getting them to listen, I followed his lead, easing down into my chair and forcing my hands back to my thighs.

Dad would've known how to handle this. He'd have dragged us all back to our old HQ for a serious beatdown or put me and Prof in the center of a ring to duke it out, fist to fist.

Hell, that was what the Powders family as a whole would've done, not so long ago. Instead of making a show with this lame-ass school board meeting.

One of the guys behind me finally spoke. "Prof, I'm with you, man. Feds're getting too comfy. We need allies to keep our operation strong."

Betrayal burned in my throat. All this time, I trusted these men to have my back, and now they were siding with the fucking Drivers over me.

Just like my sister had done.

So much for family. The Powders weren't just getting weaker with Prof driving the bus. We were falling apart, everybody getting off at their own stop.

I met his eyes, then Curtis's, and saw what I hadn't wanted to face 'til now. Curtis was embarrassed for me, maybe ashamed, willing me to keep my seat. And I heard what Prof said all over again, but it was like I was hearing it for the first time.

"Nobody told Li'l Chip, huh?"

Just like that, I saw my family leaving me alone, every last one of them heading off in his own direction, same way my dad ended up doing even if these fools weren't drowning themselves in liquor. Curtis had already known the plan that I'd been left out of, and he didn't tell me. All these guys beside and behind me had already known.

I'd been the only one of the higher-ups left in the dark.

"How could you?" My whisper died between me and Curtis, and he had the grace to look away.

My sister's smiling face came to mind, and I wanted to throw up.

Was there nobody who wouldn't betray me?

"We're stronger together," Prof cracked his knuckles, "and infighting helps nobody."

"Infighting." I let a laugh bleed up from my throat, pushing down the urge to destroy the room and everyone in it. "And what do you mean by that? Us here? Whoever of our number killed those Drivers in the alley when you want to play nice instead?"

Prof tried to silence me with a glare, but that wasn't happening. "I—"

"You remember the last time we tried to play nice with another gang? The Diamond Heads. Ring a bell?" I shifted in my seat to stare at Curtis, who'd flinched at the other gang's name. "I saved your life that day."

Prof's face softened a touch, but I could tell he wasn't about to back off. He had that look, like when a deal was happening. Whether or not it meant dead bodies, it was happening, because the money on the table was too heavy to be ignored. "That was different. That punk planned the whole damn thing."

Please don't say it. "That's—"

"This time?" He barked a little laugh, self-satisfied. "This time, I'm in the driver's seat," he laughed at his little joke, "because I went to Rails first."

My breath curdled up in my lungs and froze.

Betrayal blocked my throat like an ice cube down the wrong pipe.

Prof was serious.

And that means we're done here.

"Okay." My voice choked on the lie, so I clenched my fingers and said it again. "Okay, you're right. You say you're in the driver's seat. That's cool. I'm along for the ride."

"Don't bullshit me, Li'l Chip. You fixing to fuck things up,

I'll put you back down with the street crews. No more inner circle shit for you. I'm deadass about that."

"It's cool, Prof. I'm not starting nothing."

He nodded and flapped a hand at us like we were a bunch of flies buzzing up around his lunchtime. I stuffed my hands in my pockets, feeling my blades in their leather case, and followed Curtis and the others out. I threw Prof a smile, like I believed even half of what I'd just told him.

Let him think he's in the driver's seat. That'll only make this easier.

13

Emma and Mia both did a double take when they walked into the Starlight Lounge. It couldn't have been more different from the Night Trips club. White tablecloths, servers in black vests and ties carrying trays of steaming entrées and cocktails…the place screamed high-end dining.

Tinted glass hid the inside from the busy D.C. sidewalk, and a light-skinned hostess who looked glammed up for a night in the theater district greeted the two agents with a pasted-on smile. "May I help you?" She scanned their pants with just a flicker of doubt in her expression that they didn't meet the dress code requirements.

Emma held up her badge, willing herself not to fidget. "We'll be discreet. We're looking for someone who we believe might be a regular here."

All eyes were on them, and Emma almost hoped somebody would up and run, just to break the tension.

The hostess frowned, her fake eyelashes doing a flutter just for their benefit. "I guess it would be fine if you head over to the bar. Can you leave your badges, um…you know, out of sight? Our manager is in a meeting with the board, but Alec, our mixologist, should be able to help you. You won't bother the guests?"

Emma was already headed for the bar, talking as she moved. "Not unless you're hiding our guy. In that case, handcuffs are on the table along with the badges."

The joke was lost on the hostess, but Mia giggled as they sidled up to the bar.

Around her, the space grew colder, heavier, and Emma glanced sideways to see two ghosts, a man and woman dressed in high nineties fashion, bullet holes in their chests and tasteless martinis in their hands. The woman remained snooty even in death. She eyed them over her and her dining partner's drinks but spoke just loudly enough to be heard. "I guess they must be letting anyone in here lately. They're *cops*."

Shaking off the ghost's tone, Emma stole a seat beside Mia and focused on the bar. Her colleague was waving down a Richard Gere look-alike in a white button-up and gray vest. He moved fast to meet them as they slid onto barstools, eyes veritably sparking.

"Help you ladies?" His million-dollar smile was far more sincere than the hostess's, and although Emma judged him to be in his fifties, he carried himself like someone half that age and bucking for younger.

Emma flashed her ID again. "I'm Special Agent Emma Last, and this is Special Agent Mia Logan. Could we show you a few photos and see if you recognize anyone in them?"

"Name's Alec." His eyes lingered on Mia, who pulled out her iPad. He leaned forward, and Emma could've sworn he sucked in the slight paunch he carried. "Anything for law enforcement."

Mia's cheeks reddened as she slid her iPad in front of

him, pointedly placing it between them on the bar top. The driver's licenses of Juan Carlos Duran and Charlie Rucker stared up at him, tattoos blazing, and Alec took only a moment before he shook his head. His perfect gray hair barely shifted. "I have a pretty good eye for faces, and I think I'd remember them."

That might be the understatement of the century, but I'll take your word for it.

In another place, Emma might've pressed the bartender to look closer, but not here. Either one of these guys would've stood out like a breakdancing Santa Claus in this particular venue. "How about a young Black man, around their age and with tattoos? We understand he goes by the street name 'Snake.' Not these guys, but someone who'd fit in with them?"

Alec seemed about to shake his head, but then he clicked his tongue against his teeth and paused as if in thought. "Actually, yeah, but not for a few weeks. There's a guy who comes in to talk to one of our cocktail servers every once in a while. Hope's worked here around six months, and this guy started showing up soon after she finished training."

"Soon after. Training takes…a week? Two?"

He met Emma's eyes and smiled. "About that, usually. Hope's got a knack for it. She was quick to pick things up, has outstanding balance. I think she's tipped maybe one tray, and only lost a glass of water off the side. She caught the old-fashioned without spilling a drop." His eyes went back to Mia, and his smile turned up the wattage as he continued in a lower voice. "She likes the guy that's been coming in, I can tell you that much. They're always flirting. How about you?"

Mia's mouth opened in surprise. "Uh, taken."

Emma bit back a laugh as the bartender picked up a glass, polishing it idly. "Well, Agent Logan, I'll be here if you ever change your mind." His gaze returned to Emma then, going a touch more serious. "Hope should be in any minute if you two want to wait."

"Thanks," Emma settled into her chair as Mia pulled her iPad back, "we'll do that."

Alec flashed a grin toward Mia again, apparently not quite ready to give up. "Can I get you a drink? Something to snack on? A menu of hors d'oeuvres and cocktails? I promise we only serve the best."

Mia blushed red, fumbling for words, so Emma leaned forward and caught his eye first. "I'll take a coffee."

He looked at Mia again. The woman was going to have to speak. "Coffee for you, as well? I make a mean espresso."

She nodded, and the man disappeared toward a gleaming silver machine at the end of the bar.

Emma nudged her. "You always loved *Pretty Woman*—"

"Hush!" Mia chuckled and shook her head. "But, seriously, hard to miss someone like a Driver in this place. I mean, maybe if he's wealthy enough to buy people looking the other way…"

Emma shook her head, watching the lounge behind them via a mirror set up over the bar.

"We have to at least consider that this is exactly where a Drivers or Powders leader might hang out. They're the top two gangs in D.C., and one of them already controls most of B-more. That kind of money buys access to places like this."

"But do you see anybody in here who fits the profile?"

"That's my point. Our profile could be flawed. We're looking into a couple of street toughs who got killed. Low-level soldiers in the gang. The boss could be any of the people in this room, and we wouldn't know it because we're only looking for guys with tattoos and gold teeth."

Alec returned to slide their coffees across the bar. "On the house, ladies." He gave Mia a wink. "I'll send Hope over when she comes in."

Emma sat straighter, sipping her coffee. She didn't want to guess at what it would've cost if Alec hadn't offered it gratis. Beside her, Mia inhaled the aroma rising from her cup and took a small sip.

"Oh, that is divine. Emma, I might need you to leave me here. Tell Vance I'm sorry it didn't work out, but I found the perfect man, and his name is espresso."

She and Emma both laughed, drawing the eyes of the few nearby patrons enjoying glasses of wine and appetizers. The hostess greeted another couple at the door and flashed a glare in the agents' direction. Emma waved at her with a smile on her face before turning back to her coffee.

At the door leading into the kitchen, Alec was gesturing to a young Black woman wearing a white button-down and gray vest over dark slacks. She was tying on an apron and narrowed her eyes at Alec as he waved her toward Emma and Mia. His frown made it clear that no matter how friendly he'd been when offering them coffee, he wasn't to be ignored when it came to a direct request.

Coffee abandoned, Mia swiveled on her stool to greet the young woman with her iPad held on her lap and her ID open, revealing her badge. "Hope? We won't take up much of your time. I'm Special Agent Mia Logan. This is my partner, Special Agent Emma Last."

Hope's mouth opened in an *O*, her eyes going wide as she glanced quickly between them. "Okay...I'm...I'm Hope Jackson. How can I help you?"

Emma held out her ID as well and eyed the woman up and down. She didn't look old enough to be within fifteen feet of the cocktail lounge, let alone working there. "Hope, if you don't mind me asking," Emma lowered her voice and tucked away her ID, "how old are you?"

In truth, she didn't look more than sixteen. The idea of the petite Black woman taking down Charlie Rucker and Juan Carlos Duran, even while they were drunk, was little less than laughable. She stood maybe five-five and couldn't have been more than a hundred and ten pounds.

"I'm eighteen." The girl straightened, frowning. Her eyes narrowed so much, even her perfect eyebrows seemed to go a little harder. "And before you ask, yes, I have taken the required courses to serve alcohol. Do you need my permit?"

"No, that won't be necessary." Emma glanced at Mia, whose lips were pursed. This felt like questioning a minor. "We'd like to ask you about a young man who's come in to speak to you in the past. We believe he goes by the name Snake. Black and tall, tattooed. Possibly short hair kept neat. Maybe flirted with you. Sound familiar?"

Hope's lips tightened, her brown eyes flattening as if on cue. "I don't know who you'd be talking about."

Their friendly bartender coughed in correction, judgment radiating off him. "He's come in multiple times, Hope. I've *seen* him with you. These women are law enforcement—"

"Okay." Her nostrils flared as she swiveled to stare at the man. "I remember him, but I don't know his name." She turned back to Emma and Mia with hardened eyes. "He's come in two or three times at most. I can't help you."

Mia lowered her voice, offering the full wattage of her smile. "Maybe he talked to you about where he works, or you've met a friend of his—"

"No." Hope was quick to adjust her face to be more friendly. "I've never met any of his friends."

Alec scowled behind her, putting down the knife he'd been using to slice up an orange and stepping closer.

"Look," she took a deep breath, smoothing down her apron as she did, "I wish I could help you, but I can't."

Emma darted a glance at the bartender, willing the man to back off. "Hope—"

"I told you what I know." She shook her head, backing up a step and looking around as if someone might leap out and arrest her. "I have work to do, if you wouldn't mind letting me go. Unless there's anything else?"

Mia offered what was definitely a forced smile. "Hope, we don't want to make this unpleasant for anybody. Not you, not your boss, and definitely not for any of these very fine patrons enjoying the atmosphere of this establishment. But we need to ask you some questions. If you'd like to do that at our offices, that's something we can arrange."

The young woman deflated and took a seat beside Mia.

Alec pushed a glass of water her way and stood nearby, slicing up fruit again.

"He started coming in one day, and I thought he was cute. But, like, tell me he belongs in this building. I play along because he's cute, you know? But I always say he shouldn't be coming around here." She looked at Alec, whose eyebrows had lifted up as if to say, *Yep, nailed it.*

Emma tapped Mia's iPad, which the other agent had placed on the bar. "Hope, have you seen either of these two men before? With or without the man who comes in and flirts with you even though he 'shouldn't be'?"

Hope shook her head and reached for the water Alec had provided, taking a small sip. "No. I never seen them two before ever. God's honest truth."

"Can you tell us anything else about the man who comes in?"

"Just what I said already. He's cute and doesn't know when to stop coming around where he shouldn't be."

Mia put her iPad away. "Mind giving us your information? In case we need to talk to you again?"

Hope flinched, but with a look from Alec, she nodded. When she'd recited her phone number and address, and Mia had double-checked that it was correct, she pursed her lips and stood up from the barstool. "I really need this shift to be a good one. I'm on my weekend starting tomorrow. Can y'all let me get to work now?"

Emma sighed and dug her business card out. Beside her, Mia did the same. "If he comes in again, even though he knows he shouldn't, please call us. We just want to talk to him."

"The him I don't know. Right." Hope palmed the cards as she backed away and slipped them into her apron pocket beside her order book.

After they'd placed another set of business cards down on the counter for the bartender, Mia waved to Alec, thanking him for the coffee, and the two of them headed outside. The D.C. air was chill compared to the warmth of the bar, but Emma was still glad to be away from the hostess's glares and the patrons' endless side-eyeing.

Good thing upper-class eyeballs can't talk...I feel like I need a shower.

"Hope's nervous." Mia sighed, tapping out an update to Jacinda. "And afraid."

"She's hiding something." Emma unlocked their SUV and slid in.

Mia climbed into the passenger seat. "I asked Jacinda if we should wait until her shift ends. Kinda hoping she says yes, because I could use another of Alec's coffees."

"Careful," Emma said through a laugh, "or I really will tell Vance you've found someone else."

Mia's phone dinged. "She says it can wait until tomorrow morning. We have Hope's address, and MPD is adding it to their patrol route tonight, just in case our mysterious Snake slithers his way uptown. Did you clock where that girl's living? It's not *up* uptown, but it's not bad."

"The kind you can't get with cocktail server money?"

"No, nothing that high up. But she's living well."

"She's not working tomorrow. We should probably stop by and see just *how* well."

14

Emma had done her best to hurry home, but the end-of-day briefing had eaten up time with conjectures and brainstorming—none of it solid or all that useful in the end—so Marigold stood tapping at her phone in the hallway when Emma stepped out of the stairwell.

"Marigold, I'm so sorry!" She hurried forward while fishing her apartment key out. "It's been a day."

The woman's brown eyes all but twinkled. "For you? I have no doubt."

Emma led her inside and dropped her bag at the island. "I know I said I'd pick up taco supplies, but work got away from me. How do you feel about Chinese takeout?"

"Like I'm glad to take it in." The woman laughed, easing any worries Emma might've felt building.

Emma dug out the menu she'd last pulled out for Keaton and Neil, her colleagues from Richmond who had brought her up from the depths of her grief over losing Oren. She held it in her hands, remembering that day, and then shifted herself back to the present.

Just like Oren would've encouraged you to do, Emma girl.

She pulled up the restaurant's site. In minutes, she ordered up egg rolls, sweet-and-sour pork, seaweed salad, shrimp chow mein, and vegetable fried rice. No matter how stressful a talk they were in for, they'd eat well.

"Now," Marigold leaned forward from her seat at the island, "what's so urgent that we're talking tonight? I thought you said you wanted to take a break from thinking about the Other."

"I did." Emma placed a saucepan of water on her stove, then reached for mugs and tea bags. "But I'm ready to talk now."

While dribbling honey into the mugs and showing off the assortment of tea options, Emma proceeded to spill her guts while they waited for the food. She detailed the photo she'd found of her mother and the two mystery women—as directed by a ghost and left in her old storage unit. How it turned her fingers ice-cold when she touched it, so that her every instinct told her it was an artifact of the Other, begging to be let go. She mentioned the outdoorsy setting, their bare feet, and flowy dresses, and the writing on the back.

GT, CF, MV.

Eternally whole.

"My mom's maiden name is Gina Taylor, but I don't recognize the other women, who are also in their early twenties, or their initials."

"That sounds like a critical item, indeed. Was there anything else, though?"

Skirting over the case details, Emma filled her in on Oren's death and her spiraling descent into grief. And then, she told her about Oren's encouragement for her to embrace her talents.

Marigold, for her part, nodded along like a therapist, her brown eyes full of the warmth that had made it so easy for Emma to open up when they'd first met.

"I'm ready," Emma set aside her cup of lemon ginger tea, "finally, to find out more about my mom and those women. Especially since…oh, I forgot this part…I've been hearing that same wolf howl more often. It was loudest outside Oren's yoga studio, right before a boy's ghost hinted about where our last killer was hiding."

Marigold's eyebrows knit as she sipped her tea. "That's disturbing."

Emma waited, allowing the silence to stretch. She knew Marigold liked her time to think and didn't interrupt as the other woman enjoyed her drink.

"I thought about calling last week," Marigold pushed aside her tea, meeting Emma's eyes across the island, "because I was hoping you'd be ready to talk. I've noticed…friction in the Other that seems to be intensifying. When I try to make contact, there's…well, static. I don't know how else to describe it. It's as if various denizens of the Other are standing in my way, attempting to keep me out. And the cold is…less friendly. More formal, as if I've stumbled in rather than come intentionally."

Emma grimaced. "Like me, you mean?"

She reached one hand out to Emma. "Yes, but I'm not accusing you, okay? You must have your abilities for a reason. Don't take the Other's unfriendliness as a judgment from me or them. I think what's happening is simply larger than both of us. Now, you remember the woman who 'saw' you, according to your mother?"

Emma's heart skipped a beat, and a cold sweat broke out on her back. "How could I forget?"

Marigold offered a smile that appeared more forced than anything. "Well, I think that woman who saw you is gaining power and influence. When I'm able to commune with the Other, I get whispers that she's getting closer to you…though

I'm not sure what that means...and the way your mom warned you..."

"That can only be a bad thing." Emma sighed and moved back to the stove to retrieve more hot water. "But how am I supposed to learn more if everyone in the Other is too afraid to help me? Or even give me a name?"

"If your mother was as close as you say to those women in the photo, and it actually pains you to touch—"

"Do you want to see it?" Emma rose, but Marigold waved her back down.

"I think your instincts are right to investigate it, but not now. With both of us here, we might attract unwanted attention. One of those women might be who you need to sort all this out or be the 'she' your mother has warned you about."

Emma saw the picture in her mind and the easy smile of her mother. Her fingers tingled with the memory. "If only Dad were alive to tell me who they were, or Mom would speak up and do so. Someone in the Other has to be able to help."

"Maybe those in the Other just need a little convincing," Marigold held out her mug for more water, "to see that helping is preferable to not helping. And you may already have an ally in Oren."

Emma dipped her tea bag, spreading the essence before she drank. "What do you mean? Oren said he'd be watching, but he also said he shouldn't be talking to me any more than anyone else should."

Marigold hummed over her tea, breathing in the ginger scent. "Right, but ghosts talk to other ghosts, and we know he's on your side. Perhaps he can convince others to help you, so that you'll stand a chance in all this."

A chance?

"A chance against what?" Emma's voice had come out in a

whisper, but it was all she could manage, thinking of her mother's warning and how it had rung through the apartment like a fire alarm.

"I wish I knew."

Emma sipped her tea, immune to the cold that had suddenly seeped into the room.

There was nothing new to be concerned with, though. Mrs. Kellerly had ducked in and was snooping around the living room. "Oren. You mean that handsome yoga teacher?" She gave Emma a look. "I wouldn't mind seeing more of him around here."

Emma hid her warming cheeks behind her mug. Conveniently, the hot tea even combatted the thick, cold air that had come with the appearance of her friendly neighbor.

"Besides, he won't stop talking about you, you know. Always worrying about you." The old woman fluttered her hand at Emma's shoulder bag. "Not that we shouldn't all worry about you. FBI. Of all the careers for a sweet, young thing like you. You should be marrying and having babies. Not carrying a gun…"

Mrs. Kellerly prattled on to herself, saying nothing new, and Emma had to fight not to roll her eyes. She was just about to tell Marigold they had another guest when the bell chimed with their dinner, and she buzzed in the delivery driver.

But Mrs. Kellerly's presence had been enough to dispel some of the threat she'd felt in talking about the Other and the wolf, not to mention the unnamed women in the photo.

And, perhaps, if Mrs. Kellerly was right that Oren felt the need to keep talking about her, it meant Marigold was right, too, and Emma did have an ally in the Other.

She could certainly use one just about now.

15

Leo took another measured sip of his nonalcoholic ginger beer. Denae couldn't stand the stuff, but the extra rationing of ginger kept him alert.

He flicked the light on his watch to show it was half past ten and waved for Vance to give him a turn at the binoculars. They'd been staking out Drivers territory for hours now, ever since it had gotten dark, in hopes of catching their artist at work. So far, they'd had zero luck.

"I still think this is the most likely spot." He peered through the binoculars, searching the blocks ahead for any sign of movement.

They'd searched the neighborhood earlier and hit on this area, where the graffiti seemed to go from being prevalent and fresh to less and less visible. They speculated their artist was slowly making his way down this stretch of territory.

Vance pointed to the slats of a mostly intact wooden fence on a stretch of street littered with trash and more than a few cars that likely hadn't moved in months, if not years. "That fence is standing strong for being half rotten. My money's on that spot right there, just outside the lights shining off the street."

Leo jutted his chin to the opposite side of the street. "If I were a betting man, I'd say it's gonna be on the other side of that overpass, farther down the street and right where anyone passing by has no choice but to admire it. The guy clearly wants attention."

Vance fished a five out of his coat pocket and waved it.

Leo grinned at him. "I don't have cash on me, but I'm good for it. Bet."

Stuffing the five in the sunglasses compartment between them, Vance hummed in satisfaction. "Sucker."

And then, of course, they went right back to waiting.

Leo ranged the binoculars up and down the street. A few cars had passed.

Another half hour passed before anything changed. A bobbing light moved out of an alleyway three blocks up the street, offering just enough illumination to offset the dark figure holding it.

Leo passed the binoculars to Vance as he leaned forward over the dash. "I see him, dressed in all black. I don't think we can chance starting the car."

Vance watched for another moment, and then bobbed his head in agreement. "Looks like you win."

Leo grinned and snaked a hand out for the bill. He tucked the fiver away and zipped up his coat before Vance could change his mind.

After he carefully climbed from the car, Leo gentled the driver's side door shut, favoring his right leg still. The patellar dislocation had popped back into place a week ago, but the doctors told him to be careful. He was still recovering and could easily dislocate the knee all over again.

Vance's door clicked quietly shut as the other agent got out of the vehicle. Down the street, their person of interest had stopped in front of a concrete wall and was shaking a can of spray paint, turning his head side to side as if observing the area for threats.

And that means us. Good thing I convinced Vance to dress down for this stakeout.

At Max Stillwell's suggestion, they both wore faded jeans and work boots and had dark hoodies zipped up over their Bureau vests. In tandem, they crossed the sidewalk and moved along the edge of the properties, down a waist-high concrete barrier, past the rotting fencing, and then along the side of a building.

Stopping between a light pole and the lee of an apartment building, Leo leaned against the pole and pointed. The figure focused only on the concrete wall in front of him.

"The Rucker and Duran murders took place, what, five blocks north of here?" Leo squinted at the figure who'd begun moving his arm in a rhythmic motion, clearly working at some kind of shading.

Vance nodded, gesturing to their left to signal where the murders had gone down.

Leo was just about to suggest they continue when movement from even farther down the block caught his eye. Somebody else was approaching and keeping to the shadows too.

Their artist was between the agents and the new player on the scene, who was moving fast. Snake was in the crosshairs, it seemed.

Vance's whisper cut the air. "You see it?"

"I do." Leo was just about to pull out the binoculars when the new figure, also looking to be dressed in all black, passed near a light, and something in or around their hand glinted. "Shit. They're carrying. C'mon."

Vance was already moving forward, and Leo followed in a

light jog. The knee still twinged, but he could move well enough.

Faster than Leo would've thought possible without CGI interference, the second figure sped across the street, covering the distance to the artist in seconds. Snake whirled around to meet them, and a bright, quick flash of light erupted, along with a gust of paint.

The attacker fell back, holding their face, but sprang back up fast, lunging at the artist.

Leo and Vance drew their weapons.

"FBI!" Leo's yell broke the night apart, freezing both men in black. "Weapons down and hands up, now!"

The figures froze at the shout but remained faced off against each other for only a moment before fleeing in opposite directions. The artist abandoned his bag and his work, breaking down a side street. The attacker turned heel and sprinted back the way they'd come, straight down the street, but zigzagging back and forth on the width of the sidewalk.

When Vance holstered his gun and sprinted away, Leo followed as fast as he could, putting his weapon in its holster as he ran. But with all his attention on not torquing his knee and watching where his feet would land, he couldn't keep up with his partner.

Vance was closing on the attacker, and Leo spotted the artist racing down a side street. He had no choice. Much as they'd wanted to question the artist, the attacker could very well be their killer—he had their attention.

Leo's boots pounded down the sidewalk behind Vance, and he risked lifting his gaze to keep track of both his partner and their quarry.

The attacker was only a few steps from Vance when they swerved left into an alley, around a chain-link fence. Vance's feet went out from under him as he rounded the corner, and he went down hard, colliding with a mound of cardboard boxes and trash bags. He gave a cry, holding a hand to his face, but motioned with his other hand for Leo to keep going.

"Don't let him get away!"

Hooking an arm around the fence, Leo pushed himself to keep up with the fleeing suspect.

This dude's got some dang stamina, I'll give him that. But I'm taller.

Leo's long legs had made the difference. After another block, he was within arm's reach of the guy. With a sudden lunge, he shoved the attacker forward, causing him to stumble.

But the guy was fast on his feet and regained his balance in two steps. Leo was already back on him, though, grabbing at his upflung back leg in a two-handed grip. With a jerk, he brought the man down, but lost his grip as the attacker rolled forward into the fall.

He came up in a crouch, facing Leo, and on the man's right hand were three blades, jutting out from his knuckles just like a comic book superhero.

Leo reached for his weapon, but before he could draw, the mystery figure sprang forward and raked his clawed hand at Leo's face. He staggered back and felt a stinging line of warning on his left cheek. Leo barely deflected a left hook as the attacker retreated.

Punches and slashes came at him furiously, and it was all he could do to keep his feet without getting sliced. The guy landed a few shots with his left hand, catching Leo in the ribs, and a glancing blow that bloodied his lip.

He was outmatched in a fistfight, and the blades continued to demand almost all his attention. When the guy let his right arm cross his body, Leo surged forward and grappled his opponent, taking him down.

They landed hard. Leo had just enough time to register what felt like a vest or plate carrier underneath their dark hoodie, and it was contoured to fit a woman's curvy figure. A she.

Her right arm whipped around, and he blocked it, grappling with both hands to control the bladed weapon in her fist.

She growled and bucked underneath him, forcing him to the side. His weight shifted to the right, and his knee screamed at him. He immediately lost his grip on her bladed hand as he fell to the side, relieving the pressure on his knee.

He rolled away and assumed a crouch, bringing one arm up to protect his face and reaching for his gun with the other as the attacker lunged.

From down the alley, Vance's scream echoed off the brick buildings. "FBI! Freeze or I'll shoot!"

The threat was enough, and the figure leaped sideways rather than at Leo.

He pulled his arm down to see the attacker scurrying toward a fire escape ladder and jump, grabbing the lowest rung that hung eight feet from the ground. The ladder came clattering down, and she was already a full story above before Leo got his weapon up.

In the dim light, he had no shot, and she continued to climb.

Leo swiped at his face and came away with blood on his fingers. He was bleeding, heavily, but this wasn't the time to be precious. As long as he wasn't lightheaded enough to fall off the roof, he would damn well keep going.

Vance hit the ladder first and grunted. Loud enough that Leo called after him for a check-in.

"You okay?"

Vance looked back. His chin was ragged, bloody.

"Took some glass to the face back there. I'm fine. This

guy'll be lucky if I don't throw him off the roof." He turned back to race after the suspect, his feet pounding a staccato metallic rhythm on the fire escape stairs.

At the next level, Vance hollered, "FBI! Freeze!"

Metal clanged above them, and Leo swore it sounded like the distance was stretching. Vance continued climbing, moving faster now, and Leo fought to keep up.

Their runner landed on the roof with a thump. Leo reached the top just after Vance to see the suspect moving like a cat, bounding across the roof around air-conditioning units and under clotheslines.

Both agents were bleeding and, much as he cringed to admit it, decidedly un-catlike. In a matter of seconds, the suspect vanished from view, either sliding down another fire escape ladder or disappearing into a stairwell access door they couldn't see.

Vance paced the rooftop at one edge, staring downward at the other nearby roofs that were, given the she-cat they'd been chasing, easily within her striking distance.

Leo came up beside him. "She's gone?"

"She?"

"Attacker's a woman. Confirmed it when I tackled her. And she's wearing a contoured vest of some kind. Couldn't confirm the type, but it felt heavy enough to be Level Three."

Vance kicked at the building's ledge. He pointed toward the roof entrance near the corner, a single door that no doubt led to a stairwell heading down. He walked over to it and tried the knob. "Door's locked. Could've exited that way and locked it behind her, but I didn't hear it, so I doubt it. I think she leaped onto another building and kept running."

Leo glanced around, wishing they had more moonlight. "We'll call in backup and air support and medics."

Vance stood, staring over the dark roofs leading deeper into D.C.'s inner city and the Drivers territory. "We had her.

Dammit." He glanced back to Leo, still panting for breath. "Any chance of fingerprints, or did she have gloves on both hands? I saw the blades."

Leo grimaced, pressing one sleeve to the wound on his face. It was a deep damn cut. "Pretty sure she wore gloves. How she climbed that fire escape with those blades, though…"

Vance wiped a hand at his own bloodied chin.

Leo stepped closer to examine the wound. "Took some glass? That's a hell of a cut."

He just shook his head. "It's better than yours, or it better be. Let's take the stairs down, yeah?"

By the time they got through the very-past-its-prime lock on the door and climbed down through the apartment building to street level, they'd caught their breath, though not so much their pride. With the stinging sensation radiating from his cheek, Leo realized his knee had stopped throbbing with every step. *At least there's that.*

On the street, he called in the developments to Jacinda and Max, while Vance called in crime scene techs and backup to go over the artist's materials—assuming they were still street-side—as well as the fire escape and their attacker's path upward.

At the scene of the tagging, Leo shined his phone on the wall. A loose outline of a figure had been put in place, and although the artist had just gotten started, he'd been working from a newspaper clipping showing a mug shot. "Juan Carlos Duran. Our guy was starting up a tribute portrait."

Vance grunted agreement but pointed to the artist's bag rather than lingering over the artistry. He crouched and played his cell phone light over the outside, which was embroidered with a shiny blue cobra baring its fangs. Blood spatter marked the ground nearby as well as the tail of the serpent.

"I'd say this is solid confirmation it was Snake." Leo sighed, pointing his own light into the recesses of the bag to show a wide array of spray paint bottles and a few zippered bags, which he guessed must contain tools of the trade. "See a phone?"

Vance played his light around the area, but ultimately shook his head. "Think he could've caught her photo?"

"Our killer's photo, you mean?" Leo touched one finger to his cheek and the scratches there. The injury still stung, but the bleeding had mostly stopped.

He'd grab some ointment from the cops' first aid kit and stick around for a while.

Call their killer a cat or a wolverine or whatever moved that fast on two feet and threw punches like a prizefighter. No matter what, Leo still planned on catching her. And now that she'd officially spilled his and Vance's blood, he had no plans on calling it a night just yet.

When Max pulled up, Leo had every intention of telling him that, too, but the horror on the cop's face stopped him short.

Max held up a hand to forestall Leo and Vance from saying anything. He shined his flashlight up toward Leo's face. "How do you feel?"

"How do I look?" Leo forced a laugh. "I feel like I got attacked by a tiger, but I'm still standing. And we're—"

"Lightheaded? Dizzy? Any sort of blurriness to your vision?" Max shined his light over toward Vance. "What about you? Any strange sensations, difficulty focusing? Have either of you noticed the other acting strange?"

Vance stretched his hands, waving at an approaching EMT. "Not any stranger than usual."

Leo frowned. "What the hell, Max? We were on a stakeout, not drinking."

"Right, and our killer scratched you both, from the look

of things." He played his light over Leo's face again, then Vance's, showing off the cuts for a wincing paramedic. Leo grabbed the end of the flashlight and redirected it to his cheek.

"Just me, Max."

"What do you mean?"

"She just got me. Vance got in a fight with a pile of garbage that had some glass in it."

"Which means he's probably looking at a serious infection if he isn't treated soon. As for you, those blades could've been laced with *anything*. Hospital, now." Max looked at Vance, one hand pointing at the ambulance. "Both of you. If your tetanus isn't up to date, it will be soon. I'll get an officer to bring your car back to the Bureau. Get out of here."

Scowling, Leo accepted the attention of the paramedic, then followed Vance toward the waiting ambulance. Before he left, though, he looked back. "Our killer's a woman, Max. Did you catch that?"

"I did. Thank you for confirming. Now get going."

"She's wearing some kind of body-armor vest under her hoodie, and she fights like it's second nature."

"We're on it, Agent Ambrose." Max stared, as if waiting for an argument, but Leo only nodded acknowledgment and climbed into the ambulance with Vance.

16

Anger was an old friend, one my dad taught me to use for purpose, but tonight, my belly was so full of the emotion, I could just explode right there on the spot. I kicked at the trash around my feet.

Since getting away from those Feds, I'd been lingering around a boarded up fast-food joint left to rot.

The Powders don't even know what I'm doing, so how did those Feds find me there? And how did I let both of them get away?

Dad would be ashamed. I don't even think I got that one bad enough for a trip to the ER.

I marked him, though. Thinking of it, I ran my blades over my pants, making a mental note to get rid of them tomorrow. Much pride as I'd take in having marked a Fed, I wasn't gonna leave the guy's blood in my closet for some nosy-ass cops to dig up.

Those damn Feds. I had my hands on Snake, and now he knows I'm after him.

The course I'd set for myself was difficult enough without targeting a man who knew I was coming for him. And if he snapped my photo…

He brought his phone up just as fast as some men I knew pulled out a pole. Fast as my blades, even.

I trailed the blades along the wall beside me, watching the tracks they made in the dirty paint. I'd wanted to use Snake's blood and his paint to make a statement more than just killing him would do.

But now? It was too late to be thinking about making a statement.

I was too angry. The important thing, the only thing, was to find Snake and kill him.

Snake knew me, knew how I walked, knew what I looked like without my hoodie and blades. Dude was an artist. He saw details and remembered them, and he might've snapped a picture of me when we were fighting tonight.

My sister wouldn't stay away from him for any length of time. I knew her habits well enough to use that to my advantage, at least.

Lights sparkled from four blocks down, alerting the night to the presence of the Feds. I lost those two on the roof, but I knew they were down there with the others.

I should've circled around that rooftop and pounced on them. Finished 'em off before they could lift their guns.

It was the Professor's leadership, if anybody felt like making a joke about that term...he'd let us all get weak. Once upon a time, the Powders had been like a true family. Strong and supporting each other.

I needed to get my work done and toughen them up while there was still a gang to save.

Just the fact that the Drivers had a resident artist, and tags all over this city, was enough of an insult. The Powders had run D.C. not long ago. And then, the Drivers slipped in, slinky as a whole nest of snakes.

And Prof wanted to get all cozy with the enemy? For what?

Peace, stability, the idea that us and the Drivers could

coexist in D.C. like two sides of a coin. That was not how families operated. Giving up territory so somebody else could move in? That was like letting somebody else take up space in your own house.

I'd fix that.

I drilled my blades into the plywood covering a window behind me, anger burning a hole in my gut. Thinking of the last few months left a sour taste in my mouth—I was seeing the results of our inaction.

Me and Curtis spent our time sparring, with our so-called leader daydreaming about truces and money instead of ownership and blood. Tonight, I shied away from a fight that I would've been guaranteed to win, just because I'd been trained to run from the cops rather than stand my ground.

And this was former Powder territory.

We used to own these streets, and I would not be turning them over without a fight.

It was too risky to go after the Feds or some cop, but somebody would suffer.

And the way I'm feeling, any Driver will do.

I only wanted it to happen quickly, before Prof could get started on any so-called negotiations. If I fanned the flames, the gangs would be too lost to bloodshed—too busy outdoing each other—to think about identifying me personally, let alone coming after me based on some blurry photo that might or might not exist.

It was just a matter of making sure the Drivers believed they were all under attack, then they'd fight back. Prof wouldn't have any choice but to throw in the towel on truce-making. Then, he'd either stand up as the warrior he claimed to be, or I'd take his place and reclaim this city.

A figure lurched across the street a block down, holding their arms to their chest. For a moment, I thought it was

Snake again, come back around for his paints, but the cops were still nearby. I could see the lights flashing into the night.

I slipped out of my hiding place in the old fast-food joint and followed whoever it was out there. Maybe it was a Driver or maybe not. But I wouldn't know until I got closer.

Coming out to the sidewalk, I zeroed in on the person. It was a girl, and she must've heard me, because she started running.

That's my cue. Time to see what's got you so spooked.

I took off after her, and she sped up, stumbling a few times as she did. By the next corner, I was almost on top of her and could tell, even in the dim moonlight, that she wore blue jeans and a red t-shirt. No question about it, she was either a Driver or at least an ally of the gang. I picked up my pace and gave the girl a shove, sending her crashing down to the sidewalk on her hands and knees.

Taking a page out of the damn Feds' playbook made me feel cheap, like I was using somebody else's dirty tricks to win. But it worked.

The buildings around us were mostly dark, quiet on this Monday night, and all I heard were the sounds of distant traffic and the on-and-off sobs of the girl on the ground.

"You with the Drivers, yeah, girl?"

She flipped around to face me but didn't answer. The way her jaw shook was answer enough. She was scared, which meant I was right.

"Blue and red clothes, running around these streets. What used to be Powders' streets. You're a Driver if I ever saw one. An invader, coming around here and taking what ain't yours. Taking from me and my family."

"I ain't taken nothing from you or anyone else. I'm just doing what I have to so I can eat. Same as anybody does around here."

"Uh-huh. Same as anybody, except now it's harder

because the Drivers decided they wanted more than their share. Shoulda stayed up in B-more where you had it good and wasn't any competition. But no, y'all had to come down here, start messing around in other people's lives. Taking other people's family for your own."

Her eyes tracked down my arm to my blades, and she sucked in a breath. "You killed Jax and Rux. That was you. Because of Snake and—"

In a single leap, I landed on her. She shrieked, but I pressed her down to the ground, just like I did to that D I killed in the alley, squeezing my legs around her so she couldn't draw breath. She gasped like a fish out of water.

Just as silent, just as close to death.

I touched my blades to her cheek and drew them down, pulling up three shiny threads of bright red blood. Another sob squeaked out of her throat, but not loud enough for anyone to hear it.

The girl squirmed beneath me, but more like a protesting lover than a girl trained to fight, and I leaned into my grip on her, pressing my knees into her ribs. Her hands went slack on my arm and thigh, freezing.

Smart enough to feel death coming.

I was ready to strike, but she surprised me with more begging.

"Please, just leave Snake be. He ain't about the Drivers. They jumped him in a long time ago, but he ain't really with them. He just wants to be with his girl. That's all."

My knees pressed in on her ribs tighter, choking off her air. The idea of "his girl"—my traitor sister—took my blood from a roiling simmer to a boil.

"Snake's a criminal," I spat. "A thief, just like all you Drivers. Taking my city and my family away from me." This girl knew who Snake was with, and she clearly knew who I was too. "Snake's gonna die, girl. Nothing's changing that now. And so are you."

I had to shift my position so I could lift my arm for the kill.

"No, please…" She whispered her plea out with what little breath she could still pull in.

"She ain't *his girl*. She's *my sister*." The words came out of my mouth before I knew what I was saying, but I couldn't hold them back, not even if I'd tried.

"Your sister? You and—"

I dropped down hard on her throat, digging the lengths of my three blades into her windpipe and beyond. Blood spurted out of her, across the sidewalk as well as onto my face and my clothes.

Some of the anger in my veins eased, and I pressed the blades in harder. For a moment, I felt like I'd done the wrong thing, but she'd known who I was. She said something about Snake and somebody else. I'd cut her off in that moment. I'd let it slip, it was my mistake, but I couldn't let her go on living, knowing who I was and why I was out for Snake's blood.

Her voice echoed in my mind as I stared into her wide, dead eyes.

"That was you. Because of Snake and…"

Hope.

This would be his reward for escaping me. And the next time I saw him, he'd get his just the same.

17

Denae stumbled to a halt when she saw the rest of the team already gathered in the conference room with a box of doughnuts in the middle of the table. Jacinda glanced up and waved her in. The purely casual nature of the gesture was enough to drive any paranoia from her mind, but Denae couldn't ignore the ache in her chest.

She walked behind Leo's chair and took a seat to his left. She turned to greet him but froze when she saw his face. Leo had circles under his eyes, but even beyond that, a pad of gauze and bandages covered his cheek, speaking to how deeply he'd been cut.

"What happened? Did you find Snake? Did he do that?"

He shook his head. "Short story, I got to meet Wolverine. I spent an hour in the ER waiting for a tetanus shot, and another four waiting for a nurse to stitch me up."

Straightening her posture and relaxing the worry creasing her face, Denae patted his shoulder. "People lose limbs over tetanus, Leo. I'm…glad you're okay."

"I'd rather have had the shot." Vance flashed raw-looking hands at her and motioned to a bandage on his chin. "They gave me ointment to apply twice a day in case this gets infected."

Denae blinked, and turned her focus to Jacinda, who was sitting at the head of the table combing her fingers through her long red hair. "Can I get the whole story, not just the highlights?"

Jacinda rolled her eyes and opened her laptop. "You asked for it…"

By the time she'd finished going over the night's escapades, though, Jacinda's phone had buzzed with what Denae could only guess was another new development. The SSA finished by telling them each to get a tetanus booster that day—unless they'd had one in the last five years.

Leo met her gaze again, the stitches on his face looking angrier now that Denae had heard the story. "Our perpetrator is wearing something that attaches to her hand—"

"Her? We've confirmed we're looking for a woman?"

He nodded. "We ended up on the ground, grappling, and I was able to identify the perpetrator as female. I promise I got these scratches because she tried to kill me, not because I was getting handsy."

A joke died in Denae's throat as Jacinda held up a hand for emphasis, gesturing all of them to wait while she moved her attention between her phone and laptop. When she finally turned her narrowed eyes on the team, Denae could already guess what was coming. "We have another victim."

Leo cursed under his breath, clenching his eyes shut, and Vance slammed a hand on the table hard enough to rattle Jacinda's laptop. Any other day, the SSA would've said something. Outbursts were understandable, but not appreciated. This morning, she only glanced up at Vance and frowned.

He winced and pulled his hand back. Mia's palm landed

on his shoulder and gave it a gentle squeeze. Apparently, this morning was to be an exception to the unspoken *no couples in the office* rule.

Denae put a hand over Leo's, briefly, before removing it and opening her tablet, as the rest of the team did the same.

Vance slammed his open, earning him another look from Jacinda.

"Agent Jessup, I understand that frustration and resentment are often a part of this job. Let's remember to keep a clear head."

"Understood, ma'am. We had the killer right there. If we—"

"We tried." Leo scowled, clenching one fist above the table before snapping up a doughnut, as if to force himself into some semblance of normalcy.

Denae sat forward, ready for whatever information would come through and dreading what she was about to see on the screen. The SSA had gone to the head of the room and lowered the overhead.

"Jacinda, was the victim male or female?"

"Female, found seven blocks from where Snake was first spotted and attacked, after which Leo and Vance gave chase. Pictures incoming. Victim's name is Camilla Jones, age nineteen. Drivers tattoo on her wrist."

When the first picture flashed up on screen, Denae flinched back in her seat. The young woman was a lithe Black girl with short hair and wide-open, dead brown eyes. Her face was frozen in a rictus of terror, though tear tracks still marked streaks through what had once been expertly applied eyeliner and rouge. The girl's throat was nothing but a mass of bloody tissue.

Leo had frozen with his doughnut half-raised, paler than she'd seen him in a long time. She couldn't take her eyes off the scratches on his cheek. How close had he come to being the one whose body they were viewing?

He hissed under his breath. "You've gotta be kidding me. She's the one who told me and Vance," Leo waved between the two of them, "to find Snake and talk to him. Yesterday, at Jax's duplex. She must have been looking for him as well."

Vance grimaced. "And when our perpetrator got away from us, she found Camilla instead."

"You said the killer attacked Snake first, right?"

Vance and Leo nodded. "We announced to stop her, and they both bailed out. We pursued and lost her."

"What about him?"

Waving a hand in the air, Vance seemed unconcerned. "Our perpetrator uses blades, not paint. He's a POI, but he's not priority one."

Denae couldn't believe his flippant attitude, but he was right. They were trying to stop a killer, not a graffiti artist.

Leo took a bite of his doughnut, wincing as his sutures moved with his chewing. "Why would she kill Camilla? Just because she's a Driver? Or is it because she was seen talking to us?"

Jacinda dropped her face into her hands for a moment before meeting the team's collective gaze again. "If we're looking for a Powders member taking out Drivers, we can at least narrow the search to that gang alone. If this is someone who has it in for a particular group of Drivers, or even just one person, and she's killing anybody who talks to us…"

Denae didn't want to think about how hard their case had just become, or how hard her personal mission would be, as that possibility floated across the room.

Vance's phone buzzed, and he nudged it toward Mia. "You mind?"

She picked it up for him and read whatever message had

come in. "Fingerprints were found on the paint cans. Fingers crossed there'll be a positive match soon."

"Vance. Leo." Jacinda spoke as she added another picture beside the dead girl's, and they were all treated to another *Death by Powder* message, this one on the sidewalk beside Camilla Jones's body. "Do me a favor and remind everyone what you saw last night. You told me in the middle of the night, but let's hear it fresh now that we're all together."

Leo rubbed his left shoulder. "Female, five-five, wearing a body-armor vest. Trained fighter. She had MMA moves. I kept trying to get my gun up, but she was fast, getting inside my guard and forcing me to defend against this." He lifted a hand to his cheek.

Vance seemed to wait for the other man to go on, then finally shrugged and met Denae's gaze with a sigh. "She was a block away from Snake…assuming that's who our graffiti artist last night was…and we were about the same distance on the other side, the artist between us. Perpetrator covered that distance in a flash and attacked with no hesitation. Leo and I announced ourselves, and they both took off in opposite directions."

Jacinda rubbed her neck. "And you both followed the perpetrator?"

Vance nodded. "And I don't think either one of us is a slouch when it comes to running, even with Ambrose's knee. I fell behind when I skidded out on some loose gravel and ate a pile of trash." He held up his hands and jutted out his chin as evidence.

Leo sighed. "You want the truth, I'm lucky I didn't get more than these scratches. If Vance hadn't been there…"

The thought sent a little shudder up Denae's spine, what with the evidence of their fight right in front of her, but she turned her gaze back to Vance as he spoke up again.

"Thing is, our killer was so nimble. Disappeared up a fire escape and onto a roof, for crying out loud."

Jacinda coughed. "What the men left out is that they saw a flash of light. There's some hope that our artist caught our killer's picture. We have no way to be sure until we track him down." She glanced around the table. "That leads us to today's assignments. Emma and Mia, you two stay on Hope Jackson. Get her in here for questioning. She's suspected of being a known associate of our person of interest. Get her in here and get her to talk."

Once again, Denae sat back and did her best to appear normal, focused, and intent on the conversation. Listening for her name and an assignment.

"Denae, Max is at our newest crime scene. I want you to convene with him and stake out the area. Dress for fieldwork. Leo and Vance, that goes for you too. Pick up where you left off, canvassing Drivers territory."

Fighting down a sigh, Denae nodded at the SSA and made a note on her tablet, which she'd moved to her lap. But she didn't write anything important, just digital scribbles, because she could not ignore what she knew would be coming once she got into the field.

18

Emma headed to the break room with Mia trailing behind, thinking to grab one more coffee before they left. Leo popped in just as she was topping up with creamer.

"Emma, Mia, have you seen Denae? She left the conference room kinda in a hurry, and..."

"Restroom," Mia pointed toward the door next to the break room, "and she seemed upset. What's going on?"

He lifted a hand like he'd rub at his face but paused with his fingertips hovering over the bandage. "This case is...it's getting to her. More than other ones we've been on. Even the last one, with those kids dying. I want to help, but..."

I could give him some of Oren's wisdom, but I doubt he'd appreciate what my dead boyfriend might think.

Emma deferred to Mia with a look while she sipped her coffee. Fortunately, her colleague was armed and ready for the conversation.

"But Denae's a trained agent, Leo, just like the rest of us. She has her own methods for dealing with the stress of the job. I know you two are close, and trust me, I know how that can make it hard to separate what you want to say and do from what you know you should and shouldn't."

He rested his hands on his hips and paced the small break room, coming back to stand opposite them. "You're right. You are, and I know it. I just wish I knew what was making this so hard for her. We've seen tough things before. She grew up in this same type of environment and—"

"And it hasn't occurred to you that that could be the issue?" Mia wagged a finger at him. "Leo, you're smarter than that."

"Okay, point to you. And, yes, it did occur to me that she might be dealing with memories from her childhood, or that some of this is triggering her in a way she hasn't shared with me yet. With us, I mean."

Emma thought back to Denae's announcement during the initial briefing, when she'd revealed her upbringing, and expressed feeling like "a liability" if she were to join them in the field. "It sounds like you think there's something else going on, though. Like she's dealing with more than triggering memories."

"I do. But I can't exactly call her on the carpet."

Mia made clear her disapproval of that idea. "No, Agent Ambrose, you most certainly cannot. Not unless you want a well-deserved, one-way ticket to Single Town."

He backed up, holding his hands out. "Hey, I didn't say I was going to do that. Whatever's bugging her, she'll tell me. When she's ready."

"If she's ready."

"Yeah, that too."

"Look," Leo started, "I'm sorry to drag you into this. And we need to get on with the case. Thanks for steering me straight, Mia. And Emma, thanks for…listening."

"Anytime." Emma patted his shoulder. "You've been there

for me when I needed it. Sorry I don't know who your version of Keaton Holland would be…otherwise I'd call them in."

That got a laugh.

Hoping to maintain a focus on professional matters, Emma brought up the question that had been bothering her since she walked into the conference room. "Do either of you have any suspicion over who the perpetrator might be? We know we're looking for a woman, but who?"

Leo jumped on the question. "Vance and I met Amber the same day we saw Camilla Jones. Thoughts?"

"Honestly, I'm suspicious of her, but she seemed seriously shook up both times we spoke to her. Though the first time was over the phone."

Mia *mm-hmm*ed her agreement. "Definitely shook, but is she strong enough? Athletic enough? I mean, strippers have to be strong to do what they do, but…"

"Jax and Rux weren't small, and she took them down. Of the women we've interviewed so far, I'd say Amber's more likely than Hope, but not by much."

Stepping around Emma to reach the coffee, Leo shook his head.

"Denae's made it pretty clear that Max doesn't see the perpetrator being someone outside the gangs. Stepping in to divide and conquer, or play them off each other, isn't worth the risk for a single actor." He poured a cup and turned back to them. "That would have to be a larger coordinated effort. We just have one person, that we know of, and she seems to be targeting a specific group of people connected to the Drivers."

Vance poked his head into the break room. "Ready to head out, Ambrose?"

"Yeah." He sidestepped around Emma and Mia. "Let us know if you get anything from Hope, all right?"

Emma forced herself to nod, promising herself that Leo would be her first call.

With everything he'd done for her on their last case, she at least owed him that much.

19

Amber Wilson lived at the end unit of a long apartment building. Mia glanced at Emma. "Ah, lovely. Welcome to the Bates Motel."

Emma snorted.

The building looked more like a motel than a cluster of apartments, with battered white siding and a flickering marquee in the parking lot reading, *Vacancy*. As they made it to the end of the narrow passageway, black-stamped metal numbers, showing *112*, hung crookedly below the peephole on Amber's door. They rattled when Mia knocked.

Footsteps thumped on the other side of the door, followed by the clattering of a chain and the click of the dead bolt.

The door opened, revealing Amber in a short, silky nightgown and a long see-through robe. "I'm waiting on a… guest, and I see you two through the peephole. What the hell do you want?"

Emma shot a quick glance at Mia. That was some getup to greet company in. "Amber, we just have a few—"

"Questions? Isn't that what you said last time you

interrupted me?" Amber sighed dramatically, but then stepped back from the door and waved a hand as if welcoming them into a dinner party. "Fine. Whatever. Come on in, already."

As they stepped up to the door, Amber glared from Mia to Emma as if daring either woman to say anything about her clothing. They didn't, and she flounced backward into her place, leaving the door hanging open.

Emma led the way in after her.

What appeared shabby and tiny from the outside turned out to be a little bit larger, but no fancier. Amber's one-room home had space for a queen-size bed, a living room set with a sofa and coffee table, and a corner kitchen. A closed door beside the fridge presumably led to a bathroom.

Mia shut the door behind them, and the petite stripper dropped herself onto the sofa. Gazing at them with a pout on her lips, she put her bare legs up and crossed her arms over her chest, which pulled her nightgown a touch too far down for decency's sake.

"Well?" Amber's bright-red fingernails tapped against one elbow where she held her arms to herself in a poor attempt not to betray her nerves. "What do you want now?"

Emma remained standing and did her best to ignore the woman's state of undress. "We'd like you to go over your alibi for Sunday night. Last night also."

Her tongue darted out to her lips, and she pouted. "I came home Sunday night, right after Veevee closed up. I left around two thirty."

"You walked home? Drove?"

"I got a lift from Celine."

They'd heard the dancer's name a couple times, and it wouldn't take much to confirm Celine had both been on shift Sunday night and driven away with Amber in her car.

But we won't be talking to Veevee about that, unless he's suddenly decided to show up again.

"What about last night, Amber? Between nine p.m. and midnight?"

"I was at a friend's bachelorette party. You ask around or look at video over at the Beggar's Dream Club, you'll see me all over the footage. Didn't leave 'til after four this morning."

"Yet here you are dressed for…a guest."

"And?"

Mia nodded while her gaze roved the apartment. "So on the footage for Sunday night, we'll see you getting into Celine's car? Right around closing time?"

Amber stared at Mia, and then seemed to force a smile. "You know, you're pretty enough to do what I do. I could get you in—"

Emma chuckled. "That's a lousy attempt at changing the subject."

Called out, the blond sucked on her lower lip and shook her head. "So what if I didn't leave right away? I don't know what the cameras show or don't show. They're probably not reliable anyway." Amber recrossed her long legs and tightened her arms across her body. "Do I need a lawyer?"

"I don't know, Amber." Emma sighed. She really didn't think this stripper was their killer, but she was obviously hiding something. "Do you? You're hiding something, and you'd make it a lot easier on us if you told us what."

"People are dead," Mia lowered her voice, speaking slowly as if to emphasize the point, "but if you know anything or have a way to clear your name, now's the chance. Are you working with one of the gangs, maybe? Moving around drugs for them?"

"No!" Amber's face went red, and she sat straight up on the sofa, glaring. "I don't touch drugs! You could search this whole place and wouldn't find so much as a cigarette!"

Emma raised one eyebrow. "Is that permission to search your place?"

Amber's mouth opened in shock, then she shook her head so hard that her blond hair swept in front of her eyes and hid them until she pulled it back around her shoulder. "No, it was not. You need a warrant for that. I know my rights."

"Okay, Amber, but we know you were at Jax's house...you spoke to some of our colleagues, remember?" Emma knew they'd been over this, but Amber's explanation didn't sit quite right with her. "So there must've been a reason you went over there. Knew where he lived, for that matter. The story you gave was that Jax had your 'great-aunt's antique necklace,' but none of the jewelry recovered from the home was older than two years."

"You're just interested in the murders, right?" Amber's gaze darted back and forth between them. "That's it?"

Mia shrugged. "If you're smuggling jewelry or playing mule for the Drivers, that's not our concern. That doesn't mean you won't be getting a visit from the local drug task force—"

"I have a side hustle, okay? I pay house calls now and then. It pays a lot better than stripping, even with the tips."

"House calls?" Emma raised an eyebrow.

Amber smirked and gestured at her figure before crossing her arms again.

"Anyhow," she sat back in the sofa, "I've been trying to get the Drivers as customers since I know they have money to throw around. And I work at their bar, so it's not like I don't know who they are. I didn't really want Jax on my list...that boy couldn't keep money in his wallet to save his life, you could see from how he tipped...but he liked me enough, and I thought he might be my way into getting the gang's business in general. Maybe get one of the higher-up guys to be my man." She got a dreamy smile on her face, as if she really believed the words coming out of her mouth.

"You said Jax 'liked you enough.' Why not just stick with him and call it good?"

Amber broke out in laughter. "You wouldn't be saying that if you knew that kid. Dude was, like, so young. I swear, he probably still believed in Santa Claus and the Easter Bunny."

"And you were ready to take advantage of his youthful fascination with you so you could hop to the next highest bed on the ladder?"

Emma's comment had the desired effect of putting Amber back a step, but it came with the knock-on effect of pissing her off.

"Like you'd know a fucking thing about what it's like out here, little Miss Fedsy, all sweet and friendly. Jax wasn't my first choice, but he was a good kid, and he didn't deserve what happened to him. If I thought about him at all before, it was thinking I could help him and he could help me."

"But," Mia lowered her tablet, "he couldn't help you after he died. So why go over there?"

Amber pouted. "I thought he might have money stashed away, or maybe something I could use to get on the Drivers' good side—"

Shock almost pulled a laugh from Emma's lip. "You mean you went over to a murdered gang member's house to rob him the day after he was murdered? Breaking into a house when cops or agents were sure to be looking for evidence?"

Amber's cheeks reddened. "Uh…"

"You do know how foolish that was, right?"

She shrugged. "I didn't know it would be such a dump. Except for his video games, Jax had about fifty different kinds of shit and garbage in that place. And hey, I never broke in…thanks to your *friends*…so there was no crime. I just looked through the windows."

"So the story you told us yesterday, in your dressing room, was…a story? Made up on the spot or one you'd practiced?"

"It was…mostly true. I was trying to see if the guy who killed Jax was around, but that's because I didn't want to run into him if he was. I was just there looking for something I could sell fast, get some extra cash since him and Ruxie wouldn't be tipping anymore."

Emma glanced at Mia, who had one eyebrow raised in disbelief. They were on the same page, then. This woman wasn't smart enough to have planned, and then committed, the murders they were talking about.

"Okay, Amber, so let's get back to the original question." Emma sighed, starting to feel as if they were going in circles. "Where were you during the murders? It doesn't sound like you left work right away, so…"

"I was with Veevee. We stayed after he closed up. I was with him for about an hour. The footage of me leaving the bar later in the night will show that the two of us walked out about the same time. Close to three, three forty-five, something like that."

Mia texted the team to confirm the security footage. "If all this is true, you have nothing to worry about from us. Jax and Rux still deserve justice. Can you tell us anything else about them? About their friend you mentioned?"

Amber pouted. "Not much. I mean, I really wanted their friend as a customer, he was so quiet and respectful. Didn't want to be at the club, like I said, and I thought that meant maybe he was, like, one of the high rollers, you know? I tried to get his attention, but he was never interested. I bet it was because of some girl. I heard Ruxie tell him to 'leave her be' every time they were in, but I doubt he was listening. Dude was always texting, even while I was dancing on the pole, right in front of him."

"Did you happen to catch this girl's name? Was it ever mentioned?"

"Her name's Hope."

Emma traded a look with Mia, then turned back to Amber. "It would probably be a good idea to avoid being alone, outside, if you can. Is there someone who can walk you to your car from the club or check on you here at home?"

"What, like my big sister? Or somebody else who doesn't exist?" She rolled her eyes and stared at Emma.

"We'll have MPD add your apartment to their nightly patrols for a while. Someone's out there killing people, and their victims have all been associated with you or people you knew personally."

Amber scoffed. "Thanks so much. Send the cops around my place every night so people think I'm a snitch. I feel safer already."

"Look, this isn't—"

"I gave you that girl's name. Isn't that enough to keep me out of trouble?"

Mia put a hand on Emma's arm and nodded toward the door.

Once outside, Emma vented her frustration to Mia. "I have a suspicion that *nothing* is enough to keep that woman 'out of trouble.'"

"You and me both. But she did give us Hope's name, and that's a link between the murders and a person of interest."

20

Emma climbed into the driver's seat of the SUV as Mia read off Jacinda's text. "Amber and the manager both walked out of Night Trips at close to 4 a.m. Couldn't have been directly involved."

"Well, that's something."

Mia slid her phone back into her pocket. "Sure is. You want to question Hope again, I'm assuming."

Emma nodded, already looking up the information the girl had given her when they'd visited the Starlight Lounge.

And unlike when Emma had called Amber's number earlier that morning, Hope picked up on the second ring. "Hello?"

"Hope, this is Special Agent Emma Last. My partner and I met you at the Starlight yesterday. Would you mind if we stopped by to speak to you again?"

The other side of the call remained silent, but when Hope spoke again, all the hesitancy she'd exhibited the day before was broadcast in a second's speech. "I don't…I don't think I have anything to tell you. Good—"

"Hope!" Emma cut her off. "This is important. Please, please, don't hang up."

Hope sighed, her voice going softer when she spoke again. "You don't understand. It's not a good idea for me to talk to you."

"Because you're afraid?" Emma's guess was met with silence, but that came close enough to confirmation in her book. "Hope, people's lives are at stake. Someone else has died, and we believe you may be able to help us stop the killer before anyone else gets hurt."

Mia leaned in and spoke gently. "It'll be more discreet if we come to your apartment. If you don't want anyone else to see you talking to us…"

"Okay. Come over if you need to. You have my address?" The girl's voice sounded tremulous, and Emma only hoped she wouldn't disappear before they could get to her.

Emma confirmed they did, and Mia was already typing it into the GPS by the time Hope ended the call, leaving Emma staring at her phone.

She checked the GPS as they pulled into traffic, noting that Hope's apartment was well away from gang territory. Putting her foot down, Emma got them moving and wove around a slower vehicle straddling two lanes.

Mia gripped her *oh shit* bar a second before she glanced Emma's way. "You really might listen to Leo and slow down a touch sometimes, ya know?"

Emma frowned but made a point of lifting her foot from the gas.

When she finally pulled into Hope's apartment complex, she had to weave through a maze of mini-streets to reach Hope's building. The cookie-cutter apartment blocks were all painted in a tasteful light gray with salmon trim. Neatly manicured green shrubs lined the walkways.

Emma parked, and they got out, with Emma marveling at

the difference in their surroundings from where they had been earlier that morning.

Mia gazed around as they headed up the walkway. "I feel like I'd get lost trying to find my apartment if I lived here."

"Regularly." Emma rang the bell for Hope's apartment and waited for the buzz before opening the door up for Mia. "And I'd never find my way at all after the two of us went out for margaritas. You'd have me sleeping on your couch."

Laughing, Mia led the way down a narrow hall. At the end, a tiny elevator took them up to the fourth floor. Hope's door was decorated with a little hanger sign. *Welcome! Beware the Cat!* Before Emma could knock, the door opened.

"Come on in." Hope pulled an oversize sweater tighter around herself and stood back, waving them inside.

Mia pointed to the sign as she passed. "What about the cat? Is it safe?"

Hope nodded to a curtained window.

At second glance, Emma noted a long black tail swinging back and forth from beneath the hem of the fabric.

"More a joke than anything, long as you're not allergic. Hermit's a sweetie."

Tastefully furnished, if sparse, the small apartment had just room enough for a sectional and an armchair, with a galley kitchen. A hall off to one side of the kitchen presumably led to Hope's bedroom and a bathroom.

Hope took a seat in the armchair, and Mia and Emma sat across from her on the sectional. She glanced back and forth between them silently, sliding a hand across her brow to hold her bangs out of her eyes.

Mia spoke up first, quietly. "You sounded scared on the phone."

"Wouldn't you be?" Hope sniffed, looking younger than she was without any makeup. "Feds come around my work asking questions about…" She pressed the heels of her hands into her eyes.

Emma settled her iPad on her lap, knowing something more useful had to be coming. "Questions about the guy we were asking about. Who you know."

Hope swallowed, and then looked to the window. "Hermie. Come here, Hermie."

To Emma's surprise, the cat dropped from the window and trotted over to his owner. He weaved between her legs and out before hopping up onto her lap, where he began padding at her sweater. Hope petted him, and Emma waited. If the girl needed the comfort of her cat, and that would get them answers, she wasn't going to argue, and Mia clearly felt the same.

When the cat began purring, curling against Hope's body, she finally looked back up at the agents. "I'm seeing him, okay? And, yes, he's a member of the Drivers. But he never brings any of his buddies around the Starlight and barely comes in because he knows it could cause me trouble."

Emma waited, and then prodded her. "And his name is?"

"He goes by Snake on the street. That's his artist name," her voice cracked a bit, "but his real name is Jamaal Monroe."

If Mia had caught the name's significance, she was doing an Oscar-worthy job of not showing it. She kept her attention on Hope. "Do you know where he is?"

Hope frowned, tight-lipped. "I don't, no."

"You're seeing him, and you don't know where he is?"

"I don't keep tabs on him. We've only been dating a little while anyway. He's got some stuff here, but…" She shrugged. "I don't know where he is. Sorry."

Mia reached out a tentative hand to pet the cat. Hope nodded, and the cat purred as Mia stroked his back. Making forays into trust where she could, Emma knew. "Did you see him last night?"

Hope's head shook, fast enough that her wooden earrings dangled. "No, I haven't been able to get in touch with him for days. Not since Monday. He was here Sunday, stayed overnight. I thought about going to find him later, but… Drivers territory, ya know?"

Emma did know. Nobody was necessarily safe in gang territory these days, but a pretty girl like Hope could get into trouble fast if she ventured down the wrong street and didn't have friends there. But was that the reason she stayed clear of the area, or was something else at play?

"Do you know why anyone would be targeting Jamaal, specifically?" Emma offered what she intended as an unsuspicious smile. If Hope couldn't get in touch with her boyfriend, there was no reason for them to worry her further by telling her the man had been attacked last night.

"No." Hope scratched under Hermit's chin, gazing at him rather than facing the agents. "But the Powders are crazy. You said someone else was killed, and I guess it was them, or you wouldn't be here. They're probably aiming to start a turf war. Wait…" Hope's eyes darted up to Emma's, widening.

"What?" Emma prompted gently.

"It wasn't Jamaal, was it? Is he okay?"

Mia reached out and gripped her hand. "Hope, honey, calm down. We're still looking for him. That's why we're here. It was someone else who was killed."

Hope took a deep breath, and then another. Panic still showed in her eyes, but she seemed more relaxed. "If Jamaal's been involved in anything, it's just because he was in the wrong place at the wrong time."

Emma exchanged a glance with Mia. She hadn't particularly wanted to tell Hope about this, but it seemed there wasn't much choice if that was the line that the young woman was going to take, that Jamaal was a "good" gang member who wouldn't have enemies.

"Hope," Emma leaned forward carefully, catching her eye before continuing, "Jamaal wasn't killed, but he was attacked. Two of our colleagues interrupted someone who came after him while he was painting."

Hope's hand stilled on Hermit's fur, a little gasp escaping her parted lips. She shook her head belatedly, and her voice came out defeated when she answered. "Maybe…maybe it's the Powders' artist. Jamaal never covers up their tags, but plenty of other Drivers do. It coulda been, like, a payback move, right?"

Even Hope didn't seem convinced, but just as Emma went to speak, the girl shifted Hermit from her lap to the floor, ignoring his little meow of protest, and stood straight without warning.

"I need to go find him. If you two will excuse me—"

Emma stood and stepped in front of Hope in one motion, blocking her way to the hall.

The young woman sat back in her armchair, and her cat reclaimed his throne on her lap.

Mia leaned forward to stroke the cat again. "Hope, do you know where Jamaal might be? He may need help."

Hope's eyebrows knit together. "I…you're…"

"The Feds, I know." Emma forced a smile. "But we're not looking to arrest him, and if you've waited this long to find him, that means you had reason to be scared to go after him. So let us help. We can go searching, and we'll get in touch with you when we find him. Please. I give you my word that we're not looking to arrest him. We just want to stop any more murders."

Mia closed her iPad and ducked down purposefully, forcing Hope to meet her eyes before she spoke. "Hope, do you know where he might be?"

The repeated question hung in the air, but finally the girl stiffened, resolve seeming to come into her lips. "I think so.

There's an empty space where he goes to paint, not gang stuff…just painting to paint. He goes there when he needs to be alone. It's an old school building that shut down a couple years ago."

"Why haven't you gone there before?"

Emma knew the answer to Mia's question as the last words left her lips.

"It's deep in Drivers territory. I been with him sometimes at his friend's place. That boy who died. Jax? But that place ain't as deep in as the school."

"Is there something we should know about you and the Drivers? Did they do something to you or someone you care about?"

Terror stretched Hope's lips, and her eyes shot wide open. "I don't…no, I swear. I just don't like being around there. They are a gang, you know. That's it, I promise."

Mia squeezed the young woman's hand again. "Hope, relax. We're not accusing you of being the murderer."

She settled down after a few breaths and looked from Mia to Emma and back again. "You have to promise you won't hurt him." She then grabbed Mia's hand with both of hers. "Please? He's not like the other Drivers. He just loves to paint street art. If he's got something in his hand, it'll be a can of paint. You gotta trust me. That's who he is. He doesn't even own a gun."

Mia gripped her hand back, nodding. "Hope, somebody is out there doing a lot more than just hurting people. We only want to talk to Jamaal, to find out what he might know."

"He doesn't know anything. He can't."

"And you're so certain of that because…"

Hope's chin quivered. "He's just an artist. I swear. He's not involved in any of the violence or drugs. He stays away from all that."

"We'll go talk to him, so we can make sure he's safe. We

can have MPD send an officer around here as well, to make sure you're protected."

Where before Hope had seemed almost terrified, her entire manner shifted at the mention of cops coming around her place. "No. Don't do that. I'm fine. All I need to know is that you're going to find Jamaal to talk to him and keep *him* safe."

Mia let go of her hand. "If he doesn't try to hurt us, we won't have any reason to hurt him."

"Fair enough?" Emma waited for the young woman to nod, and when she did, Emma pulled out her phone to take down the address.

They'd alert Jacinda on the way, and with any luck, this next step might answer an awful lot of building questions.

Most importantly, it might get our whole team back in one piece. Denae's been avoiding this case, and now I think I know why.

21

Emma waited for a dog walker to cross the street with his five charges before pulling out of Hope's complex. She tapped her foot anxiously. They had to get all the way across town—again—in order to seek out the abandoned school Hope had pointed them to.

But she had a feeling they were getting somewhere. In fact, she and Mia had already put on their bulletproof vests before getting back into the SUV. She was that sure this case was about to come to a head, one way or another.

"Mia, do you want to call in with an update?"

"You just texted Jacinda, right? Why are we calling?"

"We both heard Hope's voice crack when she told us Snake's real name, right?"

Mia stared out the windshield. "Yeah, I heard it. I didn't want to believe it, and I was hoping we could find him and just ask him if he's got a sister in the FBI. But you're right." She pulled out her phone as Emma got them into traffic, heading down the street. "I'm calling her, not Jacinda."

Emma nodded and gave a slight grunt of agreement. Bringing in the SSA was inevitable and the right move no matter what. But if Denae's brother was the Drivers' graffiti artist, and their perpetrator's target, his sister deserved to know immediately. She might convince him to surrender to protective custody.

"Hey, Mia." Denae's voice didn't have its usual sparkle coming through the SUV's speakers. "What's up?"

"Denae, hey. Emma and I just left Hope Jackson's apartment. We have a lead on the graffiti artist—"

"Snake?" Denae cut in. "Do you have his real name?"

Emma glanced at Mia. Her friend looked as worried as she felt.

Denae's voice sounded strained, all the wry humor gone. "Yes. It's Jamaal."

Emma slowed the car, waiting for Denae to respond, but the phone had gone silent. "Denae, are you there?"

"Yeah." She sighed, then emitted a curse. "Just give me the address. I'll meet you there."

Emma glanced at the phone uselessly. "Denae, that's not necessary. Mia and I—"

"Give me the address. Don't make me track your vehicle."

Mia grimaced, eyes going wide as she looked at Emma, who could only shrug. Denae wasn't taking no for an answer.

"We don't have an address. Are Max and Jacinda there?"

"Jacinda's looking into the paint recovered last night, trying to find out where it was purchased. The fingerprints didn't match anything in the system, which is why you get to tell me my brother's a POI in this case. I don't know where Max is. You gonna tell me where you're heading?"

He's her brother. If the roles were reversed, you'd be just as demanding and just as insistent.

"Denae—"

"Address or GPS. Something, Emma Last. Give it to me."

"It's an old school building on the east edge of Drivers

territory. Abandoned, boarded up. Hope said it's near Tookie's Gym, on the corner of Ninth and Bell."

"I know the school. I'll text you the address and meet you down there."

Denae ended the call before Emma or Mia could reply.

"I thought Denae's only local family was her parents."

Mia picked at a cuticle. "Yeah, me too."

Emma stepped hard on the gas, veering around slower traffic to get them through a yellow light before it changed.

She knew only too well the type of mindset that could lead someone to a crime scene without it being assigned to them.

If Denae's brother was involved in all this, Emma didn't have time to stop at a fucking red light and count the seconds passing.

Mia read off the address of the school from her map search. Emma redirected the SUV there even as her friend texted Denae back to confirm they were en route. "We should at least text Jacinda. Let her know. She needs to know, right?"

"She does, but…" Emma thought of the night she and Mia's former Richmond colleague, Sloan Grant, had helped Mia take on a gang of drug dealers. They'd been acting without Bureau authorization and operating only on the tip of a shady investor whose foolhardy decisions had led to his wife and brother being killed along with Mia's brother, Ned Logan.

But that tip turned out to be accurate, and Ned's murderers were brought to justice.

"But what, Emma?"

"We got the guys who killed Ned, and we went off book to do it. I feel like we owe Denae the same kind of assist here. We're not even going in guns blazing. We just need to talk to him."

Jamaal Monroe wasn't guilty of killing anybody, as far as Emma knew. But going by the wrinkling of her brow, Mia didn't seem convinced.

"He might be the killer's primary target if the attack last night is anything to go by." Emma glanced back and forth between Mia and the road ahead as she pressed her point. "Bringing Jamaal in could be the best step, and calling in a team of agents and officers won't make that any easier. It might just scare him or get him shot if he doesn't comply."

"Okay," Mia dropped her phone into her lap, "but you get to explain this to the SSA."

"I'm fine with that."

They were at the corner by Tookie's Gym, where they had to wait for traffic to make a left turn. Several shirtless young men stood around outside the gym, flexing and trading casual jabs. They paused at the sight of the Bureau SUV, and several phones were pulled out simultaneously, some aimed to either snap photos or record video as Emma made the turn.

"Welcoming committee or early warning?"

"Little bit of both, if I had to guess."

The abandoned school was several streets deeper into the old neighborhood. As they parked, Denae pulled in just behind them.

One good thing about gang territory, parking was rarely an issue.

Emma moved to intercept Denae as she crossed the street toward the old school, but Denae offered little more than a tight smile as she sidestepped her and kept going. "Denae—"

"*Emma.* Let's go."

If the other woman was growling her name like that, Emma wasn't about to argue. Instead, she shrugged at Mia's scowl and followed Denae into an alley that ran along the edge of the old schoolyard blacktop.

Tall chain-link fencing surrounded the yard where rusted basketball hoops and weeds were all that remained of a place that must have had kids laughing and playing at one time.

Down the alley, a pair of double doors stood open, leading into what had probably been the school's multipurpose room or cafeteria. Chains hung from the handles, with a newer padlock clipped around one of the links.

Denae moved in first, with Emma and Mia right behind her.

The space was large and silent, but a glow came up on what had once been a stage. A dozen high-powered electric lanterns were set around the space, and a rainbow of art could be seen even in the sparse lighting. Murals graced the walls and even the floor. A tall stack of pallets was painted in a vibrant collage of birds on two sides.

At the back of the stage, a makeshift canvas of old sheets, stretched onto a wooden frame, had been painted to resemble the D.C. skyline, but in rainbow colors that virtually glowed by the light of an industrial-powered electric lantern.

Beside her, Denae let out a soft sigh that was entirely unlike her, totally without the woman's usual spit and vinegar.

The stage and the whole room had been empty and quiet when they arrived, but now footsteps echoed from the backstage area. A young Black man appeared, wearing headphones and carrying another canvas on a frame. He leaned it up against a pillar at the side of the stage and walked across the space to retrieve a can of paint from a supply laid out on top of an overturned fruit crate.

Emma followed Denae's lead and simply stood, ready to act. She couldn't help examining the art, though, especially on the canvas that had just been brought out.

Juan Carlos "Jax" Duran and Charlie "Rux" Rucker stood beside each other with their arms over one another's shoulders. Blue halos ringed in red hovered above their heads.

Mia came up beside Emma, whispering, "It's gorgeous. This guy's seriously talented."

Denae stepped forward, walking toward the stage and to Jamaal. Emma had to assume that was who they were looking at, because Denae had both her hands up, palms out, as if she were ready to protest or push back against something.

She's scared for him.

He still had his back to them and was now rattling a paint can in one hand and tapping out a rhythm on his pants leg with the other. His head bobbed in time to the beat as well.

"Mia," Emma leaned close, keeping her voice low, "no guns, yeah? He doesn't look armed. If he pulls something, okay, but Denae's out front. He'll see her first. Let's follow her lead."

They edged to the side of the room, heading toward the set of steps at stage right. Denae had angled herself to the other side, which was closer to Jamaal's position.

As Emma's foot touched the first step, Jamaal stood and headed back toward the crate with all his cans of paint. He shifted and spotted Denae. In that split second, which felt frozen in time, Emma saw the family resemblance. They had the same eyes, the same facial shape. But the glance was all she got.

Before any of them could reach him, Jamaal spun around, dropping the paint can and fleeing into the backstage area.

Denae screamed his name as she raced up the stairs at the opposite side of the stage and tore after him. "Jamaal, stop running! Let us help!"

Emma and Mia tore across the stage in her wake. If

Jamaal heard his sister's voice, he showed no sign of it. His footsteps faded to silence even as Emma and Mia caught up to Denae.

They emerged from the backstage area to find her standing alone in the inner courtyard of the old school. Long classroom buildings stretched out ahead of them, framing another patch of weedy blacktop with a few cracked and weather-beaten lunch tables scattered between concrete planters.

Walkways went in almost every direction, framing classroom wings and administrative buildings. Jamaal was nowhere to be seen.

Denae swiveled her head, as if searching for any sign of her brother. With a defeated cry, she crashed to her knees against a concrete planter. Emma moved to help her up, but Denae quickly pushed to her feet and yanked out her phone, hitting someone on speed dial. Had to be Jamaal.

She held it to her ear and paced around the weedy courtyard.

"Dammit." Stuffing the phone back into her pocket, she finally met Emma's gaze.

"No answer?" Emma stepped closer, but Denae only shook her head.

Fighting down the urge to question Denae immediately, Emma joined Mia in making phone calls. They reached Jacinda, and Max soon after. By the time they'd finished briefing them that their primary person of interest, Snake, had eluded capture, a pair of black-and-whites along with a forensic van had shown up.

The officers and technicians began collecting the paint and movable artwork as evidence.

As soon as Emma could get distance from the cops, she tugged Mia and Denae both into the backstage area. Denae had yet to stop tapping furiously at her phone, having pulled it in and out of her pocket nonstop since she'd last put it away.

Emma put one hand on the other agent's arm, stilling her from making a call again. "Are you going to tell Jacinda?"

Denae's gaze went to the vacant courtyard. Her face fell slack, losing much of the animation it usually held, and she shook her head with a frown. "I didn't know he was involved until you called me. I suspected, and I worried like hell, but I didn't know for sure."

"Why didn't you say something? We could've had him brought in before last night's attack."

Denae stared at her like she'd just sung the National Anthem backward and in another language. "What in the privileged nonsense are you talking about? Look around, Emma. Look at this school."

When Emma only met the other agent's stare, Denae reached out and took her by the shoulder, turning her to face the overgrown, abandoned courtyard.

"We grew up going to a school like this. Walked down streets like the ones you drove to get here."

"I know that, Denae. What—?"

"And it didn't sneak into your upper-class, private-school head that maybe I was happy to have gotten out before my life ended up looking like this schoolyard? Broken down, overgrown. Forgotten. I was one of the lucky ones, but in the back of my mind, it's always there. This childhood, the fear. Those who couldn't escape. Did your school look like this?"

That question felt like a slap in the face. Emma had indeed attended private schools with buildings that were named after men who were long dead. Denae was right. She'd been brought up somewhere far away compared to Emma's upbringing.

Emma let that sink in, choosing her next words as carefully and as thoughtfully as she could. Her friend and colleague was in pain right now. The last thing Denae needed was for her to harp about what had or hadn't been done, especially when Emma hadn't been raised in this world.

"Jamaal didn't get out, did he?"

"He moved to Baltimore after high school. I knew from Mom and Dad that he got jumped into the Drivers, but... yeah. We've been out of touch." Denae sighed, closing her eyes and leaning her head back against the wall behind her. "He's an amazing artist, as you can see. Always has been. I didn't want to believe he'd be mixed up in murder...so I didn't say anything. I should have."

Emma swallowed down a lecture that bubbled up from memory, accusations and admonishments that Jacinda had laid at her feet after previous cases where Emma had acted without thinking things through. "I get it. You hoped you were wrong and had every reason to want to be."

Denae's lips were pinched as she nodded. "I haven't told Leo..."

"I won't say anything unless you want me to. It's your story to tell."

For the first time since meeting the woman, Emma saw a tear snaking down Denae's cheek.

Before she could say anything, or even think how to respond, Mia stepped forward, putting a hand on Denae's shoulder. "Sloan and Emma were there for me when I needed help with my brother. We're a team. We're here for you, Denae. Always."

The three of them stood silently while the cops and forensic techs swarmed around the old school site. Denae's face relaxed from the tense and anxious mask she'd worn earlier, but she expressed none of the jubilance or confidence Emma was accustomed to seeing.

She's thinking about what happens next. She has to be.

Jacinda would have several select things to say about withholding information relevant to an active investigation.

That's the last thing Denae needs, of course, but Jacinda's not going to let this slide.

On top of that, their colleague had a family member smack in the middle of a possible gang war and a killer already targeting him.

If they didn't find Jamaal first, Denae could be dealing with a lot more than reprimands and disciplinary review.

She could be dealing with the same sort of debilitating grief that had nearly cost Emma her career.

22

Standing on Prof's front step, I could almost feel a clock ticking down. Telling me that this was my time to sink or swim, fight or die, growl or roll over and show my belly...all those little sayings Dad used to throw in me and my sister's faces like we were preparing for life as warriors.

Well, I was, as it turned out.

Hope, not so much.

The Professor's heavy wooden door glared at me, waiting, and finally my fist fell on it. Hard.

When he opened up, dressed in an open button-down and slacks like some half-assed businessman, his sneer said it all. I was the last person he wanted to see, but he stood aside, and I stalked past him into his fancied-up flop pad anyway. He closed and locked the door behind me, and we stood there for a moment in silence while I looked around.

His place wasn't anything amazing, really. Just an old duplex that he'd renovated by knocking a hole through to the other side, making it into one big place with plenty of room for people to occupy. Even with three rooms on the other side devoted to his workout space, entertainment, and meditation, he still had three more for sleeping in.

"Not much changed, huh, Prof? Just you living here?"

"Yeah. Something you need to say, or did you just come by to evaluate my living conditions?"

"It's all good. Just coming by to talk, like I said on the phone."

Leader of our gang and family. But his happy ass is the only one living here. Ain't that just telling.

"I'm pretty sure I told you all you need to hear at the meet. But here you come again. Understand I'm only entertaining your nonsense because of your old man's legacy. Weren't for Diamond Chip Jackson being your daddy, we wouldn't be having any conversation at all."

I nodded and followed him into the kitchen. "Yeah, I feel you. Thanks for respecting my father's memory, though. Family means a lot, right?"

He huffed and pulled out two short cans of cola from his fridge, then grabbed a bottle of rum off a high shelf. I knew where he kept the glasses, so I got them down and added ice from his fancy freezer with a dispenser on the door.

I let him mix up the drinks and went back to the front room, where I stared at the trio of chairs around a low coffee table. A stack of coasters sat at one edge. The chairs all had little round dust covers on the seats, like targets for somebody's backside so they'd know where to sit.

How did it come to this? We're supposed to be holding each other up, making sure nobody goes without.

Prof was the leader of the biggest gang in D.C., and instead of really looking out for us, he was living alone and making sure his furniture was protected while letting the Drivers roll into our neighborhoods...

Act like it ain't killing you to be sitting in this place while you know there's Powders out there who can barely keep warm at night because the heat's been turned off again.

He joined me in the front room, handing me my drink before taking a seat in the chair facing the door. I took the chair to his left, facing into the kitchen. I knew he had a pole tucked into his seat cushion, and he was right-handed, but he knew I knew those things.

Sitting on his right would've made it harder for him to draw down on me if he felt the need. I put myself at risk sitting where I did, but I still had my vest on.

God, I hope this don't have to go the way I think it does. But he's gotta know my last nerve's been worked to the end over this peace treaty shit.

I schooled my face to be fairly neutral and waited for him to kick things off like the businessman he'd become. He lifted his glass in a toast, and I did the same.

We each took a sip, then set the glasses on coasters.

"You said on the phone you had questions. All right, then, go ahead and ask."

"I want to apologize first." I waited for the lie to sink in. To see the doubt and then the slow, crinkling smile lines form around his eyes. He reached for his drink and tapped it against my glass.

"To solidarity."

I lifted my drink and repeated what he'd said, feeling the word burn on my tongue like the lie that it was. At least for now. He still had a chance to prove me wrong, but the way he smiled when I spoke those words...

"We got problems. I know you know that, and I ain't talking about between you and me. I mean the Powders. Our family's got problems, and we need to sort that shit out."

"Okay, Li'l Chip. Go ahead and sell it. If I like what I hear, I'll commit some resources your way. But don't think you can tell me how to run things. Keep respect in your mouth, we'll be fine."

Commit some resources. Here we go.

But he'd opened the door, and I had to at least try. I had to believe family still meant something to this man, because if it didn't, he was gonna find out what *Li'l Chip* was all about.

"Prof, I know you got a lot on your mind. A lot more than me and even Curtis and all of them put together. But this peace treaty with the Ds, man. How does that help us keep our family from starving? How do we look folks in the eye when they come to us for help making rent because their earners got picked up by the cops? And we gotta say we don't have enough to spread around because the Drivers came to town and took what used to be ours."

He steepled his fingers like a damn board member and looked at his front door. I forced myself not to follow his gaze and just kept watching him, waiting for his answer. When it finally came, I realized how wrong I'd been to ever think the man might come around.

"Li'l Chip, look," he laughed, "I can't be helping every poor fool living on our streets. People gotta lift themselves up. Do the work, get in the game and earn, ya know? Ain't on me if the Feds scoop 'em up. They shoulda known better and not been dumb enough to get caught."

I leaned forward, and my hand slid down to my hoodie pocket where my blades were snugly tucked away in their leather case. I took notice of Prof's hand dropping down to his hip. Before he got the wrong idea, I put up my other hand and waved him down.

"It ain't like that. Honest. I just…I think I got the answer to our troubles, and I wanted to show you what I'm working with."

I drew my blades out from my pocket and slid off the

leather sleeve I kept them in so they wouldn't snag on the fabric.

They were clean now, no traces of blood from that Drivers bitch I'd done last night. I slipped my fingers into the glove that held them, enjoying the way the padded metal frame nestled up against my knuckles.

Prof whistled low and steady, but his hand hadn't moved from next to his hip.

"You the one cut them two Ds the other night. What the fuck made you think that was a good idea?"

I looked him in the eye. "Nobody told me about the peace treaty. I was just looking out for my girl Celine. Them Ds were messing with her and were strapped. On our streets."

It wasn't the whole truth, but it was all he needed to know to pass my test. If he approved of me protecting another Powder, I might be able to call it good. If not, then it would be time for door number two.

He sniffed and nodded. "All right. I mean, it made things a lot harder, but I feel you. Just don't be doing shit like that again."

I breathed a short sigh of relief when he said, "*All right,*" because I really did not want to be killing him now. Talking with him like this reminded me of talks I used to have with my dad.

"Thanks, Ty, and yeah, I won't be doing nothing like that again. Scout's honor." I lifted my blades like a scout salute, and we both laughed.

"Where'd you get them Wolverine things anyway?"

"Made 'em myself, from my Dad's knuckle-dusters."

I held them out, and Prof admired them, even running his finger down the spine of one blade. He whistled his approval again, and there was that feeling coming back. Like I used to get when I'd show Dad some new move I'd learned or a new scar I'd earned protecting our territory.

Dad used to tell me brass knuckles were a cheater's tool. Then he'd laugh and tell me the world didn't ever fight fair, so any advantage you could get was a good one.

Welding blades to Dad's old set of brass knuckles was easy enough to do. It just took me some time down at the chop shop across town.

Making the leather sleeve to hold them had been the hard part, but it all paid off, and I could see from Prof's face that he was impressed. Then his mouth shifted from a grin to a thin line, and he sat back, keeping that hand down by his hip.

"Be straight, Li'l Chip. The fuck you come here for really?"

"Straight, yeah." I nodded fast and let my smile drop because that feeling like I was talking with my dad had vacated the premises.

"So come out with it already."

"The Powders need someone strong at the top. I don't see you doing a damn thing for our family except making yourself look good. Living fat and large up in here while others are almost starving."

His hand flinched down by his hip, but I was faster. Before he could pull that pole he had stowed in the cushions, I launched myself at him, sinking my blades into his neck.

"You like 'em?" I twisted my fist, listening to him splutter and gurgle as blood poured from his throat. It jetted out to the side, covering my sleeve, and I straddled his lap like a lover, jamming my knee against his right hand.

He spasmed beneath me as blood gushed between us and into his precious chair.

I watched him for a moment, almost expecting him to move, but he didn't.

Good riddance.

In his kitchen, I let his blood sluice from my blades, coating his steel sink in red. I didn't bother to wash it out when I was done and only wiped my blades on one of his dish towels before sliding them back into their sleeve. I was about to go out the front door when someone knocked.

I heard voices, some I recognized. Other Powders higher-ups.

"Hey, Prof. You in there?"

I stayed out of sight, in the kitchen, but felt my heart leap into my throat when I saw the curtains in the front room were wide open.

How'd I let that happen? Shit.

Without wasting a second, I ducked down low and scooted into the front room. They were still knocking on the door, and I heard one of them say, "Try the other door. Other side. Maybe he's working out."

That'd give me some time, but I was still taking a huge risk being here at all. I grabbed Prof's ankles and pulled him out of his chair. Blood kept spurting from his neck as he moved, and I had to catch his head before it thwacked against the coffee table.

I got him on the floor and dragged him into the kitchen, leaving a trail of blood behind him. If somebody looked in the window, they'd see that, but I couldn't do anything about it now.

Grabbing one of his steak knives from the block on the counter, I went back to his body and started working on him, cutting his neck good so nobody would know how many blades hit him the first time. Maybe some cop or doctor would know, but by the time they got involved, I'd be gone.

I dug the tip of the knife into the skin above his collarbone, and then pulled the blade downward along the line of his body, carving a smart *D*.

That done, I checked the front room again. I could hear the dudes knocking on the other door, but I still had to get my glass off the coffee table. It had my prints on it.

A shout from outside had me whipping back into the kitchen, out of sight.

"Hey, there's blood in there! Blood, man. Somebody smoked the Professor."

Shit. Time to get gone.

They were kicking at the door now, trying to break it. Good thing for me Prof was all about home security. He'd put in stronger dead bolts when he redid the place.

I dashed in, grabbed my glass, and spun back around for the kitchen. The guys outside kept yelling, and one of them spotted me.

"I seen him! Some dude's inside there killing Prof!"

They kicked and kicked. One of them was probably heading around the side of the house, so I had less than a few seconds to get clear. I threw the glass at the floor hard, so it shattered into little pieces, then jammed into Prof's bedroom.

I stripped off my hoodie and stole a replacement from his closet. He wore a size bigger than I preferred, but the blades were secure enough when I shifted them into my new front pocket.

I thought I should bury the old hoodie in the back of his closet. It was his blood anyone would find, but I'd rather them not find it *on* me.

But I'd worn that hoodie forever and a day. Cops'd find my DNA on it. I balled it up inside another of Prof's shirts, making sure I didn't get any blood on me in the process. I'd dump it somewhere, far away.

The front door splintered finally, and I heard them yelling.

I took a quick look out the bedroom window. Nobody was out there. I threw it open, kicked the screen clear, and jumped. I was running as soon as my feet were under me.

Prof's place was thankfully just one of many along this street, all with pretty much the same landscaping.

Bet his ass paid into a damn HOA instead of making sure every Powder had enough to get by. We all shoulda put him down a long time ago.

I went from yard to yard, tearing down the alley behind all the houses. Shouts echoed from behind me, but when I looked over my shoulder, nobody was following.

At the end of the alley, I slowed down to a jog and tossed the bloody bundle into a trash can. Somebody might find it, but they might not. I couldn't be worrying about that now.

I took a turn and headed deeper into the neighborhood. A few minutes later, when I was well away from the scene of my crime, my phone buzzed in my pocket.

I took it out and saw Curtis's handle on my screen, with a text.

Ds smoked Prof. It's war. Get to HQ.

At least Curtis hadn't forgotten me. But then another text came in, and I stopped dead in my tracks.

Need you to hold down the fort. Be ready to patch people up and shit.

I fired back a text of my own.

I should be on the street with y'all. Fighting.

He didn't reply.

I'd never felt as alone as I did in that moment. The one person I thought for sure I could count on to have my back had just left me on *Read*.

I started running again, pretending the tears on my face were born of rage, when really, they were coming from the deep well I'd been filling for years.

First, my father abandoned me when the liquor got more exciting than teaching me and Hope how to survive.

Now I'd been abandoned by Curtis twice over. When he kept Prof's plan on the down-low, letting me find out about it all on my own, and this shit with the texts, like I couldn't be any help when our gang, our family, was about to get wrecked.

I ran as fast as I could, going I did not know where. A war was starting, and I'd been the one to fire the first shot.

If anything, my challenge would be finding Snake before anybody else did, because that was one thing that hadn't changed. He was still mine for the taking. I wanted his blood on my blades.

End of discussion.

Plus, there was the small matter of teaching my sister a lesson.

Hope, you need to remember who your family is. You need to remember me. Because right now, it feels like you're my last chance at having one.

Some small part of me wondered if she'd fully dedicated her loyalty to Jamaal and his Drivers. If she had, I'd deal with her when the time came, just like I'd dealt with Prof.

My father would've understood. Before he failed to understand anything. If Hope was a coward and had no loyalty to her own blood, then she deserved nothing less than my blades, just like her new gang.

23

Leo knelt to examine the most recent message in blood that the killer had left them. Along with Vance, he'd been scouring the crime scene around where Camilla Jones's body was found. So far, they'd dug up very little beyond what was already obvious.

A dead woman, a bloody message, and nothing to indicate who's responsible.

No witnesses they had interviewed were willing to speak up, except to say they'd seen Camilla Jones around the neighborhood and knew she sold cosmetics out of her home.

Leo was just about to tell Vance they should check in with Jacinda when shots rang out down the street.

"That's over where we spotted Snake."

Breaking into a light run, he trailed behind Vance, but caught up to him at the next corner.

"Where'd it come from?" Vance turned in place.

A woman and her child were rushing in the other direction, away from an intersection. Leo didn't bother yelling at them to get to safety. They knew what they were doing, fleeing the violence.

Leo nodded in the direction they'd come from and followed Vance across the intersection.

At the next corner, Leo pulled out his phone even as it buzzed with messages. He'd been ready to call in the violence, but it seemed that someone already had. Vance's phone chirped angrily for his attention, as well, but both agents were tucked against the wall and peering around the corner, guns drawn.

Then chaos erupted.

People flooded in and out of various buildings. Some wore gang colors and carried items that could've been weapons. Leo only spotted one gun for certain.

Shouts and curses competed with gunshots, filling the air, and it was impossible to determine who was against who without nailing down colors and seeing the direct aiming of weapons. From where Leo stood, he could already see bodies lying bloody in the street, with other men attacking each other with fists and knives.

Just as he pulled back to give his phone his attention, a man clad in blue and white—Powder colors—stepped out of a broken doorway and directed a gunshot down into the forehead of a Driver who'd already lain prone on the ground. Leo flinched back behind the corner even as Vance cursed.

Taking deep breaths, Leo urged Vance to retreat away from the center of the action. They were outnumbered and outgunned. They didn't dare announce themselves and try to stop the violence. As two lone federal agents in the middle of a gang war, they'd be nothing more than prizes to whoever took them out first.

As they raced back to the relative safety of Camilla Jones's crime scene, Leo pulled out his phone and relayed Max's incoming messages. "Max is calling in all nearby units and the whole task force, but we need to alert Jacinda in case she hasn't seen this."

Vance already had his phone to his ear, dialing the SSA. "She's not picking up." He shook his head, roaming his gaze around the area.

Leo did the same, in case the battle came their way, while Vance left Jacinda a voice message. That done, Vance pocketed his phone and gestured back to the street they'd run down. "We can't go into that without backup. Sounds like Max has MPD alerted, but...dammit, I hate just standing here while people are in danger."

"Same here. What if we circle around?"

"Lead the way."

Leo jogged back along the street and took a side street that would lead them at least a block away from the fighting. Gunshots continued to crack and pop across the neighborhood, intermingled with a flood of sirens now coming from all directions. And sometimes, the gunshots came in fast enough succession that Leo worried they could be facing off against fully automatic weapons.

Ahead, an intersection was clear, and Leo was just about to attempt some game-planning when a white man wearing Powders colors rounded the corner ahead of them, gun in hand but looking over his shoulder.

He collided with Leo, and they went down. Leo grappled with the man as best he could, trying to control the gangbanger's gun hand while retaining control of his own weapon. Vance hauled the man off his fellow agent and twisted his arm around at the shoulder, disarming him.

The Powder cried out and released his gun but managed to direct a kick back at Vance's groin, sending him back a step.

Now free, the gang member dove sideways for his gun, but Leo was there first, kicking it away and aiming his weapon at the man's center mass.

"Stand down. FBI, stop going for the damn gun."

The man froze in a crouch, long enough for Leo to glance sideways at Vance.

"You good?"

Vance shifted his pants a bit and winced. "Dickhead got me where it counts. Let's cuff his ass."

When they got him braced against the wall, Leo could see the guy they'd collared was nothing but a teenager. Still, he spit the venom of a man twice his size and age.

"What's going on?" Leo held the young gang member's gaze, ignoring the sound of a cop car swerving to a halt at the end of the alley. "What started this?"

"Man, fuck off."

Leo gripped his shoulders tighter, pressing him to the wall as gunfire and sirens continued to fill the air around the neighborhood. "I'm going to ask you again. What happened?"

He shook in Leo's grasp, trying to push him off, but Leo only held on tighter. He'd be damned if he'd let a cuffed teenager go running out into a gunfight.

Leo tried to hold his eye, but the kid was in full-on panic mode. He started hollering. "I ain't talking to no Feds! I ain't talking!"

Vance and a uniformed cop trotted toward Leo and the Powder, who kept cursing and shouting about how he wasn't giving anything or anyone up to the cops. Whatever had happened, the gang war they'd all feared had finally started.

24

Emma slipped her phone into her pocket again, giving up on getting in touch with Leo and Vance to make sure they were okay. If they were in the middle of a gang war, she'd just have to trust they could take care of themselves. She had something else to focus on.

Finally, Jacinda was pulling up to the curb outside the old school. When she stepped out of her vehicle, she wore a bulletproof vest and a frown that spoke volumes. "You saw the update?"

"Jacinda," Denae stepped toward her, voice low enough that the nearby uniforms wouldn't hear, "I need to speak with you."

Jacinda shook her head, pulling her hair into a bun as she leaned against her SUV. "Not now. We're going to meet up with Max's task force a few miles away and help get this war under control."

Denae's eyes swam with panic—maybe for the first time since Emma had met her—but Jacinda wasn't seeing it, she was so focused on taking in the scene and getting a rundown from Mia. When she made a move to get back in her vehicle,

Emma stepped in close enough to keep her door from opening all the way.

"Jacinda, if there are enough people on the other side of the territory, I think you should let Denae and me follow up on Snake. Finding him could lead us to our killer and break this whole case open."

Jacinda narrowed her eyes. "You want to follow up on the graffiti artist while there's a gang war erupting?"

"A gang war at least partially caused," Emma emphasized carefully, "by the killer who attacked this artist and injured our colleagues, and who may or may not be actively participating in that war right now. Half the city's cops and agents are in Drivers territory, with mutual support coming in from as far away as Richmond. I'm just ask—"

"He's my brother." Denae's voice was rough with emotion, but her normal steel had returned to her eyes.

Emma stepped back to give her space. Nearby, Mia winced visibly, fidgeting with her own bulletproof vest.

Jacinda barely blinked. "What?"

"I didn't know for sure he was in the city, not until we found him here, but now that I do...*please.*"

Mia coughed, catching Jacinda's shocked gaze. "If things are being handled in the field, and we can spare them, I agree, for what it's worth. We have a lead on Snake...Denae's brother Jamaal...and having Emma and Denae follow it up could speed things along."

Stretching her fingers, as if she didn't know whether to clench her fists or start pounding out messages on her phone, Jacinda met each of the other women's gazes in turn before focusing on Denae. "You swear you didn't know your brother was part of this until this morning? Personal connections should've been—"

"I swear." Denae swallowed, standing straighter. "I knew he was an artist with the Drivers in Baltimore, but I didn't know he was back in D.C. When the two Drivers got killed, my radar went off, wondering if he'd know anything. But when we found out about the artist being attacked last night, that was the first time I was even suspicious he might be back in town. I didn't know his street name was Snake and didn't know he was even in D.C. until we caught him here."

Jacinda remained frozen where she stood. "How can I accept that you'll bring a professional, impartial attitude with you to this case, Agent Monroe? This is why you wanted to stay behind the scenes, isn't it? To do research instead of going into the field where you might've confirmed your worst fears a—"

"I said I didn't know!"

"But you thought about it, Denae! You thought about it, and you said nothing. Did it occur to you that those fears should've been brought to my attention immediately? All your efforts thus far could be called into question. If any of this ends up in a courtroom, the defense is going to shred the prosecution when it's revealed one of our agents knowingly withheld—"

"I didn't know!" Denae threw up her arms. "Dammit…I told you, and I'm telling the truth. I didn't know it was him."

"Interrupt me one more time, Agent Monroe, and the next conversation we have will be an exit interview. You should've said something yesterday morning. I have no choice but to pull you from this case, effective immediately. You're suspended until this investigation is completed, whichever is less. I'm sorry, Denae. The conflict of interest is too obvious and too severe."

Silence, deep and unforgiving, settled around them. Denae's mouth hung open in shock or disgust, Emma couldn't tell which. She'd never seen her colleague so distraught before.

But she knew the pain of grief and uncertainty herself.

I got through it, with her help.

"Denae, it's—"

"Don't, Emma. Just…please. Don't."

Jacinda extended a hand, palm up. "Agent Monroe, I'll take possession of your weapon and badge. Agent Last will escort you back to the Bureau, and," Jacinda leveled her eyes at Emma, "she will not be deviating from that assignment."

Emma forced herself to nod, taking some small solace from the fact that Denae readily handed over her firearm and badge. "Understood."

She stepped back to allow the SSA room to open her door. Jacinda set Denae's gun and badge inside on the center console and climbed in, motioning Mia to the SUV she and Emma had arrived in.

"Follow me, Agent Logan. Agent Last, I expect an update as soon as you arrive at the offices. I'll let you know where things stand on the ground and where you can be the most effective."

Not bothering to wait for Emma's agreement, Jacinda slammed the door. She and Mia both sped off a moment later.

Denae lifted a limp hand in farewell as the SUVs disappeared from view. "Guess I'm benched."

"Timing could've been better."

"You think? Dammit, Emma, I thought you might actually, I don't know, understand what I'm up against."

Taking a step back, Emma shook her head. "No, I didn't mean it like that. I meant we need to talk to Hope Jackson again. She's our best shot at finding where Jamaal might be, and her apartment isn't exactly on the way to the offices."

"We could take the scenic route for you to deliver me into the hands of justice."

"Denae…Jacinda's right, and you know it. You basically

suspended yourself from this case at the start. If I take you to Hope's, I may as well hand in my badge and gun too."

Denae blew out an anguished breath. "You know why I did what I did. Tell me you'd have done different."

Emma wished she could tell her that. She couldn't. And Denae knew it.

In fact, if Emma hadn't gone rogue so often, Jacinda probably wouldn't have been so strict with Denae. It was her fault. Again.

Emotion burned in Emma's eyes. "I can't tell you that because I don't know what it's like to have a brother. Or a sister. I wish I did. You, Leo, everybody on the team...you're my siblings, as close as I've ever had anyway."

They stared at each other for a few beats before Emma cleared her throat. "How about I drive and you call Hope? See if she can tell us anything."

Denae nodded and handed over the key fob for her Escape with a thin smile of gratitude curling her lips. Emma passed over her phone with Hope's number pulled up.

They got in, and Emma started the SUV while Denae made the call, putting the phone on speaker.

Part of Emma wondered if Hope would even answer. Blocking her number would've been a simple solution if she didn't want to be bothered again. On the third ring, though, Hope's breathless voice rang through the car.

"Agent Last? Did you find Jamaal?"

The bare-hearted need in her voice pulled a frustrated grunt from Denae, but it was Emma who answered. "Yes and no. He was at the old school, like you said. He freaked when he saw us and went out a back door.

"Dammit. I knew I should've come with you."

"Is there anything else you can tell us, anywhere he might go to ground? There's a war on these streets right now—"

"I know. I heard it on the news. It's crazy, what they're doing."

Denae spoke up finally. "If Jamaal's hiding somewhere, we need to be the ones to find him, Hope. Where's he at?"

"Who…who's this? I don't recognize your voice." Panic laced every one of Hope's words and her sobbing came through the phone in stuttering bursts. "Please. I know Jamaal. He would—"

"Hope, my name's Special Agent Denae Monroe. I'm Jamaal's sister, and I'm telling you that he was fine when we last saw him. Take a deep breath for me, okay?" She paused as Emma took a corner fast enough to skid the rear tires out, which earned her a warning look from Denae and a frantic plea from Hope over the phone.

"S-sister? You're l-lying. Jamaal never told—"

"I'm not lying, Hope. I wouldn't do that. Jamaal is my baby brother, and I want to help him."

"Please, are you chasing him right now? Just let him be, please."

Denae held the phone closer. "We're just on the road right now, Hope, and Agent Last is learning how to drive somebody else's personal vehicle safely."

Emma caught another of Denae's warning glares in her peripheral.

"We want to come by, okay? See if we can figure out what's going on and where to find him. And while we're on the way, you can do him…and us…the favor of thinking about whether there's anything else you can tell us that might help. That sound okay to you?"

After a pause that took the length of a block, Hope finally answered. "Okay. Yeah, that sounds good. I'll buzz you up as soon as you get here."

"I guess," Emma spoke carefully after Denae ended the call, "it goes without saying, I'll have to come up with a story for why I'm not reporting to Jacinda in the next twenty minutes. Hope's apartment is across town."

"You can tell her I was driving, and you had no choice but to go where I took you. Now if you'd be so kind as to tell me Hope's address, I'll put it into my GPS…"

"You're just leaning in all the way, Denae? This could mean the end of your career."

"Right now, the only thing I care about in this whole world is making sure Jamaal is alive tomorrow. I'll worry about careers after I've seen to my brother's safety."

Emma's fingers clenched and unclenched the wheel as if it were a stress ball.

She's right, Emma girl. You may not have a brother or sister of your own, but you'd be the first person to say family comes before everything else.

"I honestly don't know how I could live with myself if I did as Jacinda ordered. Let's go find your brother." Emma gave her the address, and Denae tapped it into the car's GPS. "Do you think…maybe your family might be able to offer some insights into where he'd be, if Hope can't?"

Denae shrugged as Emma took another turn at a slightly slower speed.

"You could still drive my car a little nicer. Bet Leo loves being your passenger."

Emma laughed at that. "He gives the *oh shit* handle a workout, that's for sure."

Part of her yearned to at least text Leo, if not call him, but if there was one thing that could make any conversation between the two of them more awkward, it would be having it with Denae sitting right beside her.

As if he could check his phone if he's got bullets flying at him.

25

By the time they reached Hope's apartment, Emma was just about vibrating with nerves. She hopped out of the Escape as soon as she switched the engine off and led Denae to the building she'd visited earlier with Mia by her side. This time, though, Hope was waiting in the lobby, fidgeting on a bench by the stairwell.

She was now clad in tight, skinny blue jeans and an oversize men's polo, which Emma guessed belonged to Jamaal. Not just for the men's fashion, but for the hand-painted cobra adorning the black sleeve.

Denae's eyes caught on the illustration, freezing her, and Hope glanced down at it. "Makes me feel close to him," she explained quietly, "and I need that right now. Also, I'm coming with you when we go after him, so know that. If you disagree, I'll go find him on my own."

"Where?" Emma had asked the question automatically, but as soon as Hope flinched, she saw the real reason the young woman hadn't already left. She didn't know where he was either.

"I'll figure it out. But...I guess I do have some stuff to tell you."

Emma glanced around the lobby, which she guessed saw plenty of traffic. "You want us to come upstairs?"

"I'm too antsy to be in there without him. The place feels too big right now." Hope's eyes were hooded, cast down to the ground. "Mind if we go outside? I was gonna go get some fresh air before you called."

Denae opened the door they'd just come through, and Hope led the way onto the sidewalk and around the side of the building. She landed at a cast-concrete picnic table tucked behind a dogwood tree and plopped onto the bench with a loud sigh.

Emma and Denae sat across from her, Denae with her arms crossed and a concerned frown that mirrored Hope's.

Emma leaned in, making it clear she was leading the interview. "Hope, you said you have something to tell us? There's a gang war going on as we speak, and there's no time to waste here."

Hope's eyebrows pinched together, and she didn't look up when she answered. "I…might know who went after him."

The air stilled in Emma's lungs. That was far more than she'd hoped for.

"Jamaal and I, we been keeping our relationship quiet because of his connection to the Drivers. I…shit." She shook her head, pressing her hands into the table hard enough that one of her false nails snapped off, and she gripped her hands together instead. "My dad was with the Powders. Not really part of the gang, but he taught a bunch of 'em to fight. Before he went to jail for being a loud, angry drunk."

Denae ducked her head to catch the younger woman's gaze. "And your dad—"

"He died in prison last year. It's my sister doing it. It's Grace."

The name hung there, and Emma pulled out her phone,

tapping a text to Jacinda.

Received contact from Hope Jackson en route to offices. Detoured. Interviewing now. Claims the perpetrator is her sister, Grace Jackson.

Her phone chimed with an immediate reply.

You are now tasked with bringing both of them to the offices. Do you need backup?

No, we're good. Denae complying.

She held back from sending and showed the texts to Denae, who gave her a silent nod of approval. Emma sent the reply and would navigate the lie she'd included if it came to that.

Denae put a hand on hers. "Just in case it comes up, I'm gonna do my best to hold off asking any more questions. No promises I don't open my mouth, but this is your show, Agent Last."

Settling herself on the concrete bench, Emma nodded and met Hope's gaze. The younger woman had a question on her tongue, as she looked between the two agents, but now wasn't the time to discuss Denae's suspended status.

"Hope, where would Grace be right now?"

"I don't know. Probably out there where they're fighting. That's always been her territory. She could never feel at home in a place like this." She waved a hand at their surroundings. "Our dad was a disaster. Just a mean-ass drunk who was always hitting us, 'making us tough' so we could 'survive on these streets.' This is all his fault."

Hope barked out a laugh that became a sob she forced back down.

"That's what attracted me to Jamaal at first." She looked at Denae. "He's, like, the exact opposite of my dad."

"Where did you meet him?"

"I'd been visiting the old neighborhood, just...I don't know why. Nostalgia? I normally don't want to remember anything about the place. And it's Drivers territory now. Jamaal was painting a whole bunch of butterflies onto some little girl's fence just because she'd asked. Girl and her mom were sitting there, watching him. All these butterflies. In Drivers colors, but still...you should see it."

Denae's lips were pinched. Emma finally gave into the impulse to rest one hand on her elbow for support as Hope continued her story.

"Dad would've spit on that fence if he'd seen me admiring it. He wanted me and Grace to be warriors, and Grace was all about that."

Emma felt for the younger woman, but needed more to be convinced Grace Jackson was, in fact, the killer they'd been looking for.

"Hope, simply being 'all about that' doesn't mean Grace is the one who's been killing people."

"It's her. It has to be. She was already getting involved with the Powders when Dad went to jail. She said she needed to provide for us. And then, when he died...she didn't look back. I think she's always been looking for an excuse to embrace the violence. It was like Dad abusing us just built up inside her, and she was waiting for an outlet so she could take it out on someone else."

"And it wasn't like that for you?" Emma spoke quietly, wanting to push Hope to hurry without interrupting the flow of the story. "So you left the gang?"

Hope shrugged. "I was never in the gang. I worked instead of going with Grace to the gym and learning how to fight. As soon as a friend offered up her couch, I moved out and kept saving money. Got the job at the Starlight, and I was able to afford this place."

Emma saw what was coming. "When did your sister find out about Jamaal?"

Before Hope could answer, Denae swept some dogwood

blossoms from the table and leaned forward. "And how did she react?"

"She saw it as a betrayal. Of her and Dad. The Powders. We haven't talked much since I moved to this place, and I made it clear I didn't feel any loyalty to the gang or Dad. That alone pissed her off, and she kept coming around, telling me I was being a bad sister. That I was forgetting my family, where I was from. All that shit." Hope closed her eyes and leaned back from the table, shaking her head. "After everything, me trying to get away from all that, and I went and fell for an enemy gang member."

Tears started scrolling down her cheeks. "She walked in one night, out of the blue. I wasn't expecting her, but I'd given her a key for emergencies, and Jamaal was sitting on the couch in his underwear. He was sketching out some new designs for the Drivers, planning out this big project. Grace saw it as soon as she walked in."

Hope looked back and forth between them, eyes shining wet. Desperation all but bled from her.

"I nearly lost my apartment that night. Grace pulled out a gun and started screaming. I got between her and Jamaal, who was trying to put me behind him, and I swear I thought she was gonna kill us both. My screaming brought the neighbors running, and they called the police. Grace ran off. My landlord told me I'm out if anything like that happens again, and I don't blame him."

"Have you seen her since?" Emma watched for any sign of a lie, but Hope only shook her head.

"I've been closer than ever to Jamaal. He tried to save me from her. But if you'd have been there...anyone would've seen it. She saw me choosing sides, him over her." Hope swiped angrily at her eyes, swatting away the tears that kept on coming. "I think I knew in my gut she'd come after one of us. I kinda just thought it would be me."

26

Emma and Denae headed back to the Bureau offices with Hope, where they set her up in an interview room and took her official statement. Emma waited there with her while Denae collected a few items from her desk.

She entered the interview room and nodded, waving for Hope to stand. Denae offered to take the young woman to the Monroe family home while Emma went looking for Jamaal.

"He might show up there, especially if he finds out you're with me."

Hope smiled, but her eyes remained hooded with concern, or maybe regret.

Emma put a hand on her shoulder. "Hope, you did the right thing talking with us. This might be the best chance we have of making sure Jamaal is safe and nobody else gets hurt."

Downstairs, Emma watched Denae depart in her Ford Escape with Hope in the passenger seat. Emma followed in a Bureau sedan on Jacinda's orders to ensure her fellow agent complied with her suspension and stayed out of the action.

They wormed their way through D.C.'s lunch-hour traffic until Denae finally turned onto a quiet suburban street lined by old shade trees. The houses were modest and mostly well-kept. The Monroes had moved from whichever lower-income district Denae and Jamaal had called home as children, but this was still an older neighborhood.

Emma had every reason to believe they were making the right choice and would be safe by staying off the street and out of any crossfire.

Unless either Drivers or Powders know where Jamaal's parents live.

She and Denae had discussed that possibility upstairs. The other agent believed it so unlikely as to be impossible.

"Jamaal didn't just keep me in the dark after he moved to Baltimore. Nobody knew where he was half the time, and he damn sure didn't tell the Drivers about his family. He's smarter than that."

Even so, Emma thought it worth suggesting that Denae's family be extra careful and had called MPD on the way over, asking that the Monroes' home be added to regular patrol routes.

Denae pulled into a cobblestone driveway, parking behind a newish SUV. The craftsman home in front of them boasted pigeon-gray siding, dark-blue windows, and a bright-yellow front door, which was a surprising flash of color.

Emma pulled to a stop on the curb behind them as they both stepped from their vehicle. She got out and joined them on the sidewalk, where they stood admiring the house.

"My parents have lived here since I left for college." Denae spoke up as if reading Emma's mind. "And they know all their neighbors by name. It's that kind of street. We'll be safe here."

Hope tapped the back of her hand against Denae's shoulder. "I didn't know we had places like this in D.C."

Guess they bonded a bit on the drive over. That's gotta be a good thing, Emma girl.

"Denae! What a surprise!" A woman hurried out of the screened-in porch, removing her glasses and letting them hang on a necklace as she stepped down the front walk. Emma and Hope moved to the side, giving the woman room to embrace Denae. She held her tight, seemingly unmindful that Denae stood stiffly against her.

"Good to see you again, Mom."

Emma waved awkwardly as Denae's mother pulled back. "I'm Emma Last. I work with Denae. And this is…" Emma glanced at Hope, wondering how to introduce her, and finally just settled for her name. "Hope Jackson."

The young woman stepped forward with more confidence than Emma felt and held out her hand. "I'm Jamaal's girlfriend."

Denae's mother froze for just an instant, so fast that Emma might've missed it if she'd blinked, then glanced from Denae back to Hope and Emma. "You kids all better come on in."

"Mom, we're not kids." Denae smiled as she followed her mom up the walk. "Emma and I are FBI agents, even if…"

Mrs. Monroe stopped and turned to face her daughter. "I'm smart enough to know that when my daughter doesn't hug me back, she's got something to tell me. Let's have that talk inside the house, all right?"

Emma understood where Denae got both her brains and intuition from. "Yes, ma'am."

With a jerk of her head, Mrs. Monroe turned around and made her way to the front steps, opened the screen door, and ushered them all inside. "Your father will be happy to see you home, Denae. And I am, too, whatever the reason might be."

Emma followed Denae through the home into a bright kitchen with white cabinets and butcher-block countertops. A man with a flat-top and a mustache sat at the table in front of a half-eaten sandwich, grinning as he took in the line of women crowding into his kitchen. "What's my daughter doing home in the middle of a workday? Denae, is this about Jamaal?"

"It is. We're trying to find him and hoped you and Mom might have some ideas."

Denae's father stood with some effort and pulled her into a hug. Mrs. Monroe rested a hand on his back, and Emma felt the love and warmth of a bonded family filling the room. Not for the first time since the case began, a pang of jealousy and sadness cut into her mood.

As Denae and her father separated, Mrs. Monroe waved them all to sit around the table.

"Mom, we don't have time."

The woman turned with shock rounding her eyes wide open. "Don't have time to eat? Well, sit down. I'll get some water for y'all, at least."

They each took a chair, with Denae sitting across from her father. Mrs. Monroe went to the cupboards and pulled out glasses and a pitcher.

Observing the scene play out, Emma found herself thinking about Grace Jackson. She'd pulled up a background check on her at the Bureau and found little more than a charge of second-degree theft last year, at the age of twenty-two. She'd been released on her own recognizance and made her court date.

Her public defender managed to get her charges reduced because her father had recently passed, and Grace had stayed off the radar since then.

Even in death, her dad managed to do something for her. And

Hope made it clear her sister values family over pretty much anything else.

Maybe that was part of what had left Grace so angry. Like Emma, she'd been deprived of anything remotely like the love and community that warmed the Monroe household. While Emma's childhood was marked by a deceased mother and a father losing himself to work, Grace's had been a looping nightmare of abuse.

When her father went to prison, Grace struggled to understand and take care of her sister. Their dad's death could only have compounded the stress she was under.

Jamaal's entrance into Hope's life had to be the last straw.

Grace was a killer, definitely, but she was also a heartbroken little girl who'd lost her family. She might have turned to the Powders out of familiarity, but probably also out of desperation.

She's watching the world take everything she knows and loves away from her. Adam Cleaver took Oren from you, Emma girl, and you know what you almost did as a result.

While Mrs. Monroe busied herself bringing them all glasses of water, Denae introduced Emma and Hope to her father. His eyebrows rose just a touch when he learned Hope was Jamaal's girlfriend.

"Haven't spoken to the boy," he met Denae's gaze, "in I don't know how long. I know you said he'd moved back from B-more, but you'd think a young man would let his parents know how he's doing. Not to mention who he's seeing." He offered a thin smile to Hope.

"Dad, please." Denae glanced helplessly between her parents. "I hadn't intended to come back today. I'm sorry I don't come around more often. That might be changing soon."

Mr. Monroe touched his mustache, fidgeting, and a sad look

dragged his features down. "Please, tell me you don't have bad news, even if you don't have good either. Is Jamaal mixed up in all that mess we're seeing on the news? Is my son…is he okay?"

Standing from the table, Emma moved to join Mrs. Monroe in the kitchen. The woman had barely faltered in what she was doing as her husband spoke, but his ultimate question froze her in place with her hands flat on the countertop.

Emma came up beside her and took the two glasses. "We hope he's okay. We just saw him, but…" She went back to the table, glasses in hand, nodding at Denae to tell the rest.

"He won't answer or call me back, and I just barely caught a glimpse of him today before he disappeared. I don't know if he didn't hear my voice or didn't recognize it because all he saw was three cops showing up where he least expected them to be."

Emma sipped from her glass as the older Monroes exchanged sad looks.

"Mom? Dad?" Denae prodded her parents back to the subject. "Do you have any idea where Jamaal could be?"

Her father gripped his wife's hand over the table and shook his head. "Haven't had a phone call in," he looked at his wife, "three weeks, maybe a month?"

Mrs. Monroe nodded. "Not a peep from that boy since before Valentine's Day. And that was just to say he'd met somebody he was taking out to dinner." She smiled at Hope, who returned the gesture, practically beaming.

"That was our first real date."

Denae's mother let her smile droop and shrugged. "There's not much more we can tell you. I'm surprised we even knew Jamaal was dating someone." Gazing at Hope again, she offered another smile. "Probably a measure of how much he likes you, that he told us."

Mr. Monroe reached out a hand to Denae. "You find him

and make sure he's safe. Please. He's always got a home here if he needs it."

Emma leaned forward and cleared her throat gently to bring the family back to the moment. "Mr. Monroe. Mrs. Monroe. Can you think of anywhere Jamaal might have gone? We found him at an old school building, but he ran."

"Sounds like my son." Mr. Monroe nodded. "I know the school you mean. He used to call it his 'studio.' Said he'd show us someday."

"There was that one boy." Mrs. Monroe looked to her husband, frowning. "The one from his art class."

"Henry Biggs. I remember. Jamaal went to his place a few times after he got in fights. Or when we tried to ground him. Emphasis is on the 'tried.'"

Emma smiled her thanks, repeating the name to herself to keep it fresh, then stood up. "Denae, I'm going to follow up with Jacinda. You're good here?"

She nodded, keeping her eyes downcast. "Yeah. Me and Hope'll stay here."

Mr. and Mrs. Monroe traded a look. He shifted in his seat and faced Emma. "Something we need to know about?"

"I'll fill you in, but Emma has to get going now. She's gonna find Jamaal and bring him where he'll be safe."

Emma didn't miss her colleague's forefinger stabbing at the tabletop.

"That's right, Mr. Monroe, Mrs. Monroe." She reached out and gripped their hands in hers, holding on longer than professional. These were her good friend's parents, and they were hurting. She'd do everything within her power to help. "I'll see if I can find Henry Biggs first, and I'll…text Denae with an update."

With the most reassuring smile she could muster, Emma gave a quick nod and exited the kitchen, leaving Denae and her family and Hope circled around the table.

The questions and raised voices started the minute Emma opened the front door.

Outside, in the sedan, Emma looked up Henry Biggs's address. It was just a few streets away, probably in the same neighborhood. She left it open on her phone and tapped out a quick update to Jacinda.

Pursuing lead on POI Jamaal Monroe. Denae confirms she will remain at home with Hope Jackson.

She hit send, then got the Bureau vehicle started up. As she pulled away from the curb, her phone chimed with a text from Denae. *He's innocent until proven guilty. Remember that and bring him where he'll be safe.*

Emma replied with a single thumbs-up emoji and drove off with only one thought in mind. If she didn't find Jamaal fast, she could probably count on Denae ignoring Jacinda's orders to sit this one out.

And that meant she'd be faced with potentially arresting her colleague for interfering with the investigation or harboring a suspected fugitive.

Or I might be telling Leo she's been caught in the crossfire of a gang war.

27

Leo yanked back the arm of a young Powder who'd been about to slam his fist into the face of a Driver. When Leo grappled him, the youth spun around and took a swipe in his direction. A quick dodge and wristlock had the teenager on his knees. A uniformed cop held the Driver in a similar position, far enough from his foe that the two boys couldn't lash out with a kick at each other.

They're barely old enough to shave, much less be throwing punches at cops.

Leo focused on getting zip ties around the Powder's wrists and holding him with a firm grip on his shoulder.

Ever since he and Vance had met up with responding MPD, it had been like Whac-A-Mole. The only upside at this point was that everyone had run out of ammunition, or the gang members who had guns were in custody or had fled the scene. One way or another, Leo hadn't heard a gunshot in a while, and the worst weapon he'd faced down in the last few fights he'd handled had been a broken-off beer bottle.

Not something he wanted to do every day, but nothing

like the blades that had left a trio of bloody scratches down his face.

Mia yelled for a uniform from somewhere around the corner, but she didn't sound desperate, and Leo barely glanced her way. This was one of those rare days when all of D.C.'s law enforcement had the same goals and were working interchangeably.

Still haven't heard Denae's voice, though. Or Emma's.

He'd crossed paths with Jacinda earlier, once responding law enforcement had gained a semblance of control. He hadn't seen her since.

A uniform headed his way from across the street.

"County lockup's gonna be full tonight. Here, I'll get that one."

The cop hauled the struggling teen to his feet and gripped him by his upper arm, steering him toward a MPD bus waiting down the block. Leo took the moment to check his phone for a text or voicemail from Denae or Emma.

Nothing. Mia said they'd headed back to the Bureau but didn't say why. What the hell's going on?

The bus full of arrested rioters and assailants roared to life and made an awkward three-point turn to aim back down the street. Two patrol cars rolled into view behind it, and a third awaited them at the next corner.

Leo watched the convoy move out of the neighborhood, taking the opportunity to gaze up and down the street. Broken glass and evidence tags littered the sidewalks among uniformed officers taking photographs or, in one case, standing around a body covered by a sheet.

Jacinda and a uniformed cop were pulling apart two young girls screaming obscenities. Their language would've earned them one of Yaya's fiercest looks and a few swats on the butt with a wooden spoon.

Farther down the block, Vance was encouraging a man to

lower his head and get into the back of a patrol car, Mia near his side.

Denae should be here.

He had a pit in his stomach. At least if she'd been there, he could've known at a glance that she was safe.

Well, no.

He'd still be worrying about her. Thinking about her, wondering what was wrong that she wasn't telling him. At least one thing had become clearer and clearer with every breath—the woman had gotten to him.

She could be right there beside him, stopping kids from hurting each other or themselves, right before telling Leo he needed a haircut.

Even if she were, he'd have been just as anxious to keep her safe.

His heart had been closed to these feelings for a long time, but Denae's wry smile, hard-nosed jokes, and gorgeous curls had cracked it open. She'd nestled inside without asking.

Not like I could've said no.

He started toward Vance, who was now halfway down the block talking to a pair of MPD officers.

Mia joined him, having seen the two misbehaving young girls into the custody of a separate MPD team. "Think we'll have time for lunch after this?"

"I sure hope so. Haven't eaten since those doughnuts this morning, and coffee only goes so far."

Leo and Mia shared a laugh. This was the first time Leo had genuinely felt relaxed since the day had started. But his guts roiled with the ache of hunger. Or maybe it was the worry about Denae still eating at him.

They passed behind a bus stop that had sheets of graffiti-covered plywood mounted where the glass had once been.

"You haven't heard from Denae or Emma, have you?"

"Nothing yet, but I've seen Jacinda on her phone a lot. I bet she's got news. We can ask—"

Glass broke two stories above the street, showering the road. Gunfire erupted from above. Leo dove toward the shelter of the bus stop. He landed on the sidewalk with a grunt.

Mia threw herself down right behind him. "Where's it coming from?"

Leo risked a quick glance around the meager barrier provided by the bus stop.

A rifle barrel jutted from a broken apartment window, popping off shots at the cop car. Vance and the two officers had crouched low behind the vehicle, flinching as bullets struck the windshield and hood.

Mia screamed something unintelligible behind Leo, but he caught her arm just as she aimed herself toward Vance.

He pulled her by his side, forcing her to stay out of the line of fire. "We can't help anybody if we're dead."

She kept looking at Vance, crouched beside the front wheel of the cop car. But she nodded. "Yeah. You're right. Somebody should call for SWAT to roll up. We're outgunned here."

One of the uniforms with Vance was shouting into her shoulder mic. Leo only caught snippets of what she said, but within a minute, an armored SWAT van roared around a corner and pulled up in front of the shooter's building.

A half dozen members of Max's task force emerged and began providing covering fire from protected positions by the van. Two of the team moved toward the apartment with breaching equipment in hand. They smashed their way into the building and stormed inside.

Beside Leo, Mia panted, muttering Vance's name, but they could both see that he and the other cops were safe, still crouched down. Bullets continued to punch into the car's hood. The windshield had spiderwebbed and fallen into the car.

Shouting and gunfire came from inside the building, and Leo snuck another glance just as the AR-15 barrel vanished from view. Moments later, their radios all crackled with a report. "All clear! All clear!"

Mia broke and ran toward Vance. Leo trotted behind her, wishing, not for the first time, that he had someone he could rush to himself.

She's not out here, so she's safe. Probably. Hopefully.

He gritted his teeth, frowning up at the window. "A blade overnight, and now an AR-15. This day can't end soon enough."

Vance patted his shoulder. "Soon, man. Soon. You okay?"

Leo nodded, grim-faced. "Just wondering what's going on with Denae and Emma."

A patrol car came down the street, pulling to a stop behind the SWAT van. Jacinda stepped out of the car with her phone in one hand. She focused on it as she approached the agents.

"Emma has another lead on the graffiti artist."

"What about Denae? Is she back at the Bureau?"

Jacinda met Leo's gaze, flashed a look at Mia, then returned her stare to him. "Agent Monroe has been suspended pending the completion of this investigation."

"She what?" He gaped at Mia and Vance, who both turned their attention to the SSA.

Jacinda nodded, not bothering to look up. "The artist in question is a person of interest, Leo, and may be central to the ongoing murder investigation. He is also Denae's brother, Jamaal Monroe. I'm certain you can comprehend the problems that might've arisen had we allowed her to remain actively involved."

Leo heaved a deep breath and nodded, only half hearing

Jacinda giving Mia and Vance their next assignment. They'd all learned how important it was to maintain professional boundaries in their work, regardless of personal connections. Yet, as Leo processed the news, a personal sting overshadowed his professional concerns.

He was surprised and more than a bit hurt that Denae hadn't shared this critical information with him. As her partner, both in the field and in life, he thought they'd fostered a bond of trust and openness.

The revelation that she had kept her brother's involvement a secret gnawed at him.

He could have helped her, protected her in some way, or at least been there for her in navigating this complex situation. The fact that she chose to bear this burden alone unsettled him, introducing a sliver of doubt into the foundation of their relationship.

He turned in a circle, looking for where he might be useful, where he could prove that his focus was here, on the case and the immediate issues facing their team. He couldn't allow his and Denae's relationship to interfere with the job in front of him, here on the street where bullets had just rained down on them all.

Not if he wanted Jacinda to allow them to remain on the same team. He knew that.

On the flip side, he was glad Denae'd been suspended. It'd keep her off the street where the bullets were flying. She was safe. As safe as she could be. Other people needed him now, and he had no choice but to be fully present to meet those needs.

But the first free second I get, I'm calling her and going to wherever she is. She needs me, too, just as badly as I need her.

28

Emma pulled to the curb across from Henry Biggs's house, searching the windows for any sign of movement. Multiple cars sat in the driveway.

The little craftsman home listed as the family's address boasted brown siding and neatly trimmed shrubs, complete with a white trellis lifting ivy up one side of the home. Maroon shutters stood out among the landscape of a neatly manicured lawn. Emma was ready to get out and head up the walk when Denae's Ford Escape raced up the street and screeched to a stop behind her.

"Shit. Shit, shit, shit."

Emma got out and stood by her driver's side door, staring at Denae through her windshield. But it was Hope who climbed out of the car and ran up to her.

"You got to let me go up there alone." Hope's quiet voice stilled Emma's hand, and she looked to Denae, who sat stiffly in the driver's seat. "You said yourself, he ran from you before. What's he gonna think when a Fed shows up at his next hiding place? He's gonna run back to the gang, and we both know what'll happen if he does."

"You're a civilian, Hope—"

"I'm his girlfriend!"

Emma's cheeks heated. "And Denae's his sister. But neither of you should be here right now. You're both risking being charged with interfering in an ongoing investigation. This isn't about being anybody's girlfriend or sister. It's about following the law and making sure nobody else gets hurt."

"That's why I need to be the one to knock on that door. You ain't heard a word I said. If he sees a Fed rolling up the front walk, he's gonna jump the back fence and be gone before you even knock. He doesn't have any reason to trust you."

Emma stared at the young woman, unable to deny she'd spoken the truth.

"I don't like it, but you're right. But you *do not* go anywhere with him, you hear me? He's being targeted, and if the two of you try to sneak out the back, I swear—"

"We won't." Hope broke eye contact and looked back at Denae, who still hadn't moved from the vehicle. "I promise I'll be back, and I'll have Jamaal with me."

A moment later, she was gone, her slim form speed-walking up the front walk, head down as if she were thinking what to say.

Denae finally emerged from her car and came to stand by Emma. "You did the right thing, letting her go by herself."

"She sounds older than she looks, like she's up to this."

"She is. Now we just need my fool of a brother to grow up a bit too."

Emma cleared her throat, itching to follow Hope now that she'd reached the front porch and knocked on the door.

A man answered. He was too far away for Emma to read his expression, but she lifted her hand in what she hoped appeared to be a casual wave. Beside her, Denae stood frozen and staring. When Hope was let into the home, they both released sighs of relief.

Emma pulled out her phone, willing it to ring with an update, but they appeared to be stuck waiting. "Am I remembering right that you have another brother?"

Denae nodded, eyes still on Henry Biggs's door. "Anthony."

"Also an artist?"

"No." Her voice had gone softer, making the monosyllabic response that much harder to digest.

Before Emma could think what to say, the door of the Biggs's house opened up. Hope came out first, holding the hand of a lanky man with short hair and skin just a few shades darker than Denae's.

Even from the street, though, Emma could see the similarities. The curls in his hair—though his were cut tight to his head, and hers were worn in a blowout style—flew everywhere, and the sharp chin and defined cheekbones. Emma would've bet money they had the same smile, even though she didn't know that she'd see it today.

They met Hope and Jamaal on the sidewalk, and he stayed a step behind her. Their loosely clasped hands hung between them. To Emma, it looked like Hope was working to maintain the contact while he was just about to flee.

"Big sis." He nodded to Denae, eyes hooded. "Been a minute."

She swallowed, nodding, and her voice cracked when she spoke. "Yeah, it has."

His nose wrinkled, like he might argue, and Hope yanked on his hand, pulling him a step closer. "She's here for you, dumbass. Don't start." Hope turned back to Denae. "He's the troublemaker in his family, like I am in mine. The one that doesn't do like everybody else, but that doesn't make him a criminal."

A touch of a smile tilted Jamaal's lips, and Emma saw more of Denae there.

"Nobody's calling anyone a criminal right now. Nobody, Jamaal. I mean that." Denae's voice cracked on his name, but she kept going. "There's a killer after you. Come home. With me, to Mom and Dad's."

He whipped his head side to side and tugged on Hope's hand as he tried to back up a step. "She'd just find me there. Eventually. Then Mom and Dad'd be in danger too. I can't be bringing this home."

Seeing the conversation spiraling away from her, Emma took a stance to one side of Denae, ready to leap after Jamaal if he tried to run. "Jamaal, our colleagues interrupted when she attacked you last night. They said it looked like you had a phone out. Did you get a photo?"

Jamaal dug his hand into his back pocket by way of answer, one arm circled protectively around Hope now. He braced his phone on her shoulder to unlock it and swiped at the screen with his thumb. He turned it around and angled it so that all three women could look at it once the agents stepped closer.

The shot wasn't great, mostly just showing a figure in a hoodie over a black bodysuit, with blades coming from her right hand, and a misty cloud of what was probably spray paint covering the bottom half of the image. But the top of her nose and eyes could be seen. The image meant nothing to Emma, but what did tell them everything was the way Hope flinched away from the phone as if it were on fire.

She cursed under her breath and turned her head into Jamaal's chest, clenching him tighter. When she spoke, the whisper could just be heard. "That's Grace. Those are her eyes."

Emma felt for the girl in front of them, who'd clearly

wished her earlier suggestion of Grace's guilt would be proven wrong.

They had what amounted to proof of that guilt now. All that remained was finding her.

"We'll put out an APB. Jamaal, can you send that photo to me…or Denae?"

He tapped at his phone, and Denae's chimed a moment later.

"I'll send this to Jacinda." Denae's expression went a little stricken. "She'll want to know how I got it. She has to understand why I'm doing this, though."

"She does, but that doesn't mean she won't toss you out on your ass for it. Denae, you have to stand down. Let me take Jamaal—"

"Uh-huh, y'all ain't taking me anyplace. Hell nah." He started to back away, and this time Hope went with him.

"Jamaal, please," Denae stepped forward, "that's not happening. I promise." She turned back to her vehicle. "Let's just get you somewhere safe. C'mon. If you won't go to Mom and Dad's, you can go back to my place. You can both stay there with me while Emma and them get things sorted out."

"How they gonna do that? Ain't none of them know where Grace is at. Hell, it's me she wants to kill, and I don't even know where she could be."

Hope cringed at his mention of her sister being a killer, but she didn't protest or challenge him on it. "What she really wants is to kill anybody who's getting in the way of her having a family. That means you and any Drivers she might find, 'cause y'all keep moving on Powders territory, taking away places she's always called home."

Jamaal's nostrils flared. "She's crazy."

"She's hurt." She looked Jamaal in the eyes and lifted up on the balls of her feet to kiss him. "Jamaal, this is personal for her. You remember the look on her face when she caught you at my place?"

He shuddered visibly. "I'll never forget it."

Hope held him tighter. "We could go back there, yeah?"

"She has a key, remember? She'll find us."

"Then let's go with your sister, okay?"

Emma waited, debating if she should just call Jacinda and have all three of them brought back to the Bureau. She dismissed the idea almost instantly, considering the betrayal that would convey to Jamaal, and probably to Denae as well.

"Denae, why don't you take them back to your place? I'll follow you, and I'll let Jacinda know once you're all inside and safe."

The other woman shook her head and laughed. "Guess you did hear what I was saying before Romeo and Juliet got the crazy idea either of them know what's best right now. C'mon, you two. Train's leaving, and you better be on it."

She opened the passenger door to her SUV and beckoned Jamaal and Hope forward.

They took sluggish steps until Hope froze in the middle of the street. The torment on her face sent a spike of sympathy into Emma's throat.

"What is it, Hope?"

"What if we go to where she is? To Dad's old place. That's where she's been staying. We could…you could talk to her. You're trained to talk to people when they're acting crazy, right? Like, with hostages and…you could make her see what she's doing is wrong."

Emma's eyes widened, and she flashed a look at her colleague.

Denae growled and slapped a hand on the roof of her Escape. "Jamaal, Hope, please just get in the car. We need to stop pretending this is a fight on the schoolyard. Grace is killing people."

"I know that." A sob escaped the younger woman. "And I hate that she's doing it. But she's still my family, just like Jamaal is yours." Her tears fell freely now, and she clutched at Jamaal's hand like a lifeline holding her from crumbling to her knees. "That's why she's doing this. She feels like she's alone and abandoned. She was screaming that at me the night she found Jamaal in my apartment. Please, can we try talking to her first? Before some cop gets his eye on her and starts shooting?"

Denae dropped her chin to her chest. "Hope, there is no world where your sister gets to remain a free woman after what she's done. But I understand you wanting to do what you can to at least keep her alive. Emma, will you let Jacinda know?" Without waiting for a reply, she waved the two young people into her vehicle and closed the door.

Emma touched her arm. "Are you sure?"

She gave Emma one last pleading look. "I'll have Hope text you the address."

"Denae, you know this isn't okay. You—"

"Save it. And tell Jacinda I'm sorry."

A moment later, Denae was gone, leaving Emma to call the SSA and give her what was close to the worst news she could imagine delivering.

She's on her own. Gangs are fighting in the streets, and she's going straight into the lion's den without her badge or weapon or any kind of support.

29

From my perch on top of an empty apartment, I'd watched the violence unfold all day, body drop after body drop. It began with gunshots and surprises. Pretty damn quick, the whole neighborhood was nothing but shooting, shouting, and fighting. Add in the police and the Feds, and it'd been an entertaining day.

But entertainment wasn't what I needed.

I needed to know who came out on top. Who was left standing after it all went down and the cop vans rolled away with their catches.

Who was left to back me up? Who was still on the street, able to claim the street and keep it in our hands?

Dad's voice came to my mind, like it'd been doing all damn day.

"Family is all that matters in the end, and you're only worth as much as you put into protecting your family from dying out."

"Keep 'em tough, 'cause life gets rough." That was what he always said before he took a swing at me. After a while, I learned to duck and dodge, to keep my guard up whenever we were alone in the house. He'd swing out with a cheap shot

sometimes and get me good, but most times, I learned to anticipate him.

He got proud of me quick. Not like he was with Hope. She never learned to duck, never saw it coming.

She's always been the soft one. Even with all Dad's trying, she never could learn the lesson.

Hope'd always been destined to get taken out. Since she chose Snake over me, she pretty much signed her own death warrant. She wouldn't even see I was trying to protect her by telling her to stay clear of that asshole.

I still hadn't dropped Snake. I'd gone down there and snuck around, staying away from wherever the cops were at. They didn't know all the ways I could get around these streets, the holes in fences, loose boards over windows in empty houses. I'd looked for Snake, but never found him.

I could hear Dad's voice coaching me on, telling me to get back into the ring, get off the ropes, and start swinging again.

The cops had their bird in the air now, circling the neighborhood and calling out trouble spots. I'd flipped them off a couple of times, but never when they were right above me. Then, I just hung out, acting like a spectator, and I kept my hands visible just in case somebody up there with a badge and a gun decided I looked suspicious enough to shoot.

Feds were still down there, too, on the street with the cops and all them dummies who took their fighting into the public square.

I still hadn't found Snake, though. Like the coward he was, he hadn't shown himself today, and I didn't much know where to go to hunt his ass down. I could maybe wait for night and look for him painting again.

But after what went down earlier, I doubted he'd even be on the streets at all, no matter the time of day. Maybe after the bodies were all counted and identified, he'd be out again, putting up another tribute mural to his fallen brothers and sisters.

I can't wait that long. Every day that goes by with him having my sister's eye is another day that one of us has to die.

And it ain't gonna be me.

Ain't gonna be me.

Frustration and anger left me feeling hollow. I had no outlet, nothing I could do to work this energy out. I couldn't go down on the street and start killing cops, much as I might want to. And I couldn't go to the gym to work out because any Powders hanging around there would want to know where I was today.

How many Drivers I'd killed and where it happened.

If I got my story wrong, or they spotted my blades, one of them would accuse me of killing Prof. They'd all seen how I challenged him at our last meeting, and I'd been hearing the gossip since before then.

They knew I wanted to run things. And I would someday, when they were ready for me.

And if they figured it out about Prof, they'd know I killed the others, too, then. So for now, I was stuck on the rooftops, but I'd come down soon enough. I'd prove to the Powders that I was all the leader they would ever need.

Just not yet.

I wasn't ready to be that warrior for them until I dealt with my own demons. I knew that now.

If I meant to prove myself to my father, to myself, and to my gang, I had to take a stand, to show them all what true loyalty looked like. Snake had earned his punishment just being a Driver to begin with. And so had my sister by choosing him over me. She abandoned her own blood family for some dick.

Punishing her would be the proof of my status as a warrior worthy of leading a serious gang and controlling this city. Nobody in Powders' town would dare defy me if they knew I'd killed my own sister for her betrayal.

Problem was, I didn't know if I could kill Hope.

The thought sent a burning shame through me because *I* still felt loyalty to *her*. Family meant something to me, still.

Maybe I could teach Hope what she should've learned long ago. That family was all that mattered, no matter how rough or tough it was. The people who had your back were the only ones you should care about.

If she was forced to watch Snake die, whimpering and begging like the damn clown he was, then she'd come around. I'd punish her with that sight, and see how she reacted, and then we'd see what would come next.

I just gotta find her and Snake to get it done.

The street was clearing, ever so slowly, but enough that I could get out of the area.

It didn't take much. Within minutes, I was down the stairs and on the sidewalk, making my way to a Toyota Camry the Powders kept in a garage.

It was a runner's car, for making deliveries. Looked like any old thing on the road driving for some rideshare hustle. Prof even had the bright idea to get knockoff window stickers made, so we'd look like drivers getting folks to and from, making ends meet.

He loved making them "drivers" jokes. Dumbass never noticed he was the only one who laughed.

We each had the app on a burner phone we carried. In case anyone did get pulled over, they could pop it up as proof they were legit. Got the cops off our asses more than once already.

I tapped a quick text from my own phone to another Powder.

HMU on my burner for a ride across town.
I need the car for something.

Dude texted back slower than I wanted, but the burner pinged with a notification a second later. I scrolled through until I spotted his request and accepted it.

There. Now if the damn cops do stop me, I can just show 'em I got legitimate business to be attending to.

Best of all, the car wasn't owned by anybody in the Powders. Prof'd seen to that, too, making up some company name and registering the car all legal and shit. But it would never be traced back to anyone still alive.

I let myself regret killing him for a whole two seconds before I rolled away in the Prius, heading for Hope's apartment across town.

Once I got there, I made my way upstairs without any real belief that I'd find her. She knew I could get in, so it'd be stupid for her and Snake to try and hole up here. Still, it was worth checking.

The emergency key she kept under her doormat was gone, but that was all right. I made a copy the first time she told me about it. The key slid in, and I opened the door. Hermit went running off to the bedroom the second he saw me. Predators recognized other predators, and he'd been some of my inspiration for the claws, the way I'd seen him tear apart mice at our old place.

Another mark against my sister. She'd taken him along with her and turned him into a spoiled, overweight house cat who was likely forgetting his instincts with every breath.

"Hope! Are you here? We need to talk." I closed the door behind me, and my call echoed around the little apartment. But it felt empty. And her purse was gone from the counter where she normally left it.

I took an extra minute to peek into her bedroom and bathroom.

In the kitchen, I took a quick look at Hope's work schedule. She still had Tuesdays off, it looked like. That was fine. Trying to get her at the Starlight woulda been a nightmare.

Hurrying back downstairs, I fought down images of Hope and Snake lying entwined in some flophouse, that bastard Driver getting his paint-covered fingers all over my little sister. I didn't know how he'd stolen her away from me, but that was a conversation we'd be having as soon as I eliminated him from the picture.

Hell, she might even be with the Feds at this point, she'd been so stupid lately. If she was, that was all the more reason to show her how wrong she'd gone.

For now, though, I'd corner some Driver and figure out where to find Snake. Or maybe I'd give Celine a call, see if she'd spotted him again.

I banged out a text at Celine and waited in Hope's kitchen until my phone dinged with her reply.

'Sup sis? I'm fixin to do this next dance in a minute.

I wrote back quick but kept it short and sweet.

Seen snake?

She was just as quick, and oh so sweet.

He's at the school by tookies where he paints.

Rails there 2, she added.

I thanked her with a heart emoji and a raised fist. The stars had aligned in my favor, finally. Now all I had to do was hope my sister would be there to watch me kill her boyfriend and the leader of his gang too.

30

Emma texted Jacinda that Denae had left with her brother and Hope for her sister's most likely known location. Her phone pinged with Hope's text first, giving her the address.

The SSA called a second later.

"She did what? How is that abiding by her suspension, Emma? What the hell is she thinking? What are you thinking letting her do it?"

"I don't think she's thinking so much as feeling right now, Jacinda. Her brother's life has been threatened, and Hope's sister is the one responsible. They're going on the assumption that she can be reasoned with, but—"

"But she's already proven she can't be. We have three bodies to confirm that. Dammit! Tell me you have the address."

"I do. Hope just texted." She gave it to Jacinda, who spoke to someone on her end of the call.

"Max is having his team head over there. I'm assuming you intend to follow Denae?"

Emma said she was and confirmed she would wait for Max's task force to arrive before attempting to engage with

Grace Jackson, assuming she was even at the address they'd been given.

"Denae says she's sorry, too, Jacinda. She knows she's going off book in the biggest way possible."

"I'd never have expected this from her, but he's her family. I have to hope the field chiefs will be as understanding when she's called in for disciplinary review. Because that will happen. There's nothing I can do to stop it now."

The SSA ended the call, leaving Emma to drive out to where Grace Jackson had been living, with worry for Denae eating away at her insides.

The drive was easy enough, at least. A few patrol cars cruised the surrounding neighborhood streets, no doubt looking for anyone involved in the rioting and fighting earlier. Emma kept her eyes out for possible threats as she entered what was clearly Powders territory.

Tags in the gang's colors of blue and white marked nearly every surface. The streets were quiet, and people sitting on stoops or leaning on cars suddenly found other places to be as her Bureau vehicle cruised through.

She spotted Denae's SUV parked against a curb and rolled to a stop behind it. Denae, Hope, and Jamaal stood nearby, in the deep vestibule of a squat apartment block.

Emma joined them all, staying on the sidewalk. "Jacinda says the task force is going to meet us here. We're supposed to wait for them before trying to talk to Grace."

A sheepish look crossed Hope's face before she laughed and put a hand over her mouth. "My bad, I guess," she sighed, leaning against Jamaal, "she ain't in there. I just checked."

Denae grunted and met Emma's gaze. "We couldn't go in without a warrant, anyway, so Hope saved us some time and trouble."

Emma shook her head and tapped a text to Jacinda, providing an update and asking for next steps. The SSA replied to say the task force was still occupied with the fighting.

Do not enter yourselves. Get whatever information you can without risking the investigation. And keep Denae from doing anything else that might end her career. She's a good agent.

"Well," Emma showed her phone to Denae, "we have our orders. We should get these two over to your place."

Denae glanced at the young people, her eyes suddenly sad. "I'm sorry I wasn't there for you, Jamaal. Maybe if I had been, you wouldn't be with the Drivers. Wouldn't be in this position."

He barely shrugged in response. "They jumped me in up in B-more. Saw me painting on a drugstore wall out back, by the dumpsters. Just started beating on me, you know? Kicking me and shit, knocked me down. Said I was a Driver now, and I'd be painting for them."

He stopped and looked off to the side. Denae stepped around to catch his gaze and lifted both hands, like she'd reach for him. He shook his head.

"Too late, Denae. I'm in the gang. Ain't but one way out of it."

"That's not true, Jamaal. I can—"

"I just want to paint. That's it. No, not even want to. I need to, for myself. The Drivers own me, though…so I gotta paint for them."

The young man's voice cracked with pain and frustration. Emma had never felt driven to art, to anything like what she'd seen him creating in the old school, but the passion in his voice couldn't be denied.

And she felt for him. He'd retreated to art, which should've at least been a peaceful pursuit, even if his chosen medium wasn't widely accepted in society…but it had led him here.

Emma let a second go by before she coughed, bringing everyone's attention back to her. "We should get going."

Gaze still on her little brother, Denae nodded and stepped down to stand by Emma on the sidewalk.

As the two young people joined the agents, Emma glanced around, feeling a sudden thickness to the air and a deep chill radiating from behind her. Which meant one thing.

Standing at the curb, beside Denae's Escape, was the ghost of Camilla Jones. She shivered, as if feeling the deep cold of the Other just as intensely as Emma did herself.

Camilla's white eyes were focused on Jamaal, and she whispered something. Emma did her best to walk normal, to conceal her interest from the others as she stepped nearer to the ghost.

"I'll follow you to your place, Denae," Emma pulled out her key fob, "and I'll let Jacinda know we came up empty here."

The other woman nodded and ushered Jamaal and Hope toward her car, extending her key ring over with the fob dangling from it. "Get in and give me a minute with Emma."

As her colleague drew near, Emma leaned over to catch what Camilla's ghost was muttering. Her voice drifted higher. "Art is safe. His art should be safe. It has to be safe."

Denae was leaning in to whisper something to Emma. As she started speaking, Emma glanced at Jamaal and Hope just in time to see him stuffing his phone in his pocket and getting into the driver's seat of Denae's Ford Escape.

"Jamaal!"

Denae spun away from her and made a dash for the back seat passenger door. But her brother had the engine turned over, and the SUV lurched off the curb, leaving Denae to stumble forward. Emma jumped and just caught her friend from falling by grabbing her wrist.

"Dammit! Dammit!"

"We can follow him, Denae. My car. Let's go."

She pulled the other woman back to the Bureau sedan. By the time they got moving, Denae's SUV was nowhere in sight.

"How are we gonna follow his ass when we don't know where he's going? He can't be heading back to my place. Probably going to hers, so—"

"They're going to the old school."

"What? How the fu…why would they go there? And why are you so sure they are?"

With only one card left to play, Emma took her chances. "He was so heartbroken, Denae, talking about his art. I think he's going back to the school where he paints, so he can get whatever's left there before he disappears again."

If her colleague accepted the explanation, she made no sign of it. "All right. You're driving, and I'm probably unemployed by this point, anyway, so just call me your willing passenger. Go wherever you think's best, Emma."

I wish I could tell you, Denae. Maybe someday I will. I just hope you don't do anything today that'll make you the next ghost I take suggestions from.

31

Leo leaned back against the patrol car and stared down the two Powders who sat cross-legged on the sidewalk. Hands tied, backs against the brick of a florist shop, uninjured, and way pissed off.

Which was fine, since that was about how Leo felt at this point.

He crouched in front of them, aiming to keep an even voice. "Look, guys, this stonewalling treatment isn't getting anyone anywhere. Tell me something, and maybe you'll get to go home faster than some of your buddies."

The older one, a Hispanic man without any ID on him, snorted and bounced his head backward, flicking braids out of his face. "What you expect us to tell you that won't get us killed on the street tomorrow?"

"You think you're gonna get killed for telling me who called off the fighting? You don't think that's what we wanted to happen?" The man's face went expressionless, and Leo stared at the other man, a younger Black man who had no ID on him. "Everything stopped, just like that. No more fistfights, no more guns going off out of random windows, nothing. It's been hours since the last outbreak, and that was hours after a shit ton of fighting. What happened?"

Both men stared at the sidewalk between their knees, apparently content to wait for the next ride down to the jail.

Leo's glare had gotten him no further than his words. He stood and, upon seeing Max walking about a block down the street, flagged him over. The liaison with the gang task force changed trajectory and headed his way. He did not look happy.

Everywhere, though, cops and federal agents were talking to witnesses or babysitting gang members awaiting rides to booking. And at least as far as Leo had seen, nobody had said much. The bits and pieces they'd gathered revealed—there'd been a gang war, maybe or maybe not set off by the murder of Tyler "Professor" Michaels, leader of the Powders. Professor's body was recovered but hadn't been sent to the M.E. yet.

Max suspected his death was the root cause of all this, but nothing was for sure at this point.

Other than the bodies. They had plenty of bodies.

Max came to a stop beside Leo and spoke low enough that nobody but the two of them would hear. "You need me? Because I think I'm about to head out here. Start questioning down at the station."

"Nothing else to do here?" Leo glanced down to the two gang members nearby, and then farther down the street to a few more awaiting transport, but Max only shook his head.

"You still think someone called off the fighting?"

Max frowned. "Until someone talks, we won't know. And it might be nobody knows, to be honest. Some of these guys were just waiting for a chance to start shooting. They did, and we showed up to put a stop to it. It could've just ended organically."

Leo caught the attention of a uniform nearby and pointed

to the two men he'd been babysitting. The cop nodded and came trotting over, standing in front of them with a hand hovering over his holster like the two of them might pull AR-15s out of their asses. Leo resisted rolling his eyes—everyone was on edge, after all—and pulled Max into the street, away from prying ears.

"And what does your informant say?" Leo kept his voice low, even though he knew they were too far away to be heard by anyone. "She giving you anything? Or have you not had a chance to catch up with her yet?"

Max's lips thinned, lines going deeper into his brow. He pointed down the street to where some body bags were lined up near a bus stop, also awaiting transport. "You got someone who can talk to ghosts, feel free to ask her. Tamila got shot down early, it looks like, but we just found her body."

Shit.

Leo closed his eyes and tried to gather his thoughts, feeling what remained of his hope for answers waning. "Do we know if she was outed?"

"I don't think so. She'd have been…a lot worse if that was the case. It was just a single shot to the chest."

"Sorry, man."

Offering only a tight nod, Max took the opportunity to loosen his vest. "You need me for anything else? Looks like everything is pretty well in hand here, but I need to start working on where this leaves things with the gangs."

Leo raised an eyebrow. "This war change things that much?"

"Well, the Powders clearly lost, based on what we're seeing in terms of bodies. If what Jacinda told me is correct, that the killer's also a Powder, that means the gang is imploding." Max frowned, eyes focused on some body bags being loaded into a van down the street. "Things might be scattered right now, but the Drivers' drug structure is unaffected. They could use this to expand their territory, expand their reach…it's hard to tell what's coming, but we need to be ready. And that's gonna be hard, since we still don't know where the Drivers are getting their meth. So yeah, work to be done."

All Leo could do was wipe a hand down his face. Battle grime stuck to his sweaty palm.

Max refocused on Leo. "I'm gonna touch base with Jacinda before I go. You good?"

"Yeah, go ahead." Leo waved the man off, aware of the weight of his steps as he headed back toward his car. He should've seen how beaten down Max was earlier and guessed at the informant's fate, but there was just too damn much screaming for attention in his head.

Denae most of all, now that the gang war had run its course.

With things so clearly wrapping up, Leo moved into the middle of the street and pulled out his cell phone. Barricades were set up to block off the street, which meant this was just about the quietest space available. He hesitated for only a moment before calling Denae.

"Leo, hey. You okay? I was gonna call." Denae stopped there, as if she'd given some major revelation, and Leo's gut clenched. She was definitely up to something, with or without Emma.

"I'm fine. So is the rest of the team. Where are you?"

Denae remained silent, enough so that Leo could hear her breathing. A car engine revved, and her breathing shifted suddenly, like she'd just sucked in a mouthful of air in surprise.

"I guess that means Emma's driving, huh?"

"Leo, I need to tell you something."

He took a deep breath. "I think Jacinda already did."

Denae was silent for a moment. "I guess that makes sense. She was right to tell you. But...I'm sorry I didn't tell you before. I honestly didn't know for sure until today. I'm sorry—"

"You haven't been yourself since the case started. Jacinda suspended you, but you're still working, aren't you?"

"I am."

"This...you could be jeopardizing everything."

"I know." Something that might've been a sob broke from Denae's chest, and it was such a foreign sound, Leo flinched. "I know, okay? I was praying it wasn't him. Last I heard, he was in Baltimore, and he's so much younger than me, we never developed enough of a relationship, and I'm sorry I didn't say anything, but—"

"Stop. Stop, it's okay." Leo took a deep breath, counted to three, then breathed out. Denae was safe, and it seemed her brother was too. *That's the important thing, right?*

A job was a job, and it wasn't something to take lightly. But family always came first. Leo would drop every ball and miss every meeting to help his brothers get clear of whatever trouble they'd gotten into. If Aleksy were caught up in something like this...the thought nearly stopped Leo's breath.

Denae said something on her end of the line, probably to Emma, but he couldn't make it out. He wondered again where they were and where they were going. Before he could ask, she was back on the line.

"I've been with Jamaal all afternoon. Emma and I found him, with his girlfriend's help. I need to be there for him right now. That's why I haven't called."

"And I need to be there for you." Leo's response hung in the air, weightier than it should've been. They hadn't talked much about the future, or even their feelings, but he knew she'd heard all of that in his voice. Yes, he was a federal agent who could back her up. He was also falling in love with her. "Where are you? Right now?"

Denae sighed. "You're not needed there?"

"I'll talk to Jacinda." He was already walking her way, hurrying. "But, no, I don't think so."

"We're heading to Jamaal's studio…an old school building he paints at. It's on the other side of Drivers territory from where you are."

Leo sped up, already wondering what Denae wasn't telling him. *Why* they were going there.

But he'd rather ask in person.

"Text me the address. I'll be there as soon as I can. Don't either of you do anything stupid until I get there, all right? No running yellow lights, even."

Denae chuckled, but it sounded forced. When she spoke, Leo could swear he heard worry warring with relief over the prospect of him coming. "Promise. No yellow lights."

She hung up on that note, and Leo tucked his phone away just as he reached Jacinda, who looked exhausted. Her long red hair was flatter than he'd ever seen it, pulled from her bun and hanging limp and sweaty.

The SSA held a hand up to stop him from interrupting her, pointing needlessly to the phone at her ear.

He heard the barest broadcast of her lips tightening and a fast-talking voice coming from the device. Couldn't make out who.

As Jacinda closed her eyes, she brushed a hand through her hair as if in pain. "It's a stupid plan, Emma. But fine, it's worth a shot." Jacinda glanced up at Leo, talking as she did. "We have an APB out for Grace Jackson and a BOLO for Denae's vehicle. If you're right, let us know. If you're wrong, MPD will hopefully find them before they get themselves or anyone else hurt. And remind Agent Monroe she's suspended and is to be operating strictly in a bench-warming capacity. That means she stays in the car. Cuff her to the damn steering wheel if you have to."

Jacinda ended the call.

Before she could say anything, Leo jumped at the chance. "Jacinda, I was coming over to ask to be reassigned to help Emma, so whatever she's up to—"

"Stop, stop." Jacinda waved her phone as if to remind him what he'd just heard, and he obediently shut his mouth before she could change her mind. "You're in. Emma's got a harebrained idea that our killer's going to end up at that school building tonight, and—"

"Then we should all be heading over there!" Leo waved at Vance and Mia, who stood near a cruiser a block down the street. "If she needs backup—"

"Leo!" Jacinda stared at him.

"Sorry. Shutting up."

"Really?" Jacinda rolled her eyes. "If you'd let me finish, I'd have explained that it's extremely unlikely she'll need backup. Most likely, she'll be staking out an empty building that isn't going to get any more empty as the night drags on, but you and Max's team will be there just in case."

Leo smiled tightly, happy enough with the clear long shot of things. Goose chase or not, he'd be joining Denae and Emma to make sure they stayed safe. The concern he'd heard in Denae's voice still rang in his ear, so that was the important thing. Maybe Emma had simply gotten to her, convincing her this plan had more merit than it did.

"All right, then, get going, and if you get there before Max and his team, let 'em know he'll be there shortly. I'll send the address to your phone," Jacinda pulled out her phone, "and Vance can ride with us. He and Mia can help me finish cleaning up the mess here, and we'll all meet there when we finish up. But keep a low profile on approaching their location, all right?"

That means they're already up to something.

Leo offered Jacinda a quick nod before turning away. He started out jogging toward the area where he and Vance had left the car, then allowed himself to break into a run, despite the ache it put on his knee, as soon as he got off the main street and past the police barricades.

He needed to get to Denae before whatever was about to happen actually went down.

Because the more he thought about it, the more he wondered if Emma's instincts didn't have some sort of third eye. Meaning that what Jacinda thought was a long shot might be the opposite.

32

Leo found Denae's SUV just a block from the address Jacinda gave him for the old school. Her Ford Escape was parked driver's side to the curb, facing down a narrow one-way street. A Bureau sedan sat in front of the car, and two figures were visible inside it. Leo parked his Bureau ride a few spots away, behind a Subaru that might've been from the 1980s.

He got out and pulled his jacket on over his bulletproof vest, scanning the area for movement or any approaching figures. The street was quiet and empty as early evening light cast long shadows everywhere. Bits of trash blew from an open set of cans in front of an apartment block across from the school.

The chain-link fence around the school had mostly been pulled down or cut to allow access to the old blacktop playground area. Two rusted basketball hoops stood sentinel there.

Leo tried to imagine children playing in the area, their laughter echoing off the buildings nearby.

When he reached the car, he could tell Emma was trying to convince Denae of something. They were arguing, hands flying and slicing at the air to punctuate whatever points they were each trying to make. Leo tapped on the window by Denae's face. She turned to look at him, and he froze. He had never in his life seen a face so deeply etched with agony and conviction at the same time.

Whatever was driving her thoughts, Denae Monroe would not be discouraged by anyone.

But I have to try. I have to.

"Denae—"

She was out of the car in a flash, wrapping her arms around him and squeezing him as if he were a pillar and the street around them a raging tempest. Her heart raced against his chest. She pulled back from him just as fast and took a step into the street, in the direction of the school.

Emma was out of the car and on a trajectory that would cut off Denae's route to the building.

Denae must've heard Emma's footsteps, because she raced across the sidewalk and did a quick jump over a row of scraggly bushes that bordered the abandoned property.

"Denae, please," Leo called, moving after her. But she kept moving.

"He's my baby brother. He's run off to this school, and I swear he's in there right now, about to get himself killed. I need to go in and stop that from happening. I don't care what Jacinda says."

Leo opened his mouth to respond, but Denae's tight expression held him off for a moment. If this hadn't been her brother, he would've railed against the idea of letting her take another step...

If it were Aleksy in there being an idiot, what would you do? What would Yaya say if you didn't at least try to keep him safe?

Denae's eyes gleamed with anxiety, waiting for him to accept what she was dead set on doing, or hoping she wouldn't have to turn her back on him. He couldn't tell which, and he wasn't sure which he liked less.

If the killer was inside already, then her brother was in danger, and he couldn't live with himself knowing he'd delayed an attempt at saving Jamaal's life.

"Let us help you here. Max and his team are on the way too. We can go in as a force and save Jamaal and his girlfriend together instead of you risking your life alongside theirs by rushing in on your own."

"Not gonna happen. We've been hearing about Grace Jackson all day. She gets up close and personal, with blades. You know that. I know that. But I'm the one who trains at the gym almost every chance I get."

Leo felt his own eyes widen, horror at the nonchalance of her words bleeding out into a cold sweat on his back. "We're talking about your *life*. This isn't a street fight."

"And I know this type of person. She wants blood, yeah, but she wants it her way. She wants revenge. And right now, I want to go stop her from getting it. So if you don't mind…"

A bubble of air caught in Leo's throat as he met Denae's gaze. Her stance, the look on her face, the bulky vest she wore over her shirt…she looked wholly different from the woman he'd woken up to on Monday morning, her hair tousled and his college t-shirt clinging to her figure in all the right places. "Can you at least let me go in first? You're not even supposed to be here, let alone going into an active operation. You're suspended, Denae. This could mean the end of your career. The end of…"

He hadn't wanted to say it, and only just stopped himself from letting the word "us" creep past his lips. But she must've heard it in his sigh.

Denae's lips pressed together, the tiniest sign of nerves coming through. "I'm gonna be okay. I promise. And so are we. When this is all over."

Emma shook her head, silently telling Leo to not press.

Denae sprinted away toward the school.

With terror for her safety gripping his heart, Leo gave chase, shouting her name as she crossed the barren lawn and pushed through the broken chain-link fence. Emma was right behind him, heading into whatever might unfold within the darkened ruin.

33

Rails Foster paced the stage inside the school auditorium, doing his best to ignore the stripper cowering in the corner by one of Snake's murals. It wasn't easy to do. Not with what Veevee told him about that stripper. Dude called an hour ago and said he'd be skipping out of D.C. for the foreseeable.

And he dropped that Celine had been working the Night Trips for the Powders. She was probably getting word back to their leader, Prof, about deals going down, where the Drivers would be moving into next. All that kinda shit.

Rails gave Veevee some hell about that for damn sure.

"The fuck you been doing at that club, then? I thought I told you to keep an eye on the place."

Veevee was quick on the defense, saying how he'd kept the place running fine and with no cops coming around to give the Drivers any headaches. But the dude still blew himself into the wind the minute the cops did show up.

So on top of dealing with a Powders informant dancing at Night Trips, Rails had to find a new manager for the club.

Can't be me, and Rux is dead. Gotta be somebody else,

somebody who can take the heat and won't cause no fuss with the dancers.

Snake might be the man for the job. Rails texted him a bit ago, telling him to come down here because he had something to show him. He figured seeing Celine, learning that she was the reason Rux and Jax got killed, that might be enough to get Snake thinking about taking over at Night Trips.

The girl was fast with the info the minute Rails had his gun in her face.

"Them two was hassling me on the way home the other night. That's why they got smoked, for messing around like they shouldn't have been."

Sure they were. Rails figured his boys were just catcalling like anybody else who saw a stripper walking down the street. And that was enough to get them killed over?

"Hey, girl. Tell me again how it went down with Rux and Jax."

She met his gaze, still with some of the fire she'd had in her when he found her in the dressing room at Night Trips. But she was ready to talk too. Fear had her eyes wide open.

"I told you. They were hassling me, so they got smoked."

"Uh-huh. And who cuts up a man's throat like that just for paying a pretty girl the compliment of his attention?"

Celine scoffed and spit on the floor next to where she sat. "Compliment. As if. Them two was treating me like I was just a good time waiting for them to show up and have me. Ain't no surprise to me when I heard they got killed for it. She don't fuck around when it comes to family."

"*She?*" That was a surprise. "You telling me it's a bitch been killing my people?"

The stripper laughed at him, loud and proud, like he wasn't the one holding a gun. He aimed it at her chest, and she stopped laughing, but the smile didn't leave her face.

"Yeah. That's what I'm telling you. Girl has beef with your artist. That's why I told you to send them texts to her when you grabbed my phone, so she'd come down here and know where he hangs out. She's gonna get him, Rails. Killing me ain't gonna stop that."

He'd heard enough. Knowing she'd played him, and had him send texts that would bring his enemy right where she'd wanted to be all along…on top of spying for the enemy, Celine might've put Rails in harm's way himself.

He lifted the gun to her face. "Guess this is goodbye, Cee."

She turned away from him, fear shaking her chin now, until an expression crossed her face that put Rails's hackles up.

He looked in the direction she was turned but didn't see anything. The stage was wide open in both directions and empty. Still keeping his gun trained on Celine, he stepped to his right and slowly rotated in place to take in the auditorium beyond the stage. The sun had dropped lower outside, sending slanting blades of light across the floor.

Rails turned back to Celine. She sat surrounded by Snake's paintings. They were all on big sheets of plywood he must've pulled down from the old school buildings, where they'd covered up windows into the empty classrooms and offices.

The rasp of metal on metal came from somewhere outside, slow and steady, like something being dragged across a pipe.

"Who's out there? Somebody coming up in here? You better show yourself." He got no answer, and the metal sound stopped short, like somebody was planning their move. "Who is it, Celine? Tell me now, or I'm putting you down."

He aimed the gun at her face again, and a shout sounded from the auditorium behind him.

"Rails, no, man, don't."

He spun around to see Snake and some girl coming across the floor. He had his hands up, like he was surrendering or something.

"Why you got your hands up like that?"

He and the girl drew closer to the stage, and Rails stepped over near the wall, so he could keep Celine in his peripheral view. Snake reached the stairs leading up to the side of the stage. He came up with the girl behind him.

"The hell'd you come from, Snake? This the bitch who killed Rux and Jax?"

"No! Shit, man. This's Hope. Me and her are together, and she's cool, Rails. I swear it."

Heart beating like rolling thunder in his chest, Rails strove to keep his voice steady. "Still don't answer how you got in behind me like that."

"Side door back there. I keep it covered with plywood outside. I got a few ways in and out, in case cops or somebody put extra locks on the doors. Happened when I first started using this place."

"Uh-huh, and so you used one of them ways and come up behind me. You ever think before you do things, or just go with whatever comes to mind in the moment? Shit, I coulda smoked your ass." Rails wiggled his gun in the air, then aimed it back at Celine. "Fitting you should show up now, when I'm about to solve a little problem we been having at the Trips."

"Rails, man." Snake moved up, still hugging on the girl he'd come in with. "This ain't necessary. It wasn't Celine's fault. It was mine."

"The hell you talking about?"

"Just listen. Celine ain't had nothing to do with all this... really. Let her go, man. I'm the one she wants. That's why she killed Jax and Rux. She saw me with them and thought they'd know where I was at."

Celine snorted, and the sound fired the fuel of rage inside Rails's heart even more. Teeth clenched, he stomped across the stage to stand in front of her, still aiming his gun at her face. "Something funny over here? Powders bitch got a joke she wants to tell?"

She stared up at him, almost like she was daring him to pull the trigger. "Just thinking how funny it is your boy there doesn't know the real reason them two got killed. It was because of me, but not because I told her to kill them. Like I said, she took them out because they was hassling me while I walked home."

"Who is this 'she' you keep talking about? I need a name, and I'ma count to three."

Celine shifted away, and he tracked her with this gun. She moved to sit with her back against Snake's mural. The image of a sunrise above a garden loomed over her in the darkness, like a backdrop of stains and blood spatters on the old auditorium's wall.

"One."

With immense satisfaction, Rails saw that the girl had started shaking. She knew he meant it, but still, she didn't give him a name.

Fine, then. Let's get to counting.

"Two."

A tear fell from her eye, and she shook her head. "You don't get it, Rails. She's not like you, and that's why the Powders will always be on top in this town. Because we look after our own like family. That's what she was doing when she killed your boys that night. So go on and shoot me if you need to. It'll just give her one more reason to come after you next."

His aim wavered, just for a second, as footsteps sounded on the stage behind him. Snake's voice came from a few feet away.

"Rails, man. Please don't shoot her. She ain't the one doing all this."

"Sounds pretty clear you know who it is, and since this bitch over here don't seem inclined to talk, I'm thinking I might just kill her, anyway, unless you can give me a real good reason not to."

A voice he didn't know piped up, and Rails turned to see the girl with Snake staring at him. "She's my sister, Rails. Her name's Grace."

"Your sister. That means you're a Powders girl. And that means," he looked at Snake, "you're a traitor."

For a second, Rails envisioned Snake behind the bar at Night Trips, pouring for the crew when they'd come in, keeping watch over the clientele, and making sure nobody got handsy with the dancers.

That second came and went, and he knew he'd been wrong about the Drivers artist. He was good for one thing and one thing only. Dude could paint. He could make a wall look like a place you could walk into. He could show you people who'd died, and you'd swear they'd come back to life.

"You got skill, Snake. Real skill. Mighta got you somewhere someday. But if you don't tell me right now, not your damn girl, who it is been killing Drivers with some blades, I'm afraid your career will have to be cut real short."

Rails lifted his gun and aimed at Snake's face. Instead of showing fear, the man actually turned his head sideways and clutched at the girl at his side.

A scream behind Rails had him looking at Celine, but the stripper was still curled up against the wall. Rails caught a flash of movement in his peripheral. He spun and popped off three shots, but all he saw was an empty room.

A sudden, furious burning pain exploded in his side, and he roared, clutching at his ribs. Hot blood poured from his body as another burst of pain erupted in his gut, and then another.

Hope screamed. "Grace, stop!"

They kept coming, the bursts of fiery, flaring torment ripping into his midsection and his lower back as he fell. His attacker screamed at him as the blades continued to slice into him, draining his lifeblood and his strength more and more with each strike.

"He's mine! My kill! Mine!"

Rails slumped onto the stage, his face turned to watch Celine bolting away and out a door at the back. Another set of feet appeared in front of his eyes as blood bubbled up from his throat. He coughed it out.

Snake and his girl had run in the direction Celine took, but the dark figure was just behind them, her right hand held at the ready with the set of three blades sticking off her knuckles, Rails's blood dripping on the floor like some comic book monster movie shit.

"Sna…run, man. Just…"

Rails coughed one more time, feeling blood fill his mouth. He tried to swallow and ended up choking on it, his chest heaving with an effort to breathe.

Snake and his girl were still all wrapped around each other, but the killer was moving closer, pointing with the blades now.

A voice Rails didn't recognize rasped out of her as she stalked forward.

"Let my sister go, you Drivers piece of shit."

With his last breath, before his eyes closed forever, Rails watched Snake and the girl spin away and run into the shadows at the back of the stage.

34

Emma and Leo sped after Denae through a gap in the chain-link fence surrounding the abandoned school building. They'd heard some shouting moments ago and three fast gunshots, but now the only noise came from passing cars on nearby streets.

The schoolyard was deadly quiet. Blacktop and rusted basketball hoops stood to their right, in front of what had been an administration building. All the windows were boarded up now, except for a few where the plywood had been pulled down, likely by Jamaal to use as canvases.

"Denae, please go back to the car and wait while Leo and I go in. Please. Think about what you're doing here."

"He's family. My little brother. I know you don't know what that's like, so I don't expect you to understand. Leo should, though."

When Denae turned to face them, Emma's fists clenched as tightly as they ever had. "No, I don't know what it's like to have a brother. Or a sister. While we're talking about it, I'm not sure I know what it's like to have a family at all, since the only one I've had was short-lived and nearly nonexistent.

That doesn't mean I don't get to weigh in on your bad judgment here."

Leo stepped forward and gestured as if trying to encourage the two fighters to back away from each other and wait for the bell. "Let's remember we're here to protect innocent lives and stop a killer. Denae, I understand why you're doing this. Trust me. But I also know that you know better than to be doing it."

"I'm not leaving him to die."

"Nobody's asking you to. You've been told to stand down by the SSA. If you'll let Emma and me take the lead, we can get in there and protect both you and your brother. Max's team should be here soon too."

Emma stepped aside and monitored the area while Leo and Denae continued the conversation up close.

Let them have a private moment, Emma girl. It might be the only thing that keeps Denae from doing something that can't be undone.

Not for the first time, Emma worried if she would someday soon be faced with the prospect of seeing one of her colleagues in the Other. Oren had been taken from her so recently. Was she about to lose yet one more of the people she considered the closest thing to family she'd ever known?

With the advantage of a quiet night and no immediate threats, Emma observed the abandoned school in more detail than she had on her first visit. Of course, that had been in the daylight. The empty grounds, blacktop yard, and boarded-up buildings now held multiple signs of potential threat as the urban canyons around them cut off sunlight.

Growing shadows concealed doorways and what few windows were visible where boards had been removed. The empty rooms within were all but completely shrouded in darkness.

If they were going to seriously search this area for

fugitives or defend against an attacker, they would need light.

"Leo, Denae, I'm going to get flashlights from the car. You'll wait for me here, right?"

Her colleagues replied with silent nods before getting back to their hushed conversation.

She retrieved flashlights from the Bureau sedan and hurried back to Leo and Denae, who'd finished whatever chat they'd been having. Denae now stood to the side and gestured for Emma to join Leo ahead of her on the walkway leading into the school.

"After you, Agent Last."

"I hope we can get back to first names after this, Denae. I mean that."

"Me too. I still need to get you down to the gym so I can show you how it's done."

With a sliver of a smile on her lips, Denae ushered them both forward.

Emma nodded at Leo, drew her weapon, and moved into the empty schoolyard.

35

I went after Hope and Snake as they took off down a walkway. We passed boarded-up classroom windows and wide-open doors that had long ago been smashed in. Funky smells came from one classroom, like an alley out back of a club late at night after the drunks got done pissing away all the booze they drank.

Hope slipped and scrambled to hold on to Snake.

He pulled her up, and they kept running, feet slapping the concrete, until they hit the end of the walkway and went around the corner.

But I caught up to them. I got a hand out and grabbed Hope's shirt, pulling her back. She had to let go of that shithead she was with, and that was my chance.

I put on the speed, running double time, and latched onto Snake's sleeve with my left hand. My blades came around as I pulled him to me and went in for the slice.

He slid right out of his unzipped hoodie—and just like that, I was left holding his damn clothing in one hand while my blades hit nothing but air. I screamed his name and charged ahead, but Hope got in front of me.

"Dammit, Grace! Stop!"

Too late.

With a fast jab, I shot my left fist out and hit Hope on the button, right on the chin, snapping her head up and back. She staggered, and before Snake could get his slimy hands on her again, I wrapped my left arm around her, pulled her in close, and set my blades at the side of her neck. She barely struggled in my grasp, just whimpered.

"Grace, please," Hope pleaded. "Just let us go. Please. We don't want none of this life. Jamaal and me just want to be together."

"Jamaal, huh? That's your real name? Okay, then, Jamaal." I snarled the name. "Here's how we're gonna do it. I'ma let Hope go, then you and me are gonna finish this, one to one."

He stared at me over Hope's shoulder with murder in his eyes. I knew that look because it was the same look I had on every time I thought about him when I boxed with myself in the mirror. I'd seen his face so many times, always full of blood and tears, beaten up, swollen and messy. Because of me.

Now, though? He looked mad. He looked mean. And I knew I'd been right all along. This little punk was nothing but a Driver, an enemy, and he'd been trying to steal my sister from me.

Somewhere behind us, in the schoolyard, I heard shouting, like a cop letting you know they were there.

"You hear that?" Jamaal jerked his chin toward the shouting. "My sister's a Fed. She's out there with them, probably. She got a whole team of them coming. Task force cops and shit. You should just let me and Hope go and take off yourself. Just go."

"You got some big-ass balls talking to me like that, Driver. Don't think I'm fooled for one second. Now, we gonna go into this classroom here, nice and quiet. Let's go."

I pulled on Hope and kept my blades up at her neck so Mr. My-Sister's-a-Fed knew I meant business as I dragged her into the nearest classroom. "Follow us in, punk. And pull that door closed when you do."

It wasn't really a door, but it still hung on the hinges even if it was half broken and didn't have glass in the little window anymore. But the classroom windows were all boarded up on this room, so I knew we'd have cover enough to hide from any Feds or cops that might come through.

Sure, they'd do a whole search. They'd find us eventually, but before they did, I was gonna make sure my sister understood what I was doing and why.

We got inside, and I could hear more voices out there now, more cops saying they were coming in, calling my name and Hope's too. Somebody even called out for the asshole Driver.

"Guess your sister really is out there, Jamaal. Think she really cares about you, being that you're in a gang and she's a damn Fed? I bet family dinners must be a real shitshow in your house, huh?"

I'd hoped to at least get a laugh out of him, something to show me he could take a dig. It almost would've been easier if he'd started crying or looking hurt, like I'd cut him with my words. Anybody that weak and spineless had no business being around Hope, and killing him would be doing her and the whole world a favor.

But Jamaal just kept mugging at me, glaring with that look on his face that said he was in this until the end and he didn't really care which way it went.

Gotta respect that. Maybe there's something real in him after all, something like the warrior our dad used to be.

I shut that shit off as fast as the thoughts came to me. Couldn't be feeling weak right now. It was time to finish this.

With a jerk, I spun Hope around and shoved her to the

side. She went sprawling onto the floor, leaving me to face off against her Driver boyfriend. He had his hands out to the side, like he was ready to fight or surrender. I couldn't tell which, but probably the latter.

I knew you were a candy-ass. Just like Prof. Probably thinking you can ask me for a peace treaty right now.

"Grace," my sister scrambled to her feet, "you gotta stop. You gotta let us go. Please."

"Like you let me go? Left me to flap around on my own, living in that old house Dad gave us, like some forgotten piece of furniture? We had a family once. You, me, and Dad." To my horror, tears sprang to my eyes, which pissed me off even more. "When he was gone, I figured it was gonna be the two of us and the Powders, because they're the ones made it possible for us to survive without Dad in the first place."

"They're drug dealers. And criminals."

"They're family. My family. Our family. And you just had to shit all over everything they did for you and me. All the times we had Powders dudes walking us to school when we were little, looking out for us like the big brothers they were. All the times they helped us fix stuff in the house. They taught us, like Dad taught us, and we survived because of it. And you treated them, and me, like garbage. Throwing us away for some dick."

Hope swiped tears off her cheeks. "It wasn't like that. You know it. I left because I didn't want to end up like Dad or…"

I knew what she was going to say, so I finished for her. "Or like me. Right? That's what you're thinking by hanging around with this lump of shit in a shirt? He's only got one thing he knows how to do, I bet. So he can paint. So what? Can he teach you how to change the oil in your car? Can he fix a broken toilet? Can he fight?"

Hope was crying harder now. "Grace, just stop. Please. Look at me, Grace. Look at me."

I did, and I found my sister on her knees, hands up like she was praying, tears rolling down her face.

Each tear that dropped off her chin was like gasoline fueling my disgust and hate.

"Stand up. That ain't how I want to remember you. If this goes wrong and the Feds get me when I'm done here, I need to at least have an image of you I can love."

"And you can't love me like this? When I'm on my knees begging you? I still love you, Grace, even after all this. You're still my sister! I thought for sure you were gonna kill me out there when those blades touched my neck. But I still love you, and I always will."

"Because I'm family." I pounded my fist into my chest. "That's right. And family doesn't betray you. Family doesn't leave you in the wind."

She wiped her face on her sleeve. "You're right. Family doesn't do any of that. Family is two little girls running down the lane and into their daddy's arms after school. Family is those same little girls dressing up for trick-or-treat like a couple of superheroes, using any old thing they could find for a mask. Family is me, Grace. It's me. And I'm begging you, please, put those knives down and let it end."

I had to fight back the tears that started climbing up my throat. Hope was hitting below the belt with those memories, but she was right. I looked back at Jamaal and felt my shoulders sag. My blades came down a few inches, so I wasn't looking at him over them anymore.

I could see his whole face now. His goofy haircut framed his eyes. If he wasn't a Driver, I might've even called him fine.

But the man I was staring down belonged to the Drivers, so just like I tested Prof, I'd have to test Hope and Jamaal too.

What choice did I have?

"All right. Say I just stop, like you're telling me to. What happens with us? With me and you? Because maybe I can accept that this man ain't my enemy. Maybe. But that don't mean I intend to share airspace with him. And I can't be having you going off with him somewhere and leaving me behind."

My sister didn't have an answer for me. But he did.

"I'm thinking we'll just keep doing what we're doing, and you keep doing what you're doing. Ain't no reason we need to be up in each other's lives and shit."

Wrong answer. Wrong fucking answer.

I lunged, taking a swipe at his chest, but he skipped back a step. I followed, bringing my blades around in a backhand slice that just caught the baggy shirt he wore. Three slices showed now, revealing his skin underneath, but no blood.

"Got lucky, Snake. Guess you earned that name. But I still ain't see you trying to fight back. I figure you must be one of those dudes likes to look all hard and tough, but really, you're just a candy-ass."

Dude had the guts to shake his head and put up his fists. "Okay then. Put them blades down and let's go. Fair fight. You win, I'm gone. But I put you on the ground, then I win, and you leave me and Hope be."

My sister was on her feet and jumped up close to him. "Jamaal, no. She trains every day, baby. She can kill you with or without the blades."

I had to smile at that. "Little sister, speaking the truth. Finally. But it ain't gonna come to that because there's no way I'm putting these blades anywhere but in his chest."

With that, I sidestepped to the left, aiming to get behind her. But she backed up and raised her hands like she might block me. For a second, I saw the woman she could have been, a warrior by my side, but her eyes weren't in it.

I put out my left hand, like I'd throw a punch at her, and she leaned away from my fist. That gave me my opening.

Jamaal had his hands on Hope's shoulders, pushing her to the side, out from in between us. I dodged back to my right to finally face him now that my sister wasn't in the way.

Jamaal lifted his hands and was watching my face like a good fighter should, looking for my tells to know which way I might break and come in for a punch.

I flicked a glance to his left, and he shifted his weight, lifting his hand to defend.

With a predator's precision, I swept my blades in low, targeting Jamaal's vulnerable stomach. His eyes went wide with the dawning realization of his mistake, mirroring a scene of impending doom.

Letting out a primal scream, a symphony of rage and triumph, I lunged forward with all my might. But fate twisted cruelly in that split second. Hope, my sister, the girl who had always been everything I wasn't, threw herself between me and my target, shielding the man she continued to choose over me.

My blades, their deadly dance interrupted, sank into my sister. The shock of the connection jolted through me, a cold wave of horror following. I'd been moving too fast, too furiously, and only at the last, irreversible moment could I wrench back, retracting the deadly steel from her flesh.

Hope, with a gasp that tore at the edges of my conscience, clutched my wrist. Our eyes locked in a silent, desperate communion.

"Grace, no…you…" Hope's voice was a fragile whisper, laced with disbelief and pain.

I recoiled, as if her touch burned me with the truth of what I'd done. She dropped to the floor, her knees buckling under the weight and shock of her injury. Jamaal went down beside her, pressing a shaking hand over the wounds I'd created.

"Hope, baby." His voice was a raw edge of panic and

desperation. "You gonna be okay. You will. We'll get you help."

The world seemed to pause, the air thick with a silent scream that refused to escape my lips. I couldn't breathe. Couldn't think.

That's my sister's blood all over the glove. Hope's blood on my blades...

I stared at my blades, once instruments of my wrath, now stained with my sister's blood, with her suffering. They felt alien in my grasp, like some kind of cursed artifact from a nightmare.

Revulsion shivered through me, an overwhelming urge to cast them away, but my body refused to comply. My fingers, locked around the hilt, were traitors to the horror of my own creation. The straps that bound the weapons to my hands had transformed into chains, sealing my fate as the bringer of this tragedy.

"Grace."

I just killed my sister. I killed Hope. All hope.

"Grace!"

In the background, Hope's ragged breaths and Jamaal's frantic murmurs were a haunting melody, the soundtrack to a reality I could no longer escape.

"Dammit, Grace, wake the hell up!"

Jamaal was looking at me.

I blinked, trying to understand. "What?"

He wasn't wearing a shirt anymore. His hands held it wadded up over Hope's stomach. Tears fell down his face as he stared at me.

"Grace, we need help. You gotta go find somebody. Please."

He was right. I needed to save my sister. "Yeah…yeah, I'll go find…"

Shouting and the beat of a helicopter filled the air outside. They'd be here any second. They'd find me and...

I was out the door with Jamaal yelling my name behind me. Flashlight beams were cutting across the schoolyard from every direction, aiming into all the doors. I still had the walkway roof over my head, so the helicopter couldn't spotlight me, but they were roaming that beam around the courtyard between classroom wings.

Cops were running in from every direction. I couldn't see them, but I heard their boots and all their yelling, even with that damn helicopter chopping at the sky above. I spun around and raced down the building to the corner.

The chain-link fence was up ahead, and it was still intact, not like the parts out front. But on the other side was freedom. I just had to get around the next corner and see if the fence there was broken or cut. I didn't hear any cops yelling from that direction.

But then, I whipped around a corner as fast as I could and came face to face with two of 'em. I opened my mouth to tell them about Hope, but they reached for me. Without thinking, I put my blades into one of their necks, and he dropped, gurgling on his own blood. The other guy had his hands on me, twisting my left arm around. I stomped hard on his boot, twice, and jabbed back with my blades at his leg.

He let out a shout, and my arm was free. The fence was in front of me, but it didn't have any holes in it, and the other cops would be coming.

Shit. Shit, shit, shit. Where the fuck *do I go?*

If I tried to hide, they'd just search every room until they found me.

I'd just killed a cop, maybe two. They weren't going to take me alive if they saw me.

I ran back the way I'd come, moving on the balls of my feet as fast as I could. I tried to stay quieter than all the cops in their heavy boots and shit. The helicopter made that easier.

At another corner, I waited and listened. All I could hear was the damn helicopter and shouting from around the front of the school and over by the auditorium where I'd killed Rails. I looked around the corner. It was clear, and the room with Hope and Jamaal was the first one down this side of the building.

Had my life always been a path laid out without my consent, every twist and turn leading to this inevitable end? Choices, those fleeting illusions of freedom, had they ever truly been mine to make?

As I stood there, the weight of a destiny I never chose pressing down on me, it seemed all roads had led to this moment—a tragic finale written long before I took my first breath into this shitstorm of a world.

I can go out on my own terms.

Taking a deep breath, I got ready to head for the door as shouts and stomping boots and sirens raged at me from everywhere.

I have to get back to Hope and end us both. At least we'll be together.

36

Leo had followed Emma's lead into the schoolyard, with Denae trailing behind them. Shouting and sounds of violence came from the direction of the auditorium, and Denae bolted before either he or Emma could stop her. She was tearing across the open ground between the auditorium and the first classroom wing when two figures emerged from the back of the auditorium building.

They ran along a walkway that connected to another classroom wing, and Denae shouted her brother's name. If he'd been one of the people running, he didn't hear her or ignored her if he had.

Based on the third figure to emerge, Leo had to guess at the latter.

That was Grace Jackson. There's not much light around here, but there was enough to glint off the blades on her right hand.

Max and his task force had shown up, with air support providing more light. A perimeter had been established, and roving teams of officers were scouring the school grounds for any sign of Grace, her sister Hope, or Jamaal Monroe.

Emma and Denae moved off around the side of the

classroom wing that the three figures had run toward. Leo stayed behind in case they came running around the other side of the building. Max and one of his officers headed in that direction in an attempt at tightening the cordon.

Additional task force members remained on the outer perimeter to catch Grace if she hopped the fence ringing the property.

A shout and scream from the classroom wing had Leo running for the building. It came from the direction Max had taken. Leo neared the structure, Glock at compressed ready and flashlight up as he drew tight against the wall and edged toward the corner.

From his position, he could see the back of the auditorium, where two double doors stood open.

Would she try to get back in there? She has to know we have her surrounded.

In the darkening night, and with so many avenues of approach, Leo couldn't be sure where Grace Jackson might be or where she'd run to.

Leo spoke into his mic. "Possible location of our suspect, classroom wing behind the auditorium building."

The air-patrol chopper above cast its searchlight into the open spaces of the schoolyard, sweeping around in arcs on either side of the auditorium, then moving up to the classroom wing. The light revealed nothing more than overgrown, weedy patches of ground, cracked and broken blacktop, and boarded-up buildings.

Breezeway roofs and covered walkways offered too many places for concealment.

Leo slid closer to the corner and announced from where he stood, "Grace Jackson, if you're there, this is the FBI. We have you surrounded. Surrender now, please. Nobody else needs to get hurt."

He got no answer for his trouble but caught the muffled sounds of someone in pain.

Weapon and light up, Leo spun around the corner, ready to parry a knife attack that never came. The walkway was empty but for two slumped forms on the ground at the far end. Leo was already running and keying his mic as he moved.

"Officers down! Officers down!"

He gave his location as he sped forward. He slid in a growing pool of blood and nearly crashed to his knees beside the two bodies. One of them was no longer moving. Deep gouges in his neck revealed the officer's gruesome fate.

The other man was Max, and he clutched at his right leg above his knee. Thick gouts of blood flowed up from between his fingers. His face was almost ashen, and he was barely breathing.

Leo holstered his gun and reached for his belt as Max's body went limp and slid to the side. With a hand on Max's cheek, Leo helped the man gently to the ground. Blood pooled around his body, soaking into his clothes.

Unable to hold in his anger, Leo roared at the night. "Dammit, Grace!"

Footsteps echoed from somewhere on the grounds, heading in his direction. They were the heavy tread of boots, multiple sets. Help was coming, but it was too late.

Leo stood and reached for his mic when he heard Denae's voice raised in a shout from around the other side of the building. He sped in her direction, reaching for his weapon as he rounded the corner.

Not five feet from him, crouched on the walkway like a stalking cat, was Grace Jackson.

"Freeze! FBI!" Leo yelled, bringing his weapon around. She moved without even looking at him, rushing to the side, then back to the wall as he fired twice. His shots missed, and she was inside his guard before he could get his weapon trained on her.

She slashed upward, and he knocked her blades aside with the muzzle of his weapon, bringing his hip around and bodychecking her. She fell back, rolled over her shoulder, and was up and running as he shouted at her to freeze and fired two shots that missed as she whipped around the corner and out of sight.

Leo was close behind, racing for the corner.

She's heading for Denae. Emma, please still be with her. Please, please, please.

He came around to the next walkway, staying back from the building to give himself plenty of space to draw a bead on Grace if she leaped out at him.

The walkway was empty, but Denae's voice was raised inside the nearest classroom. He sped for the door hanging off its hinges and halfway blocking the entrance. Pushing it aside, he aimed his flashlight beam into the room, revealing a horrific scene.

Emma was crouched over two bodies on the floor in the middle of the room while Denae and Grace traded kicks and strikes in the far corner. Leo wanted to shoot, but as fast as the two fighting women moved, his best shot might still hit Denae.

His flashlight beam cast stark shadows of their forms on the wall as arms lashed out, swiped, and parried and legs lifted in kicks. Denae grunted when Grace landed a solid blow to her side but was quick enough to block the blades from raking across her face as the shorter woman sliced at her.

With a shout, Grace launched a flurry of kicks and punches, driving Denae back a few steps, and then shot a straight jab with her blades, aiming for the taller woman's face.

Denae caught her wrist and folded her hand over, twisting her arm at the same time. Grace howled and kicked out, but Denae already had a foot up to stomp the younger woman's leg back down. Giving a twist of her hips, she had Grace moving under her control now, still manipulating her blade hand.

A final motion had Grace going to the floor, where Denae wrenched her arm up behind her and dropped onto her back with a knee to pin her down.

Leo rushed forward, skirting around Emma and the huddled figures she'd been protecting. He had cuffs in his hand and immediately slapped them around Grace's wrists.

Convulsing with sobs intermingled with screams of fury, Grace struggled between Denae and Leo on the ground, but her eyes were shut against the night. She could pull at her cuffs and rail against them all she wanted.

It was over.

37

Emma dropped down to the asphalt beside Leo. He and Denae had taken seats on the blacktop when EMTs arrived to tend to Hope Jackson. Some feet away, task force officers stood in a ring around Grace. She sat with her back to the chain-link fence, staring up at the night sky, weeping.

A bullet-proof vest she'd been wearing was on the ground a good distance away from her, along with the fabricated weapon she'd used to commit her vicious crimes.

The officers around her all held their weapons muzzles down, but Emma could feel the anger radiating from the group. They'd lost two of their own tonight, and one of them had been the task force leader.

The man who lost his son to gang violence met the same fate himself.

Max's ghost stood behind Grace, his white eyes blank and unforgiving as he stared down at her. "So much wasted. And all for the wrong kind of family."

Emma wanted to ask Max's ghost what he meant, but the EMTs were wheeling Hope out of the building on a gurney.

Jamaal walked beside them, holding her hand until Denae called to him.

"You need to stay here, Jamaal. You're a witness, and still a person of interest as far as this case goes. Might as well pull up some blacktop by your big sister, because they'll be talking to me, too, before the night's over."

He reluctantly released Hope's hand and watched until the EMTs disappeared with her into the back of a waiting ambulance that had pulled into the schoolyard. The chain-link fence was now breached in multiple places to provide access to a SWAT van, the ambulance, and three MPD patrol cars.

Flashing lights and the helicopter's searchlight lit up the night. Where before the abandoned school had been a cemetery of shadows and regrets, now it looked more like a big-top circus.

At least nobody's trying to kill anyone here, much as some of them might like to.

Jacinda approached from the direction the ambulance had taken. Her red hair stuck up around a headset she wore as she conferred with someone via radio. She paused in the middle of the blacktop, far enough away that Emma couldn't hear what was being discussed, but she could guess.

She looked around Leo's shoulders at Denae and saw her colleague monitoring Jacinda's every motion, nodding her head as if she knew exactly what was coming.

Leo reached out a hand and placed it on Denae's knee.

Emma nudged him on his shoulder as a second gurney, followed by a third, was wheeled down the walkway behind them. Unlike Hope's, these two were both covered by sheets marked with dark splotches and stains of blood.

The task force officers standing around Grace stiffened, and one of them stepped away to set down his weapon. He removed his helmet and began slamming it into the ground as he shouted and raged about their losses. Another officer joined him and helped him stand, trading quiet words of sympathy with him.

Ending her radio conversation, Jacinda stepped up to stand before them, taking in their faces one by one, ending with Jamaal Monroe.

"Mr. Monroe, you'll need to provide a witness statement and fingerprints. We also understand you might have information pertaining to the disposition of one Celine Austin."

He shook his head quickly. "I ain't seen her since she ran off. Honest."

"Be that as it may, we'll need to confirm that, along with your statement about what occurred here tonight. An officer will escort you to the station shortly. Will you cooperate, or will you need to be officially detained?"

Jacinda lifted a set of flex cuffs and wiggled them in the air.

Before Jamaal could speak, Denae stood and reached a hand to help him rise as well. "We'll both go, SSA Hollingsworth. Willingly. No need for cuffs."

The SSA met Denae's gaze, and Emma could do nothing but watch whatever was about to happen unfold according to protocol.

Was she going to lose her colleague and friend? Were all those promises of gym dates and sparring practice going to evaporate into thin air?

In front of her, Jacinda reached a hand for Denae's and shook it. "I understand you were central to apprehending Grace Jackson tonight, and without causing further loss of life in the process. That should help with the forthcoming disciplinary review. And I assure you, I will be speaking in your favor to the Bureau chiefs."

"I'm sorry, Jacinda. I know you said to stand down, but—"

"I understand, Denae. I wish that were all it took to move forward, but rules are rules. Just be honest and be respectful. We'll see you in the conference room for a briefing again soon, I'm sure of it."

Emma stood, and so did Leo. They both gave Denae a hug and watched as she and her brother departed with the SSA.

At least Emma didn't have the agony of seeing a new ghost with a friend's face. Losing Max and the other officer had been enough of a blow.

Honestly, I don't know if I can take seeing another ghost after this. It's bad enough Mom never comes around, and the one I'd like to see most right now just makes me miss him all the more.

38

Leaned back into her overstuffed couch, Emma rubbed at her wrists and elbows and, for the moment, simply appreciated the silence.

Exhaustion weighed on her, heavier than it had in a while. Just twenty-four hours ago, she'd been sitting in a Bureau sedan with Denae and doing her damnedest to convince her colleague to stay behind, not to rush in and try to save her brother.

Since then, the paperwork and the body bags and the emotions had come at her and the team nonstop. When she'd finally returned to her apartment that evening, she'd been so excited for the silence, she simply dropped onto the couch and stared at the wall.

Her phone buzzed, and Denae's name popped up.

Mom and Dad want you and Leo to come over for dinner soon. Next weekend maybe? Gotta find time to introduce Leo first.

Emma smiled and typed out a quick reply in the affirmative. Denae and Jamaal's relationship might still be shaky for obvious reasons, but it seemed like they were on a good path, and Emma wouldn't turn down a chance at spending more time with the Monroe family.

Thinking of how Leo had embraced Denae back at the Bureau, Emma felt some of the warmth she'd known with Oren returning to her heart. Her colleagues were good for each other. And from what she'd seen, Leo cared about Denae more than he'd let on. He might not be in love with her yet…but he was getting there.

Emma only hoped Denae would let him into her heart, the way he'd clearly let her into his.

She just needs to get through the disciplinary hearing that's headed her way. She will, but getting back to normal isn't going to be easy after this case.

If she were being honest, Emma wasn't sure what normal even meant now.

Gang activity hadn't really changed, and Max's task force still had their work cut out for them. With leaders of the two most prominent gangs dead now, it was hard to tell what might happen next. A power vacuum at the top only meant that someone else would rise to fit the bill and take control.

Someone would be willing, eager even, to pick up the pieces.

Thinking of what the city might be faced with in the coming weeks or months, Emma's exhaustion tugged at her. She leaned her head back, eyes still closed. It was too early for bed, and her nerves remained on edge.

I just have to relax. Like Oren always said.

Emma breathed deep and imagined her whole body going limp, like Oren had instructed her in his classes. Bone by bone and limb by limb.

Relax, Emma.

Piece by piece.

Breathe deep and let it out. Slow and even, not forced, not held back.

Anchored in her soft couch, in the safety of her living room, Emma imagined Oren there beside her, his deep voice reverberating the calm she'd always felt when near his side.

The air chilled around her, and a thrill of shock ran through her. She took two more deep breaths, hoping against hope that he'd be there…and to her surprise, he was. Faint, less clear than so many of the ghosts she saw from day to day, but there.

White-eyed, he sat perched beside her on her couch. The chill of the Other spread out around them, but despite that, Emma still felt the warmth of Oren's attention.

"Oren," she whispered, "I miss you."

"I'm doing everything I can for you, Emma." He raised one ghostly hand and pushed some loose strands of hair behind his ear. He reached forward, as if to touch her, and seemed to realize the impossibility just in time to pull his hand back. Lacing his fingers together in his lap, he leaned toward her instead. "Just be patient. Be careful."

She swallowed, the cold of the Other slipping into her throat, down to her heart and lungs. Holding him closer. "Thank you. I miss you so very much."

He smiled, the same peace he'd had in his studio radiating from him.

And then he was gone.

With a last bit of energy bestowed by Oren's appearance, and her ability to call him to her—somehow, amazingly, she had, hadn't she?—Emma forced herself to stand up and make a fast dinner of leftovers. Then, after one last shower, she collapsed into the luxury of her bed.

Light from a streetlamp shined in through the window, just as it always did. Emma had placed her mother's photo in such a way as to allow the light to hit it and make it visible even when the room was dark. Tonight, the picture remained standing, facing the middle of the room so that it could greet

Emma whenever she entered. From that angle, Emma could just see her mother's smile.

I need to figure out who those other women in the picture are. I can't keep putting it off.

As if cued by her thought, the picture suddenly twirled in place, upended on one corner, and spun in a blur. Before Emma could react, it came to a wobbling stop.

Emma's mother now faced her directly, as if demanding her focus.

But her face was kind, loving…and too familiar to make Emma fearful, even after that little tantrum the photograph had displayed to get her attention.

Closing her eyes, Emma crawled into bed, promising herself she'd look into the identity of those women the next day. But even as sleep began creeping in, the familiar sound of a howling wolf drifted in with it, so slow and haunting that Emma couldn't even be sure whether it was the beginning of a dream, or the last trace of reality before she fell into sleep.

39

"Eight dead police officers?" Emma stared at the document in front of her, working to process all the destruction and violence that Grace Jackson had wrought.

Jacinda sighed and flipped through the paperwork before her, sitting across from Emma at the conference table. "That's the tally from the rioting and fighting in the daylight. It doesn't include Max or the man killed with him, Officer Emile Zafon."

"Or the gang members who died and the bystanders struck by stray rounds fired blindly."

"We have no reports of children being injured or killed in this case, small mercy though that may be."

Emma glanced out to the bullpen, where Mia and Vance were sorting through call records. Family and community members wanted to know whether their loved ones were dead or in jail, and MPD hadn't been able to get answers to all of them yet because of the chaos and the number of lives lost. "The newspaper said at least a dozen died on each side. Do we know if that's accurate?"

Without looking up, Jacinda *mm-hmm*ed a reply. "Best

guess based on tattoos providing evidence of gang affiliation. The M.E. is still completing autopsy reports and will be for quite some time, I imagine."

"Makes me wonder if we've solved anything or just made things worse."

Nodding, Jacinda sorted papers into separate folders. "It's a mess. A tragedy." She closed the two folders she'd been sorting papers into and pushed one toward Emma. "This is yours, and the other's Leo's. I need your eyes on this to make sure the details are right, and a rundown of exactly what happened after you and Denae found her brother and Hope Jackson in that classroom. Today, if you can. Leo'll be in within the hour, and—"

Jacinda's phone buzzed at her elbow.

She glanced down at the number, frowned, and picked it up. Her eyes narrowed in confusion, but she pulled the phone from her ear and put it on speaker.

"...listening? You're going to be sorry for what you've done." The disguised voice chuckled darkly.

It chilled Emma's blood just as effectively as the presence of the Other could.

"Do you understand? You will be sorry. Rails, the Professor...they're nothing compared to me."

"Who the hell is this?" Jacinda leaned into the phone, glaring at it. "Identify yourself!"

"Oh, you'll find out very soon. I'll spell it out in the blood of one of your agents."

Before Jacinda could respond, the call ended with a jingle, and Emma was left staring at the phone along with her SSA. The *Unknown Number* label sat before them, as if mocking their confusion.

Jacinda cursed, stalking to the door and slamming it open, on a warpath to determine where the threat had come from.

Behind her, Emma could only tell herself to breathe, to focus, but none of the calm she'd felt the night before remained within her grasp.

A wolf's howl erupted in Emma's ears, angry and close. She jerked to her feet.

She wasn't fleeing, either the phone or the wolf—not really, she promised herself—but as the howl came again, resounding as if inside her own head, there was no way to pretend otherwise.

Whatever was coming for her and her team, from the Other or from that dark voice on the phone, they were running out of time.

Emma had never been surer of anything in her life.

The End
To be continued...

Thank you for reading.
All of Emma Last series books can be found on Amazon.

ACKNOWLEDGMENTS

The past few years have been a whirlwind of change, both personally and professionally, and I find myself at a loss for the right words to express my profound gratitude to those who have supported me on this remarkable journey. Yet, I am compelled to try.

To my sons, whose unwavering support has been my bedrock, granting me the time and energy to transform my darkest thoughts into words on paper. Your steadfast belief in me has never faltered, and watching each of you grow, welcoming the wonderful daughters you've brought into our family, has been a source of immense pride and joy.

Embarking on the dual role of both author and publisher has been an exhilarating, albeit challenging, adventure. Transitioning from the solitude of writing to the dynamic world of publishing has opened new horizons for me, and I'm deeply grateful for the opportunity to share my work directly with you, the readers.

I extend my heartfelt thanks to the entire team at Mary Stone Publishing, the same dedicated group who first recognized my potential as an indie author years ago. Your collective efforts, from the editors whose skillful hands have polished my words to the designers, marketers, and support staff who breathe life into these books, have been instrumental in resonating deeply with our readers. Each of you plays a crucial role in this journey, not only nurturing my growth but also ensuring that every story reaches its full potential. Your dedication, creativity, and finesse have been nothing short of invaluable.

However, my deepest gratitude is reserved for you, my beloved readers. You ventured off the beaten path of traditional publishing to embrace my work, investing your most precious asset—your time. It is my sincerest hope that this book has enriched that time, leaving you with memories that linger long after the last page is turned.

With all my love and heartfelt appreciation,

Mary

ABOUT THE AUTHOR

Mary Stone

Nestled in the serene Blue Ridge Mountains of East Tennessee, Mary Stone crafts her stories surrounded by the natural beauty that inspires her. What was once a home filled with the lively energy of her sons has now become a peaceful writer's retreat, shared with cherished pets and the vivid characters of her imagination.

As her sons grew and welcomed wonderful daughters-in-law into the family, Mary's life entered a quieter phase, rich with opportunities for deep creative focus. In this tranquil environment, she weaves tales of courage, resilience, and intrigue, each story a testament to her evolving journey as a writer.

From childhood fears of shadowy figures under the bed to a profound understanding of humanity's real-life villains, Mary's style has been shaped by the realization that the most complex antagonists often hide in plain sight. Her writing is characterized by strong, multifaceted heroines who defy traditional roles, standing as equals among their peers in a world of suspense and danger.

Mary's career has blossomed from being a solitary author to establishing her own publishing house—a significant milestone that marks her growth in the literary world. This expansion is not just a personal achievement but a reflection of her commitment to bring thrilling and thought-provoking stories to a wider audience. As an author and publisher, Mary continues to challenge the conventions of the thriller genre, inviting readers into gripping tales filled with serial killers, astute FBI agents, and intrepid heroines who confront peril with unflinching bravery.

Each new story from Mary's pen—or her publishing house—is a pledge to captivate, thrill, and inspire, continuing the legacy of the imaginative little girl who once found wonder and mystery in the shadows.

Connect with Mary online

- facebook.com/authormarystone
- x.com/MaryStoneAuthor
- goodreads.com/AuthorMaryStone
- bookbub.com/profile/3378576590
- pinterest.com/MaryStoneAuthor
- instagram.com/marystoneauthor
- tiktok.com/@authormarystone

Printed in Great Britain
by Amazon